DEATH
ON THE SET

A BRENNA FLYNN MYSTERY

ROSE KERR

Relax. Read. Repeat.

DEATH ON THE SET (A Brenna Flynn Mystery, Book 1)
By Rose Kerr
Published by TouchPoint Press
Brookland, AR 72417
www.touchpointpress.com

Copyright © 2022 Rose Kerr
All rights reserved.

PAPERBACK ISBN: 978-1-956851-15-1

This is a work of fiction. Names, places, characters, and events are fictitious. Any similarities to actual events and persons, living or dead, are purely coincidental. Any trademarks, service marks, product names, or named features are assumed to be the property of their respective owners and are used only for reference. If any of these terms are used, no endorsement is implied. Except for review purposes, the reproduction of this book, in whole or part, electronically or mechanically, constitutes a copyright violation. Address permissions and review inquiries to media@touchpointpress.com.

Editor: Kimberly Coghlan
Cover Design: ColbieMyles.com
Cover Images: Kitchen TV Show Recording Home Recipes, Cartoon by Viktoriia (Adobe Stock); gold retriever by Colorfuel Studio (Adobe Stock); female avatar by Volha Hlinskaya (Adobe Stock)

Connect with the author:
@rosekerrauthor @rkerrwriter

First Edition

Printed in the United States of America.

For Gary, this book would never have happened without you.
Your encouragement, love, and support mean the world to me.
Thank you for being you.

CHAPTER ONE

"Come on, hurry up!" The light was taking forever. Brenna drummed her fingers against the steering wheel. Monday morning traffic should have been over by now. A glance at the clock on her Jeep's dashboard showed she had less than ten minutes to get across town. She couldn't be late for this interview. Finally, a lead on a job. The light changed, and Brenna hustled to her meeting. It had been a rough six months. Her husband's sudden death and then losing her position at the school. Coming home to Bayview City in Northern Michigan seemed like a good idea at the time but work as a high school guidance counselor didn't come easily. Most of the school boards had been impacted by the cuts to education funding.

For the last month, Brenna had been working with Jackie Randall from the Randall Temp Agency to find a temporary position. There wasn't a lot available, but this position popped up this morning. Jackie had called before eight this morning to let Brenna know about the posting and had secured an interview for her. This job promised good pay and interesting work, even if it wasn't in her field. How on earth could she translate her skills to a cooking show? Helping high school students deal with the challenges of being a teenager and navigating their futures demanded specialized knowledge, compassion, good listening and speaking skills, and being well organized. Jackie had told her the posting indicated no experience needed. She had to at least try.

Arriving at the studio, she noticed a publicity poster on one side of the door. The poster featured the three chefs starring on the show, *Bayview Cooks!* She paused for a moment, recognizing two of the chefs. She'd eaten in both of their restaurants. The food and the atmosphere were excellent. Walking into the lobby, she stopped and took a breath. She felt rushed and out of control—not how she wanted to present herself. *Come on. There's nothing to lose. I've got this.* She squared her shoulders and went to the reception desk.

The receptionist asked Brenna to have a seat. She took deep breaths to settle herself. Looking around the reception area, she noticed large windows overlooking the harbor. Lake Superior was calm today, and she saw a few pleasure boats heading out toward Pebble Island. The reception area had comfortable seating and a low coffee table with the local paper. Brenna sent Jackie a quick text letting her know she had made it in time for the interview. A few minutes later, Brenna heard footsteps coming down the hall.

"Hello, Ms. Flynn? I'm Tim Harris, executive producer for *Bayview Cooks!*" He held out his hand.

Brenna stood to greet him. At five-two, Brenna had to tilt her head back a bit to see him. He was probably just over six feet tall, and his dark brown hair was cut close on the sides. With his round tortoiseshell glasses and casual sweater and pants, he reminded her of a former college professor. On his feet were a pair of black Keds.

"Nice to meet you." Brenna clasped his hand.

Tim smiled as they shook hands. "Let's go to my office. The producer is waiting for us. We'll talk there." He pointed down the hall.

Brenna picked up her brown leather tote bag and followed him. They arrived at his office door, and she could hear someone speaking.

"To be clear, you're saying you've completed the job even though I'm telling you the lights don't work? And you aren't coming back? What kind of bullshit is this? You can't do this. No, your contract doesn't specify a date. I have it right here in front of me." The man's voice rose as he spoke.

As Brenna and Tim walked into the office, Brenna could see his face was red. A vein in his neck was bulging, and he was scrunching up some papers in his left hand.

"Fine. We'll see what happens! I'll be taking this up with our lawyer."

The man banged the handset down on the phone's base. He ran his hands through his black hair, making it stick straight up.

Tim cleared his throat. "Mathew, what's wrong?"

Mathew put his hands on his hips. "We've got a situation. The electrical contractor isn't coming in to work on the lights on the set. He says the contract is to do the wiring only. Any issues aren't his problem. I've never heard of such crap." Mathew's voice vibrated.

Tim shook his head. He addressed Brenna. "We've had some challenges with this contractor. Less than quality workmanship and now refusing to fix the mistakes his employees made. It's holding up production. Without the lights, we can't film."

"Which contractor did you use?" Brenna asked.

Mathew checked the contract. "Bayview Electric."

"And what does the contract say about them having to fix mistakes or issues that come up as a result of their work?" Brenna's gaze moved from Mathew to Tim as she asked the question.

Mathew threw the contract on the desk. "Nothing! You'd think a reputable company would do it without question, but these guys are impossible to deal with." His brow furrowed as he stared at the contract.

"I might be able to help you out with this." Brenna glanced at Mathew and Tim.

"If you can get the lights working again, the position is yours," Mathew stated.

"You might want to read through my resume before you make that kind of promise." Brenna reached in her bag and handed each of them a copy of her resume. She pulled out her phone and moved by the table at the back of the office to place a call.

"Hi, Mary, Brenna here."

"Brenna, how are you?"

"I'm well. Mary, I'm at Studio One. They have a problem with the lighting on their set. Are any of the electricians available today to come by and see what the issue is?"

"Let me check the schedule. I just had it open a moment ago. Did Flynn and Family have the contract? I don't remember seeing anything from Studio One."

"No. It was Bayview Electric."

"We have a team of electricians available this afternoon. I can make certain they know to be there by one today."

"Sounds great. I'll let management know to expect them. Do you want to talk to someone here about the invoice?"

"Yes. We don't have anything in our system for Studio One."

Brenna turned around. "Who does she need to speak to about invoicing?"

Tim glanced up from skimming her resume. "You found someone to come in today?"

"Yes. My family owns a contracting company. They have most of their own tradespeople. The contract with Bayview Electric is completed, right? Otherwise, no one else will come in to do any other work."

Mathew held out his hand for Brenna's phone. "Yes. That's the reason why they aren't coming in again. I can talk to her about the invoicing."

Brenna smiled and held up a finger. "Mary, I'm going to hand you off to one of the producers from Studio One. He'll let you know about the invoicing. We'll talk soon." She handed the phone to Mathew.

Tim put her resume on the desk. "Well, I'm impressed. Are you that good with anything else that can go wrong?"

Mathew finished up with Mary and returned Brenna's phone to her. "I agree. Can we expect the same results with any other problem that may come up?"

Brenna wondered what problems they might be referring to. "I have a lot of personal connections with contractors and people in the construction business. My grandfather started the company, Flynn and Family. My father and one of my uncles run it now. I grew up in Bayview City and studied at the university here. I worked for the city for a while before leaving four years ago. There have been some changes with the city council, but the city employees haven't changed."

Tim pointed to her resume. "Which city department did you work in?"

"I worked in marketing and public relations. The position crossed several departments."

Mathew interrupted. "Is this necessary? As far as I'm concerned, she has the job. Brenna, welcome to the team. You've proven to me you can deliver when we need it."

Tim frowned at Mathew and adjusted his glasses. "Yes, well then . . .

Brenna, let's get you signed up. We'll go over some of the duties you'll be responsible for."

Mathew's phone pinged. "I'm needed in the studio. Tim, can you make sure Brenna has all the information regarding the position?"

"Of course. I'll make sure our expectations are clear."

Mathew was already out the door.

Tim shook his head and sighed. "People skills aren't his strength. He's always thinking ahead to the next task. That's not a bad thing, just makes life interesting, that's all. Let's sit at the table. Do you want a coffee or water before we start?"

"No thanks. I'm good. I'm curious about what the position entails." Brenna pulled out a chair and dropped her bag on the floor.

Tim grabbed his laptop and sat across from her. "Right. Let's go over the basics. As the only production assistant for the show, you're going to be doing some of everything—and everything includes office work, running errands, picking up supplies, and working with everyone involved with the show."

"So, is there a schedule I'd need to follow?" Brenna asked.

"Monday and Wednesday are rehearsal days. Tapings take place on Tuesday and Thursday. Those days are scheduled pretty tightly. We have a studio audience that comes in for the tapings. They come in at twelve-thirty, and the show begins taping at one. It can take as long as four hours to tape the show." Tim took a drink of water. "The rehearsal days aren't as tight, but the chefs and judges are expected at about one in the afternoon. The host and the rest of the crew all have to be here from about ten-thirty in the morning. Those days are spent on blocking and going through the script. Any changes to either the script or blocking need to be made then."

"When is the show televised and where?"

"The show we tape on Tuesday is broadcast on Thursday evening, and the Thursday show is broadcast on Sunday evening. We distribute through the local television station here, and the show is seen across the state. We don't have a wider distribution yet. We're working on something with Public Broadcasting, but nothing is confirmed."

"That sounds busy! And what happens on Friday?" Brenna wondered out loud.

"Most of that day is spent in meetings, getting supplies for the next week, and making sure everything is organized for the coming week. You're also going to have to make certain the cleaning crew that comes in during the evening accomplishes what they're being asked to do." Tim tapped his pen on the table. "We've had a few problems there, and it may mean you'll have to stay later on occasion."

"When do they come in?" Brenna opened her calendar app on her phone.

Tim pulled up a file on his laptop. "Let's see. They don't come in until eight in the evening, and they're supposed to take no more than two hours. I don't expect you to be here tonight. I've already spoken with them about the problems I've seen, and the owner has assured me things will be better. We'll see how things are tomorrow morning when we come in."

"Okay, and what time should I plan on being here in the morning?" Brenna asked.

"It's probably best that you're here by six or six-thirty at the latest."

Brenna winced. That was early.

Tim chuckled. "Sorry if that's early, but you're going to be really busy most of the time you're here."

Brenna shook her head. "It's not a problem. I'm used to getting up early. I just didn't have to deal with people that early in the day. As a counselor at the high school, I learned the students didn't come in for meetings before nine-thirty."

"Well, there won't be a lot of people here at that time. Mathew and I usually show up at seven or so. But you'll need to get the set ready and verify the call sheets for the day. And that can take some time."

"It's fine. Don't worry about it." Brenna smiled. "I'll manage."

"Now, your salary. It isn't a unionized position, but we don't want to lose you to another position somewhere else. The show is scheduled to run for six weeks, so we won't have time to bring someone else on." Tim looked at her and named a weekly remuneration that was quite generous. "Is that acceptable to you?"

"Yes, it is." Brenna was surprised at the wage. She wouldn't have to tap into her savings now, and that made her feel much better.

Tim spent a few more minutes going over her duties. Although they weren't what she was accustomed to doing, Brenna was confident she'd be able to address the varied tasks.

Tim glanced at his watch. "Any questions?"

Brenna shook her head. "I can always ask if I'm not sure what I should be doing. It seems pretty straightforward."

Tim gathered his papers. "Excellent. We have a production meeting scheduled over the lunch hour in the conference room. It's a great opportunity for you to meet the crew. I'll touch base with Margo Ryan, our associate producer. She'll set you up with all the necessary gear."

"Sounds good. I'll be right back. I need to add money to my meter." Brenna grabbed her bag.

"You're officially on the payroll, and one of the perks is parking in the back lot. Let me introduce you to Sally Marshall, our front desk receptionist. She'll make sure you have the appropriate parking pass and the information needed to access the building."

They went back to the reception area, and he introduced her to Sally.

Sally took her glasses off and let them swing on the bejeweled cord around her neck. "Glad to have you with us. I'll just get the keys and security code for you and print out a parking pass."

Tim said, "You're in good hands. I'll see you shortly."

Brenna watched as Sally efficiently typed some commands on her computer. A printer off to the side whirled as it spit out some papers. Sally walked to the cabinet next to the printer and took out a set of keys. Then she picked up the printed papers and walked back to the desk.

Sally put the papers on top of the desk. "Now, I just need you to sign here and here. That lets us know you have the keys to the building and a parking pass. I have to get a security code for you for the doors, and you'll be all set."

Brenna signed where Sally had indicated. "I hope I'm not out of line, but your rings are beautiful."

"Not out of line at all. Thanks. The ring on my right hand is from our thirtieth wedding anniversary. My husband insisted I needed a new wedding band. I liked the one he had originally given me, so I had the new one sized for my right hand." Sally's eyes crinkled as she spoke. "Now, the security code. You need to know that it is unique to you and can't be changed. It's randomly selected by the computer system. You'll need to enter it when you come in every morning and if you leave here after six at night."

Brenna chuckled. "From what I've learned about my position, I may be leaving after six most nights. And I think I'll be one of the first ones here in the morning."

"Are you concerned about being here early in the morning or late at night?"

"No. The hours are okay. And I take it only people who have the keys and an access code can come into the building, right?"

"Yes. Entering the code keeps a record of who's been in and out of the building. I come in at eight in the morning, and when I arrive, I disarm the system for the day. If you're in before I am and leave before I come in, you'll have to enter the code again when you exit. In the evening, the system automatically arms itself at six." Sally was filing the forms Brenna had signed.

"Sally, what are all the keys for? They can't be just for the front and back doors."

"Hmm, there are office keys and some for the storage units in the building. Would you like a labeler to identify them?"

Brenna sighed. "Someone after my own heart. Yes, I love being organized. The labeler would be a huge help. I'm going to move my Jeep, and I'll do that next."

Brenna moved her car to the parking lot. She closed her eyes and smiled. Hopefully, life would now start to improve.

She texted Jackie Randall, at Randall Temp Agency.

> B: Got the job! It's six weeks and good pay.
> J: Excellent! I'll touch base with you tomorrow after work to see how it's working out.

Then, Brenna texted her closest friend, Emily.

> B: Got job as PA on cooking show.
> E: WTG! What's a PA? Dinner 2nite?

Brenna chuckled as she texted back. She and Emily had a standing date on Monday evenings at the local pub.

> B: Tell u @ 7ish.

Taking advantage of the few minutes she had before the meeting, Brenna checked out the sound stage. Her footsteps echoed across the wooden floor. The stage was bigger than she expected. It was set up with three separate kitchens.

"Three chefs, three kitchens, that makes sense," she said aloud to herself. Looking around, she saw an immense semicircular desk with three high-back leather chairs. *This must be where the judges would be sitting.* She walked to the desk and noticed three monitors built into the desktop. *I wonder if that's so the judges can see what the audience sees? I'll have to ask someone about it.*

Turning to the kitchen area, she realized they were equipped with restaurant-quality appliances. *Wow, this could be my dream kitchen. Well, if I was a cook, it would be. Hmm, wonder if the chefs would be open to giving cooking lessons.* She skimmed her fingers along the marble countertops and sighed. "This feels so cool and rich."

Brenna made her way behind the stage. *Ah, this must be the pantry area.* One of her areas of responsibility. The shelves were almost empty, and there was a mess on the floor. It looked as if flour or sugar had been spilled. "What happened to all the supplies? There's nothing here and what's left isn't organized. That's not good," she muttered to herself.

A glance at her watch had her making her way back to the conference room. She pulled out a notebook and jotted some reminders about the state of the pantry as she sat waiting for the meeting to start.

CHAPTER TWO

About fifteen people attended the meeting. Brenna was introduced to everyone present, and she made note of Margo Ryan, the associate producer. She would connect with Margo after the meeting. Tim and the director, John Simms, discussed the schedule for the remainder of the week. John was a short, portly man who appeared to be well respected by the crew. Tim deferred to him on many of the questions the crew asked.

"Right, people, let's get out there and make this week great." Tim dismissed the group.

Brenna gathered her purse and notebook. When she stood, Margo approached her with her hand outstretched.

"Hi, I'm Margo Ryan, the associate producer. Welcome to the show. Tim asked me to get you set up with the gear you'll need for your job."

Brenna shook Margo's hand. Margo was dressed casually in jeans and a long-sleeved flannel shirt. Her dark brown hair was pulled back in a ponytail. Margo's nails were short and unpainted. Brenna felt overdressed in her charcoal dress pants, long-sleeved cream shirt, and charcoal blazer.

"Hi. Nice to meet you. I'm looking forward to working with you." Brenna smiled at Margo.

"There's lots to learn, and if you get stuck on anything, don't be afraid to ask for help. That's how most of us learned our way around." Margo led Brenna to the back of the studio.

Brenna stepped up her pace to keep up with Margo's longer stride. "Have you been working in television for a long time?"

"Almost five years. I like being able to take on new projects. I started in the news department and then did some special interest programs." Margo unlocked a tall, wide metal storage cabinet.

Brenna's eyes took in the assortment of electronics, clipboards, and tool belts with all kinds of different attachments. "Wow! There's a lot of equipment."

Margo laughed. "Yes, there is. You'll be working with almost everyone associated with the show, from Tim and Mathew to the talent and most of the crew. I'm going to set you up with a lot of technology, but, trust me, you'll use it all."

"Tim did mention I'd be the main contact person for the show. Why do I need all this stuff?" Brenna leaned in and picked up one of the tablets.

"This 'stuff' is going to be your lifeline. It'll keep you and everyone you have to work with organized and on top of everything. We use the radios in the studio, and the headset has to fit comfortably; otherwise, you'll get a headache. You'll need a phone as well. Sally at reception can give you everyone's contact information."

Brenna watched as Margo pulled items out of the cabinet, checking off the inventory sheet attached to the inside door. "Why do I need a tool belt?"

"It has compartments that will allow you to carry most of the equipment you'll need. Can you put it on so I know it fits? You'll also have a backpack to carry larger items. Both need to be properly fitted to make sure the weight is well distributed." Margo added a clipboard, notebook, pens, pencils, and markers to the backpack. The last two items she included were a first aid kit and a small sewing kit.

"I need a sewing kit?" Brenna's voice rose in a mild panic. "Tim didn't say anything about being a seamstress. We're in trouble if I have to sew a button." She took her blazer off and put the tool belt on. It fit perfectly.

Margo shook her head and chuckled. "I don't think you'll need to sew anything. We do have a wardrobe department. This is just an in-case item."

"Well, that's a relief. And what about first aid? I'm certified in basic first aid and CPR." Brenna wondered what she had got herself into.

"That's all you need. Most of us have the same certification. Again, it's just in case."

"Good. I can handle small mishaps. I worked in the school system, and kids were always getting into some sort of scrape or other."

Margo verified Brenna had all chargers for the electronics and then locked up the cabinet.

Brenna grabbed her blazer and waited until Margo had secured the cabinet. "Is there additional security I need to know about? Sally gave me keys and a code for the doors."

"Small electronics seem to grow legs around here, so we keep them locked up. The building has an alarm code connected to a central office." Margo shrugged. "We haven't had any problems so far."

"Just one more question. Tim said he would be sending me the revised scripts for distribution. Who has the email lists I need for that?"

"Sally has them. We can go see her now. Did Tim tell you who gets the scripts?"

"The chefs, sous chefs, judges, host, director, assistant director, and all the producers."

"And you should send a copy to yourself as well. That way, you'll always have the most current one available. And Sally needs a copy so she can upload it to the teleprompter. Oh, I almost forgot. The crew lockers are back here as well. You can use one of the empty ones. I'd be careful not to leave anything valuable in it since they don't lock. Most people just leave their coat in one." Margo pointed out the lockers. They looked like standard-issue high school lockers.

Margo's phone vibrated as they were making their way to the lobby.

"Are you okay to get to the front? I have to meet with Tim and Mathew."

"Yes. Thanks for all your help."

"Not a problem. See you later." Margo headed toward the office area.

Brenna continued to the reception desk. "Hi, Sally. I just found out I'm going to need some email distribution lists and the contact information for the cast and crew. Margo said you could help me out."

"I just got off the phone with the IT company we work with. They're setting up an email account for you, and as soon as that's done, I can send you all the contact information you need."

"That's great. Do you know how long it'll take?"

"It should be done in the next hour. I'll be notified when you're added to the system, and I'll send you a text when it's been taken care of."

There was a commotion at the front door. Brenna turned around and saw the three chefs dressed in their street clothes. Each carried a bag resembling a soft-sided briefcase. They were an imposing group. Brenna recognized them from their restaurants and the poster on the front door.

The three chefs stopped at the reception desk. Chef Mike looked at Brenna with her tool belt. "Ha, a new hire! Who are you replacing?"

Brenna bit her lip to stop from laughing. Chef Mike's manner reminded her of her older brothers. "Hi, Chef Mike. I'm Brenna Flynn, the new production assistant for the show. I'm not sure who I'm replacing."

Chef Mike nodded his head. "Thought you seemed familiar. I've seen you in my restaurant. And are Jim and Brady Flynn your brothers?"

"Yes. You all played football in high school."

Chef Rosa asked Brenna, "Is today your first day?"

"Yes. I've never done anything like this before. I'm sure I'll figure out what needs to be done—or someone will tell me."

Chef Aaron had been quiet up until now. "The crew's great. Everyone works well together. We've completed one show, and the ratings were pretty good. With just that one episode, we've seen an increase in reservations at each of our restaurants."

Chef Mike added, "And the local paper has written a couple of articles too. Who knew we're becoming media stars? All that translates to busier restaurants, which is good for our bottom lines."

Chef Rosa said, "One of the radio stations interviewed us and asked why we're doing the show. We all attended the same culinary school and then went our separate ways. It's fun working with these two again. It's not a huge time commitment since it's only a six-week schedule."

Chef Mike piped up, "Well, it does make us look at different ways to prepare food. We've all had different experiences in the kitchen. I like the idea of working in front of a live audience and preparing a meal. We can be as inventive as we want or we can pull out our favorites."

Chef Aaron said, "The host was asking us quite a few questions on the last show. I'm wondering if he's going to do the same thing for this episode."

Chef Rosa leaned against the reception desk. "I think he is. The show's trying to build on our reputations, and we need to 'sparkle.' At least that's what I've been told by that Mathew guy."

Chef Mike rolled his eyes and hooted, "Me 'sparkle'? As if."

Chef Aaron snorted and shook his head. "I'm with you. I'd rather pay attention to the food we're preparing than try to 'sparkle.' So long as they don't expect us to argue and fight with each other. With the host asking questions, you really have to focus on a lot of different things. It would be nice if we had an idea on the topics he's going to talk about."

Brenna was fascinated with the conversation. Here were the chefs, the stars, talking about the show, and now they were gossiping about the host.

"Well, maybe they want you to sparkle to bring in bigger ratings. Isn't that the whole idea?" she asked.

Chef Mike looked at the other two chefs. "Yeah, it is. But none of us are looking to be reality stars. We've known each other for about ten years. We've been there for each other through our growth in the food industry. We decided to do this because we thought it would be fun and a great way to promote our restaurants. And Aaron's right, there's no way we'd stage fights with each other. We have too much respect for each other."

Brenna glanced at her watch. "When are you supposed to be in the studio for the rehearsal?"

Chef Rosa sighed. "Probably now. Let's go, guys, before we're officially late."

Chef Mike said, "Yeah, that Mathew guy is pretty intense. Always wanting us to be 'at the ready,' as he says."

The three chefs trooped out toward the studio. Chef Rosa lead the way with Chef Mike and Chef Aaron following her.

"Wow, they're just regular people, aren't they?" Brenna asked Sally.

"Yes. They're pretty nice about everything. I know they aren't getting much money to do the show, and they've been giving a lot of their time for publicity too." Sally picked up some papers as she stood.

Brenna grabbed her backpack. "I'd better get to the studio. I'll watch for the lists from you."

Brenna hurried to the studio. John Simms, the director, and Mathew were with the crew. Two electricians from Flynn and Family were working on the lights. Temporary lighting had been set up for the afternoon. Margo was sitting in the empty studio audience seats. She waved to Brenna and indicated a chair next to her. Brenna made her way to the section Margo was in. As Brenna sat next to her, she noted the judges were seated at their large desk, and Tim was right behind them. She hadn't seen them come into the building and wondered how they gained entry. Three other people were standing with the chefs in the kitchens, but she didn't recognize them.

Brenna nodded toward the man walking on the set with a script. He was wearing a blue dress shirt, a striped black and blue tie, and black dress pants. "Is that the host?"

Margo frowned. "Yes, Sean Jamieson. I'm not sure why he didn't show up for today's meeting. Mathew wasn't happy about that."

"Oh, how come?" Brenna raised an eyebrow.

"Mathew likes to run a tight crew. He expects everyone to come in for all the meetings and to be ready to work. Sean's new. He's from the Southwest and hasn't clued in that he isn't the star of the show—just that he's part of the show."

"And who are the three people with the chefs?"

"They are the sous chefs. Each chef was told they were to bring one person in to help them out. They arrived a few minutes ago."

John walked to the kitchen area. "Okay, folks, we're going to get started. Chefs, I need you in your kitchens. Sean, are you ready to go?"

"You bet. All right, everyone, let's make this rehearsal sing."

Chef Mike raised his hands as if leading a choir, "La la la la la la la."

Chef Rosa laughed out loud, and Chef Aaron's shoulders shook.

Tim rolled his eyes. He was sitting behind the judges and didn't look pleased.

John rubbed his beard. "If the comedy act is done, maybe we can begin."

Sean smiled. "Sorry, John. We're good to go."

Chef Mike raised his hands up. "No disrespect intended." He smiled, and the dimple in his left cheek was pronounced.

John moved toward the judges sitting at the semicircular desk, just off stage. "I need you to stay focused on what the chefs are doing in the kitchens. Use the monitors in front of you if you have to. Sean's going to ask you some questions during the next taping. They'll be added to the script. If you get lost during the taping or forget what's going to happen next, look at any of the cameras. The teleprompter feeds onto each of them."

Mr. Harlow, a judge and the food critic for the *Bayview Times* said, "Good. We'll be able to prepare for tomorrow's show."

"Can we talk amongst ourselves?" Mr. Fitzgerald was another judge and the mayor of Bayview City.

"You can if you remember that you're miked and if you speak too loudly, it could disrupt the flow of the show." John made a note. "We can always turn your mikes off until it's time in the script for you to speak."

"That might be easier. I know last show there were a few times I wanted to make a comment to Mr. Harlow and felt as if I couldn't," Ms. Keene, the final judge and president of Bayview College added.

"Right. I've made a note here. Brenna, where are you?" John looked around the studio for her.

Brenna waved her hand. "I'm here, John. Did you need something?"

"Yeah. I'm not sure if anyone's told you, but could you take notes of the rehearsal? I'll need them sent to me after we're done here. And Tim and Mathew will need copies as well."

Brenna pulled out her tablet. "Not a problem."

John walked to the kitchens. Chef Rosa was looking through the cupboards in her section.

"Chefs, I'll need you to be focused completely for the rehearsal. Chef Rosa, is there a problem?"

Chef Rosa put her hands on her hips. "Well, yes. I can't find any of the pots and pans. I know we don't need them today, but where are they going to be?"

Chef Mike spoke up. "Mine were in the drawers right below the cutlery. And that's not where they were last week."

Mathew said, "Brenna, make a note. I'll need you to verify that all cooking utensils and equipment are in the correct locations for tomorrow's taping."

John took charge of the rehearsal. "Okay, everyone, we're about to start. Sean, let's get the rehearsal underway."

Sean walked to his mark on center stage. "I think having the audience ask questions last week worked well. I'm planning on doing the same tomorrow. Any objections to that?"

The judges shook their heads. Chef Mike answered for the chefs. "I don't have a problem answering questions. And last week we all kept talking to each other while we were taping. I think that's pretty important. Communication is key when you're working as a team."

Sean said, "I'd like to use the line about communication in the kitchens tomorrow if I can."

Tim said, "I'll add it to the script."

The rest of the rehearsal was relatively easy and went by quickly. At the end of the rehearsal, John clapped his hands together twice. "That's it, everyone. We're done for today. Good work, chefs and judges. We'll see you here tomorrow at eleven. You'll have time for makeup and to get settled. The studio audience will start coming in at twelve-thirty. Taping is scheduled to begin at one. Crew, finish up your tasks for the day. You'll need to be here for the eight-thirty meeting in the morning. Have a great evening, all."

Brenna looked at her tablet. There were ten pages of notes with changes that would need to be incorporated into the script.

"Was that a normal rehearsal?" she asked Margo.

"Pretty much. Why?"

"There's a lot of notes for the changes. I didn't think there'd be that many."

"It may slow down once the show's been taping for a while. The chefs are still finding their way. Are you going to be able to get the notes done up and distributed?" Margo sounded concerned.

"Oh yeah, it's not a problem. I used a note-taking system I developed in grad school. And Sally just sent me the distribution lists. I'll get these done in less than an hour. But before I do that, I want to check with the chefs about the pantry setup."

Brenna walked to Chef Rosa's kitchen.

"Could I trouble you all to come to the pantry and let me know exactly how you want it organized?" Brenna asked. "It makes sense to me you'd have some say in this, and it'll make my job a bit easier."

The chefs followed her to the pantry.

"Wow, it's pretty empty. What happened?" Sous chef Tina worked with Chef Mike.

"From what I was told, anything that wasn't used was donated to the Community Care Kitchen. I've been told to replenish the supplies. I have a list Tim and Mathew put together. But what I need from you is some feedback on where you want them set up. And that includes everything from baking soda to the wrap you'll use to cover the food you're preparing," Brenna said.

Chef Aaron asked, "Would it help if we sketched out a diagram and let you know where all the supplies should be?"

"That would be perfect." Brenna pulled out her tablet.

Using the drawing app on the tablet, the chefs quickly produced a sketch she could work with.

The chefs filed out of the pantry, and Brenna heard them making plans for drinks before going home for the day.

CHAPTER THREE

Brenna made her way to the reception desk. "Sally, is there an office or a desk I can use to do some work? Tim didn't let me know where I can set up the laptop."

Sally shook her head. "Sometimes I think he has too much to think about. There's a small office with a desk, a chair, and a filing cabinet behind the larger conference room. And it has a door. No one uses it on a regular basis, so if no one's in there, I'd suggest using that."

"Perfect. If anyone's looking for me, that's where I'll be." Brenna smiled her thanks and soon found the room in question. It was small, not much bigger than a broom closet, but there was a decent desk chair and a desk. "This will work. And I can close the door if things get noisy."

Grabbing her tablet, she opened her laptop and set it up on the desk. She adjusted the chair and began transcribing her notes from the rehearsal. Her fingers flew over the keyboard. She checked for any errors and then sent the notes to John, Tim, Mathew, and Margo.

With that task completed, she took some time to get the pantry in order. She was getting ready to leave when she overheard a man's voice.

"I'll need the shipment delivered on Thursday evening. Is there going to be a problem?"

At first, she thought he was speaking to her but realized he was on the phone. Brenna peered around the doorway. She saw a man moving away from her to the left but couldn't determine who it was. Turning her head to the right, she noticed Sean Jamieson. He was putting something in his jacket pocket.

Sean saw her and called out, "Hey, Brenna, what did you think of the rehearsal?"

"I thought it was fascinating. I can't wait for the taping tomorrow. I imagine things move quickly then. You and the chefs seem to have a good rapport."

"Tomorrow will be today on steroids. Pretty intense. I'll need to make sure the judges are engaged with the show." Sean strolled over to where Brenna was standing. "Last week they didn't participate enough, and even though the chefs are the stars, the fans need to get to know the judges too. I get along well with the chefs. I've gone to their restaurants a lot since I moved here from Kansas. I like all three of them, and the sous chefs they have working with them are pretty talented as well."

"The only restaurant I haven't been to is Chef Aaron's. I'll have to try his soon." Brenna said.

"Well, maybe we can grab a bite there soon. I'll see you tomorrow."

"See you then." Brenna didn't want to commit to going out with anyone at this time. She quite simply wasn't ready.

Glancing at her watch, she saw it was almost six. She walked around to see if anyone was still in the studio. Finally, she heard someone in the office area. She knocked on the open door before walking in and found Tim and Mathew discussing the script.

"Excuse me, I don't mean to interrupt, but I'm done for the day and checking to see if there's anything more you need from me."

Mathew looked up from his laptop. "We'll be sending you the script revisions in about an hour and you'll have to get them out tonight. And you know you're at the farmers market in the morning to pick up the supplies?"

"Yes. I made a note in our meeting this morning. And I have the email groups from Sally. I'll get the revised script out as soon as you send it," Brenna said.

"Well then, have a good evening. Nice to have you on the team," Tim said.

She went back to the studio to make sure she had all her equipment and heard footsteps coming in her direction. She walked around the corner and ran into Chef Mike.

"Hi, Chef Mike. What's up?" Brenna was surprised to see him here.

"Brenna, hey. I wasn't sure if anyone was still here. I think I left my tablet in the kitchen." Chef Mike raked his fingers through his short, black curly hair.

"I haven't seen it, and I was just cleaning up the kitchens. It might have been handed in to reception. I can check for you."

Brenna dropped her blazer on one of the audience chairs and hurried to reception. She found the desk drawers and cupboards closed up and locked. She returned to the studio.

"Everything's locked up, and I don't have a key. Are you sure you left it here?"

"It's the only place it could be. I'll check with my sous chef, Tina. She may have picked it up."

"Okay. Are you going to stay around? Because if you are, you'll have to lock up when you leave. I'm on my way out."

"No. I'm going to head out as well. We don't have keys to the building. And I need to get back to my restaurant. I'm testing a few new recipes."

They walked out together. Brenna had to check for the alarm code she had saved to her phone. She found it in the notes app and then entered it to arm the system. Chef Mike waited to walk her to her car.

"Thanks for waiting for me. How did you get in just now if you don't have a key?" Brenna asked.

"Sean was just leaving, and he held the door for me. Otherwise, I would've had to call someone. None of us have keys or alarm codes. I didn't realize the doors were locked so early."

"Sally told me the doors are locked at six and are armed until eight in the morning when she gets in." Brenna's Jeep chirped as she unlocked her door.

"Have a good night. I'll see you tomorrow." Chef Mike continued toward his dark-blue Toyota.

Brenna drove home satisfied with her day. She had work and, so far, the people she was working with seemed to be an interesting group. A six-week contract would fly by. And when the contract was finished, she was confident Jackie Randall would be able to find her something else.

The drive home wasn't too long. She caught glimpses of the lake on the drive. It shimmered in the sun, and people were walking along the shore.

The city had developed a couple of parks by the lake, taking advantage of the natural cove that had been carved out centuries before. One of the parks had running trails that Brenna and Emily used regularly.

Pulling into the driveway of the refurbished Victorian house, she let out a contented sigh. She felt happy for the first time in a long time, and for once, she wasn't worried about the next few weeks. She pulled into her assigned parking spot and locked up her Jeep after she got out. The sun was still shining through the large oak trees lining the property. The doctor that rented out the apartment on the first floor was outside barbequing something on the community grill. It was a nice fall evening.

Her cell phone rang. Checking the display, she saw it was Emily. "Hi, Em, what's happening? Don't tell me you're stuck at work."

"No way! Just connecting with you to see if you mind giving me a ride home afterward. My car's in the shop until tomorrow afternoon."

"Sure. Not a problem."

"Thanks. Oh, and Kate's going to join us. She's on her first day off. The hospital's moved her to the emergency room for a bit."

"It'll be good to see her again and catch up. I just got in and need to change out of my work clothes. I'll see you at Charlie's shortly. You're okay to get to the pub?"

"Yep. It's just a short walk from the office. I'll meet you there in about twenty minutes."

Brenna entered the foyer of the old Victorian house. The double doors leading into the house had leaded glass inserts, and the side panels were leaded glass as well. The foyer had a row of mailboxes above a mahogany sideboard. In a large rattan basket next to the sideboard was a recycling box to discard flyers and unwanted mail. On the opposite side of the wall, a large, oval mirror with two sconces was the perfect place for checking on your makeup before leaving. Brenna considered herself fortunate to be able to manage the building with its four other apartments. The arrangement with her father and her uncles meant she was the person the other tenants contacted if there were issues, and she, in turn, contacted her father. He took care of anything that needed to be done. It was a good arrangement for her. She lived rent-free, and the tenants were great. One was a doctor, two were lawyers, and the last one was a university professor in her forties. They were friendly and quiet.

She walked up the wide wooden staircase to the third floor and unlocked her door. The sun hit the stained-glass windows her father had put in next to the fireplace. The colors danced across the wooden floor. The apartment was starting to feel like home.

Brenna put away her things and headed for the shower in her master bathroom. The quick shower was refreshing. The body wash she used had a light, fresh fragrance. Changing out of her dressier clothes to comfortable jeans and a nice sweater, she thought out loud. "Everyone at the studio wears jeans or khakis. That's a bonus for me. I can dress down a bit." She pulled her reddish-gold hair into a messy bun and added taupe eye shadow. Her green eyes popped with the color. A gloss of color on her lips and some blush on her cheeks finished the look. She slipped her feet into some ballet flats and grabbed her leather jacket and bag.

Brenna drove the short distance to Charlie's Pub and arrived a few minutes before seven. Monday evenings weren't busy, and there was plenty of parking available in the lot.

Brenna walked in through the front door, pausing for a moment while her eyes adjusted to the light.

"Hi, Brenna, looking for Emily and Kate?" asked the hostess.

"Yes. Are they here already?"

"They just got here and are in the far booth on the right-hand side."

"Thanks. Catch you later." Brenna made her way to the back booth. She could hear the television at the bar broadcasting the start of Monday night football. No doubt, some of the local fans would show up soon. The bar was on the other side of the pub, away from the booths and tables. That allowed for families and couples to have a quieter meal.

One of the servers was at the booth handing out menus. As Brenna moved closer, she heard Emily say, "Brenna should be here in a few minutes. We'll wait to order drinks when she arrives."

"No need to wait. I'm here, and I'd love a vodka tonic, please."

Kate looked at Brenna, "Are we celebrating?"

"Well, I am. I started a new job today, so the first round's on me." Brenna took off her jacket and hung it on the hook by the booth.

Kate clapped her hands. "That's great news, Bren! I'll have a glass of the house red, please."

Emily said, "I'll have a vodka tonic as well."

The server said, "I'll leave the menus here and be right back with your drink order."

"So, tell us all. How did you hear about the job and how is it?" Emily distributed the menus, her movements quick and efficient.

Brenna filled them in on her day. She finished just as the server returned with their drinks and took their food order.

"You know the show's filmed in front of a live audience. You should come by. The host will be going into the audience and asking them to participate."

"What time tomorrow?" Kate asked.

"At one. But you should come to the studio around twelve-thirty to get a good seat."

"I might be able to get there for tomorrow's taping. My next shift at the hospital isn't until Thursday. You wouldn't mind if I showed up? I don't want to add to your stress level, but I've never been to a live show before. I think a cooking show would be fun."

"You won't add to my stress level. I think you'd enjoy it, and you might get selected to ask some questions."

Emily shook her head, her short, dark hair falling in place. "Well, I'm in court tomorrow at ten, dealing with a nasty divorce. The couple we're working with is quite the piece of work. Going to the taping would be a lot more fun than dealing with that, so I wish I could go."

Their meals arrived, and they gave their attention to the food. The meals at the pub were always good, and the chef liked to change things up a bit. Brenna's meal was a pulled pork sandwich with a side serving of fries and coleslaw. Emily had the cashew chicken with generous portions. Kate had a beet and kale salad.

Kate looked at her meal then at Emily's and Brenna's. "Seriously, you guys. How is it you can eat all of that and not gain an ounce while I have to be careful of absolutely everything I put in my mouth?"

Emily was silent for a moment. "I don't know. Maybe our amazing metabolism? Or our ancestors' genes?"

Brenna's shoulders shook with laughter. "Or it could be we actually work out every day. While you're hitting snooze, we're out for our morning run."

Kate shook her head. "That sounds like too much work. I think I'll stick with my salads and sleeping in."

The evening went by quickly with plenty of laughter and great conversation. Brenna's work phone pinged with an email from Tim.

Kate asked, "Is that a new phone?"

Brenna shrugged. "It's my work phone. I have to carry two phones now. I just got an email I've been waiting for. I have to forward it to some people. It'll only take a minute." Brenna checked the message. Yes, it was the revised script. She made sure to send it to the correct individuals and then put her phone back in her bag.

They left shortly after nine. Kate beeped her horn at them and waved as she drove her Volkswagen Beetle out of the parking lot.

"The job sounds like it will be good, doesn't it?" Emily asked.

"It does, but it's only a six-week contract. At least it gives me something different, and the pay is good. I'm going to be putting in long days. Tomorrow morning I have to get to the farmers market for some supplies before getting to the studio by seven. So, this is going to put a snag in our running schedule."

"Wow, I thought I worked long hours, but I don't start quite as early as you do. Are you going for a run anyway?"

"Yes, but I don't expect you out that early. Oh, for Pete's sake!" Brenna smacked her forehead. "I just remembered I forgot the list for the market in the office I was using."

"Hey, don't be so tough on yourself. It's only a list, and you've had quite the day, you know."

Brenna shook her head. "I know, I know, but it isn't 'just a list.' It's a huge list of items I have to pick up. It won't take me long to get it. I can see it on the table next to the printer. I'll go right after my run in the morning and grab it before going to the market."

They arrived at Emily's apartment building. Brenna pulled as close as she could to the front door.

"Thanks for the ride. I'll see you soon. Good luck tomorrow with the taping."

"No worries. And I'm looking forward to tomorrow. I think it will be fun. We'll catch up tomorrow night."

Emily got out of the car. Brenna waited until she saw the lights flicker on in her apartment before she left.

BRENNA GOT HER run in early the next morning. A quick shower and taking her cue from Margo's wardrobe choices, she put on a pair of jeans and a flannel shirt. She pulled her hair back in a low ponytail and applied minimal makeup. She hurried to the studio to get the list before heading to the market when it opened at six-thirty.

Pulling into the studio parking lot, she noticed a car parked in the spot usually reserved for Tim or Mathew. It looked similar to the car Chef Mike had been driving last night. "Why is he here this morning? And how did he get in? Or did his car break down last night?" Brenna thought out loud. She shook her head and made her way to the front door. She unlocked the door, walked in the vestibule, and entered her code for the alarm. The tiny lights on the alarm panel flashed from red to green.

She went through the reception area and walked to the back of the building, turning on lights as she made her way down the hallway. She saw the list on the table in the office and grabbed it, stuffing it in her purse. As she walked out, she noticed the lights were on in the studio. *What are those lights doing on? Is Chef Mike here? No one else is supposed to be here, and the cleaning crew should have turned everything off when they left.* Brenna sighed. *I better go check.*

She entered the studio and called out, "Is anyone here?" Hearing no answer, she started making her way toward the light switches. She caught a whiff of an unpleasant odor. "Ugh, what is that? I thought Tim said the cleaning crew used environmentally friendly cleaners." She turned the corner and walked into the studio kitchen and stopped in her tracks.

On the floor, behind one of the counters, was Chef Mike. There was a large kitchen knife in his chest, and he wasn't moving.

CHAPTER FOUR

Brenna took a deep breath and made her way behind the kitchen counter. She leaned over and looked at Chef Mike closely. His face was colorless, the freckles across his cheeks standing out like specks of dirt. There was a puddle of dark, inky liquid on the floor and around his chest where the knife was. Was that blood? She opened her mouth to say something, but no sound came out. She was pretty sure he was dead but had to make certain. She drew in a breath and whispered, "Just do it."

Moving closer to Chef Mike, but being careful where she stepped, she put her hand on his cheek. It felt cold and waxy, and his eyes were open and cloudy. She pushed her fingers on his neck, checking for a pulse. Nothing.

She backed away, pulling her phone out of her tool belt. She called 9-1-1 and waited for the call to go through.

"Nine-one-one, what is your emergency?"

"He's dead. I came in, and he's dead. He's just lying here on the floor." Brenna gasped as the words forced their way out of her mouth.

"Ma'am, did you say someone is dead?"

"I'm pretty sure he's dead. I just came into work, and he's on the floor, flat on his back. There's a big knife in his chest, and, and, and he's all pale and cold." Brenna was having difficulty making sense of what she had found. Her breathing was loud and shallow.

"Ma'am, you have to stay calm. Take a deep breath. Now, can you tell me where you are? I need your location to send help." The operator's voice was cool and authoritative.

Brenna took a deep breath and willed herself to calm down. "I'm at Studio One, five nineteen Harborview Road. I'm in the sound stage area, in the kitchen, at the back. The man I've found is Chef Mike Jones. He's one of the contestants on the cooking show I'm working on."

"Are you alone in the building?"

"I think so. Well, there's a car in the parking lot, but I think it might be his."

"I need you to step outside and wait for the police to arrive. They'll be there shortly."

"But then he'll be alone. It isn't right. I can't just leave him here." Brenna's voice cracked.

"Ma'am, you don't know if anyone else is in there. You have to get out. The police will arrive in a few minutes, and the ambulance is on its way too. We need to ensure your safety. Please, leave now. Go wait outside, at the front door of the building."

Brenna finally understood what the operator was saying and, although she didn't want to leave Chef Mike, she knew she had to. She made her way to reception and then out the front door. She stumbled down the steps. The operator stayed on the phone with her. A few minutes later, Brenna saw a police cruiser come to a stop in front of the studio.

"They're here. The police are here," Brenna told the operator.

The operator terminated the call, and Brenna watched the police as they came up the stairs.

"Did you call nine-one-one, ma'am?" the first officer asked.

"Yes." Brenna quickly explained what she had found.

"Ma'am, I'm going to ask you to go stand by the cruiser while my partner and I check out the building." The second officer, a woman, took Brenna by the arm and made sure she was standing by the cruiser before going into the building.

Brenna leaned against the police cruiser. She knew she had to let Tim know about this. Her hands were shaking. Fortunately, Tim's number was in her contacts and easy to find. His phone went directly to voice mail and she left a message for him to call her immediately. She called Mathew and left a message for him as well.

The ambulance arrived a few minutes later. The EMTs slammed the doors of the ambulance closed and then hurried into the building.

Brenna's phone rang. She glanced at it and saw it was Tim calling her back.

"Brenna, what's happening? You sounded upset." Tim's voice was choppy and garbled as if he was in a car.

Brenna gulped. "I, I, I found Chef Mike on the set. He had a knife in his chest, and I'm pretty sure he's dead. I called nine-one-one and the police. An ambulance arrived a few minutes ago." The wind had picked up and blew some of her hair out of her ponytail and across her cheek.

"What do you mean you found Chef Mike? Where are you?"

"I'm at the studio. I forgot the list for the market and came in to pick it up. I got the list and then noticed the lights were on in the studio. When I went to turn them off, that's, well, that's when I found Chef Mike."

"Did you call the police?" Tim fired the question at her.

"Yes, the police are here and so's the ambulance."

"I'll make my way to the studio. Don't speak to anyone about this. I'll get ahold of Mathew as well. We're going to have to do damage control."

"What? Damage control? Chef Mike is dead!" Brenna's voice rose.

"I'm aware of that. But it doesn't change that we still have to keep the press away from this. I'll be at the studio shortly. Mathew will join us, and we'll take charge of the situation." Tim disconnected the call before Brenna could say anything.

She looked at the phone and muttered, "You jerk! You don't care about Mike at all."

One of the police officers was making his way back to the cruiser. "Miss, is everything all right?"

Brenna shook her head. "I had to call my boss and tell him what's happening. He's not happy."

"People react to a crisis in different ways. There's no right way to handle things."

The quiet of the morning was broken by the sharp snap of car doors closing and footsteps coming toward her. Brenna turned around and groaned. *Oh no. Could today get any worse?* The detective assigned to the case was her cousin Bob McLean.

Bob spoke to the woman with him, and she headed up the building stairs. Bob continued toward Brenna.

"Brenna, what are you doing here?" Bob put his hands on his hips; his shield, hooked on his belt, glinted in the sunlight.

Brenna sighed. She didn't need any hassle from Bob. Since he made detective last year, he thought he had the answer to everything. He was even bossier than she remembered him as a teenager. She waited until he was closer to her before speaking. "I just started working at the studio as a production assistant. And I'm the one who found Chef Mike."

Bob was next to Brenna by now. He put his arm around her shoulders. "You found the body? Are you okay?"

He waited while she pulled herself together.

"I'm not hurt, but it was upsetting, to say the least. Not a nice way to start the day." Tears formed in her eyes, and her voice shook.

Bob reached in his pocket and handed her a handkerchief. "No, it wouldn't be. Listen, Bren, one of the officers will speak with you soon, but my partner and I will have to go through it as well. Just a quick question, for now. Did you notice anything out of the ordinary in there?"

"Other than Chef Mike with a knife in his chest?" Brenna wiped her eyes. "I don't know. This is my first full day. I know the door was locked. I used my key to unlock the door, and I entered my code for the alarm. I was supposed to be at the farmers' market this morning, but I forgot the list of supplies. I came in to pick it up. When I saw the lights on in the studio, I went to turn them off. That's when I found Chef Mike."

Bob asked, "How would someone gain access to the building once the doors are locked?"

"Well, you need a key for the front door, and you have to know the alarm code to get in. Everyone who works at the studio has his or her own key, and you have to sign for it. And the alarm code is different for each person. I know because I just had to go through this yesterday."

Bob looked around the street.

"So, what happens now?" Brenna leaned back against the police cruiser.

"Now my partner and I go in and assess the situation. You stay put. We'll be back to speak with you shortly." Bob opened the trunk of the police car and pulled out an emergency blanket. "Here, wrap up in this. I don't need you going into shock and not able to remember anything." He smiled as he wrapped Brenna up. "You'll be okay, kid."

"Thanks for the blanket. And for not being a jerk."

"Don't worry. It's still early. I'm sure you'll find a way to let me know I'm a jerk."

That brought a smile to Brenna. Bob might have been a pain, but he was family, and he'd look out for her. Brenna watched as he and his partner signed in at the top of the stairs and grabbed some paper booties to cover their shoes. They pulled on gloves as they entered the lobby. Brenna noticed the uniformed officers were setting up a perimeter around the building. The perimeter reached down the steps of the building and on the sidewalk. She was outside the perimeter.

Brenna's phone buzzed with a text.

> E: Just finished my run. Didn't beat your time yet!

Emily reporting in on her morning run. "I need to let her know what's happening before she hears it on the news," Brenna mumbled. She quickly composed a text.

> B: At studio. Stumbled onto Chef Mike's body in kitchen.
> E: OMG! R u ok?
> B: Yes
> E: Be there in 10. Don't argue
> B: Tks

Brenna heard someone calling her name and she turned toward the sound. "Oh great. Tim. Just what I don't need," she muttered under her breath.

"Brenna!" Tim called her name again and waved his arm.

Brenna raised her arm. "Tim, I'm here."

She watched as he made his way to her. She saw him pull out his phone and put it to his ear. She could hear him speaking to someone.

"Yes, you need to get here as soon as possible. We're going to have to do damage control. Brenna found him." Tim paused, glanced at Brenna, and sniffed. "Yes, the new hire." He disconnected the call and looked at Brenna.

"Hi," she said.

"Right. Mathew just got your message. We're going to meet at the coffee shop across the street. We'd like you to be there as well."

"The police want to speak with me about what I found. I'm afraid the meeting will have to wait."

One of the patrol officers came out and made her way to speak to Brenna. "Ma'am, I have a few questions for you. Please come with me. Sir, you need to move off this sidewalk and over to the other side of the street. If you're involved with the studio, we'll have to talk to you as well."

The officer pointed to a bench, and she and Brenna walked away from Tim.

They sat on the bench, and the officer opened a notebook. "Now, we'll start with your name and why you were here at the studio."

"Brenna Flynn, I'm the production assistant for the show, *Bayview Cooks!* I started working here yesterday. I came by to pick up a list of items I need from the farmers market for today's taping."

"And then what?"

Brenna recounted what she had seen and done to the officer. She paused to take a breath. "He's dead, isn't he?"

The officer watched her carefully. "Yes, ma'am. The paramedics have pronounced him dead. The medical examiner will be coming in, as will the crime scene technicians to work the scene."

"That's awful. He was just lying there."

"Now, ma'am, I need to know what you touched in the kitchen."

Brenna's brow furrowed, and she pulled the blanket closer. "All the light switches and the kitchen counter. I might have touched a couple of the chairs. And well, I did touch Chef Mike's face and neck. I touched his face 'cause he seemed pale—and his neck, well, I was trying to find a pulse."

"Did you touch the knife, ma'am?"

"No! Why would I do that?" Brenna gasped at the question.

"That's all for now. Please stay close by. The detectives will want to speak with you as soon as they're done inside." The officer closed her notebook, rose, and started walking back to the building.

The street had been blocked off by two patrol cars, and crime scene tape surrounded the perimeter. Several officers were taking names of individuals who had come in for work at the studio and directing them to an area across the street to wait to be questioned.

Brenna walked across the street, where Tim was standing off to the side. He was busy on his phone. He looked up as she approached him. "What did the police want?"

"Just wanted to know what happened and why I was here."

Tim nodded. "And remind me why you were here? I thought you were going to the market this morning."

Brenna explained why she'd come in. "Did Mathew say when he'll be here?"

"He was getting home from his run. He was going to come straight away. We'll need you at our meeting at the coffee shop," Tim reminded her.

"I understand that, but I don't know what I can contribute to the meeting."

Mathew arrived as Brenna finished speaking. "I'll tell you what you can contribute. You can tell us what you found, and then we'll need to work with our PR firm on damage control."

Brenna shook her head. "I don't think the police are going to let me talk to anyone about what I found."

"You're right about that." Bob's voice cut in before Mathew or Tim could say anything.

"Who are you?" Mathew asked.

"Detective Bob McLean and my partner, Detective Clare Morris. And you are?"

"Mathew Smith, producer of *Bayview Cooks!*"

"Tim Harris, executive producer."

Detective Morris looked calm and fully in control of the situation. Although it was early in the morning, she was dressed in a black suit and a red shirt. Her long black hair was pulled back in a bun. She wore flat shoes but was almost the same height as Bob, and he was six feet two.

Detective Morris pulled out her notepad. "We're going to need to speak with both of you. Bob, why don't you take Mr. Harris, and I'll chat with Mr. Smith here."

Tim glared at Bob. "We have a meeting planned with our PR agency. Is this going to take long?"

Bob pointed in the direction of the patrol car and led Tim away from Mathew and Detective Morris. Brenna could hear Bob say, "It will take as long as it takes. And your PR agency will need to cool their jets."

Detective Morris nodded her head at Mathew. "Follow me, please."

Mathew looked at Brenna. "Stick around and when the PR agency reps show up, ask them to wait for us in the coffee shop."

Brenna simply nodded her head. She couldn't believe these two. Chef Mike was dead, and they were worried about PR.

CHAPTER FIVE

"Brenna, Brenna!"

Brenna turned around and saw Emily waving at her. She had just stepped out of a cab and was making her way to Brenna. She watched as one of the patrol officers stopped Emily. They exchanged a few words, and then the officer permitted Emily through. Emily was still dressed for her morning run. A hoodie, ball cap, running pants, and her running shoes. She certainly didn't look like a lawyer this morning.

Emily wrapped her arms around Brenna in a hug. "Are you okay? You aren't hurt, are you?"

Overcome with emotion, Brenna couldn't say a word. Emily pulled her away at arm's length and took a good look at her. Emily's brown eyes looked worried.

Brenna nodded. "I'm fine. I'm not hurt, just really upset. This is the first time I've found someone dead. And it isn't fun."

Emily pulled Brenna close. "Come on. Let's find a place to sit." Emily led Brenna to a bench, away from the crowd that was starting to gather. "So, do you want to talk about it?"

Brenna put the heels of her hands on her eyes. She felt as if she'd been at the studio forever, but, in reality, it had been about ninety minutes. "Yes, I guess I do. I need to put this in perspective. I didn't know Chef Mike well, but I'm really rattled."

"Have you spoken with the police?"

"One of the patrol officers asked me a few questions. My cousin Bob is on the case. He spoke to me for a bit when he got here."

"And you found Chef Mike?"

Brenna nodded. "What did the patrolman want from you?"

"He wanted to know why I was here. I told him you were my client."

Bob and Detective Morris arrived just then.

"Brenna, we're going to want to ask you a few questions. Emily, what are you doing here?" Bob asked.

Emily stood and dusted off the seat of her running pants. "Brenna contacted me. She's my client."

Bob raised his eyebrow. "I don't think Brenna needs an attorney at this time. And you aren't a criminal attorney." Bob knew Emily almost as well as he knew Brenna. Growing up, Emily had spent a lot of time at Brenna's house.

Detective Morris spoke up. "Ms. Flynn, I'll be speaking with you. Since Bob is your cousin, he's going to have to step away from interacting with you about this case."

"Is that true, Bob?" Brenna asked.

"Yes. But Detective Morris is first-rate. You're in good hands with her."

"This won't take long. I just have a few questions for you, and then you'll be free to go." Detective Morris pulled out her notebook.

Emily stood next to Brenna. "I'm not going anywhere."

Brenna looked at Detective Morris. "Any objection to that, Detective?"

"Not at all. Now, was there anyone else in the building when you got here?"

"I don't think so. The alarm was on, and the hallway lights were off too. The only reason I went to the studio was because the lights were on and they shouldn't have been."

"Why were you here so early this morning? Are these normal working hours for you?"

Brenna explained again about the missing list.

"Do you know why Chef Mike would have been here?"

Brenna looked at Detective Morris blankly. "No. Last night he came in looking for his tablet before I left. He might have come back. But he doesn't have keys to the building."

"When did he leave last night?"

"He left with me at around six-thirty. And he told me he was going back to his restaurant."

"And have you seen the knife before?"

"I don't know. The chefs had their knives for the rehearsal yesterday, and there are knives in the kitchen drawers. They all look the same to me."

"Did you touch the knife or any of the knives at the rehearsal yesterday?"

"Well, I didn't touch the knife in Chef Mike. But, I had to make certain all the cutlery in the drawers was in the correct location. That was yesterday after rehearsal. Apparently, someone had moved everything around. The chefs kept their personal knives in their knife rolls."

"Anything else you can add?"

Brenna thought for a moment. "I don't think so. I started here yesterday, and I don't know the people very well. Chef Mike seemed like a nice guy. I've been to his restaurant before. And he and my older brothers went to high school together."

"Detective, if we're done here, can I take Brenna home?" Emily asked.

"We're done for now. We may have some more questions for you later today, so don't be surprised if you get a call from me." Detective Morris closed her notebook and started walking toward Bob.

"Emily, I can't leave yet. I have to meet with Tim, Mathew, and the PR people." Brenna's voice was hushed. She didn't want anyone to overhear her.

"I don't think so. You're wiped out and need to get home. I don't care what they say. You don't have to meet with anyone." Emily's voice was firm and unwavering. "I'll deal with those two for you."

Emily strode toward Tim and Mathew. Emily might have only been five feet tall, but she was a fighter. Brenna followed her.

"Excuse me. Which one of you is in charge?" Emily asked.

Tim looked at her. "I am. Who are you?"

"Emily Connors, Brenna's attorney. I'm also the person who's going to make sure Brenna gets some rest today. So, any meeting you had planned is going to have to wait."

Tim raised his eyebrows, and Mathew smiled. "I guess she told you, didn't she?"

Brenna didn't want to lose her job. "Em. Please, I can deal with this."

Emily shook her head. "I don't think so."

Tim raised his hands. "Okay. Enough already. Margaret Shaw, from the PR agency, has been delayed, and we can't meet with her until later this morning. The reporters are here, and they aren't getting any information from the police or us. And I need to connect with John, and he isn't answering his phone."

"Is there anything that needs to be done about the crew coming in? There was a meeting scheduled for eight-thirty this morning," Brenna reminded him.

Mathew looked up from his phone. "We need to let them know the studio is closed and the taping canceled for today. I also have to connect with the college to let them know the students can't come in today, either."

"What students?" Brenna asked.

"We have students from Bayview City College who are doing co-op placements here. They're working in the editing department. Tim, I'll need to talk to the student advisor from the college."

"Do you have the number?" Tim asked.

"Yes, in my contacts. I'll be as discreet as possible. I'll deal with them if you can deal with the crew. We really need to get this out soon. And we also have to deal with the sponsors." Mathew's shoulders sagged.

"What sponsors?" Brenna felt out of the loop on who was involved with the show.

Tim pressed his lips together in a straight line. "The sponsors we have for the show. All the appliances are provided by local merchants, and some of the farmers and stores are giving us lower costs on the food and other supplies in return for advertising with us. Gawd, this is a nightmare."

The two detectives arrived in time to hear Tim's comment.

Bob spoke up, "We're going to need a few more things from you before you leave."

Detective Morris added, "We need a liaison from the show who can work with us. Someone who'll be able to provide us with the contact information for everyone associated with the show. Can you recommend anyone?"

Mathew glanced at Brenna and then nodded at Tim. "I think Brenna would be well-positioned to do that. Brenna, you have all the contact information for everyone associated with the show?"

Brenna frowned. "Well, after hearing about the students and then the sponsors, I'm not sure I know everyone who's involved."

"The distribution lists and the contact lists Sally provided you with should include everyone. Can you check it now so we can be certain?" Tim asked.

Brenna pulled out her phone and checked to see what information was available. "Yes. It appears I do have all the contacts, including the sponsors and the contact for the college as well." Brenna looked at Detective Morris. "What else will I need to do?"

"We'll connect with you when the studio and offices are available for you to use."

"Sure, that's fine. I don't have a problem with being the liaison."

Detective Morris handed her a business card. "Can you send me a message so I'll have your contact information in my phone?"

Brenna quickly sent a text to Detective Morris. "Bob, your contact information is the same, right?"

"Hasn't changed. You should have it," Bob replied.

"I do, on my personal phone. I'll transfer it to the work phone shortly."

"Detective, what happens now?" Tim asked.

Detective Morris cleared her throat. "Right. A few more follow-up questions. Can you let us know how many people would have had access to the studio last night?"

"Anyone who has a key. That must be about twenty people," Mathew said.

"Does anyone who isn't working here have access?" Bob asked.

Mathew shrugged and said to Tim, "Frank Simons. Did he turn in his keys, or were they picked up?"

Tim shook his head. "I don't know. We'd have to check with Sally Marshall at reception. I think she's the person who would have received them. If they were returned."

"Who's Frank Simons?" Detective Morris asked.

"He was the production assistant here, and last weekend, he was arrested for drug possession. We haven't been able to get any of his equipment back, and I'm not sure we have the keys he was assigned," Tim answered.

Brenna spoke up, "Even if you don't have the keys, the IT company should have deactivated his alarm code."

Bob made a note. "When can we speak with Sally Marshall?"

"I saw her speaking with one of the uniformed officers a few minutes ago," Brenna said.

"Good. We'll touch base with her shortly." Bob made a note in his notebook.

"Thanks for the information. We'll continue to work the scene with the CSU. We're going to have the rest of the crew come to the police station. Officers will question them on anything they may have seen or heard. The ME will take charge of transporting the body and performing the autopsy." Detective Morris was definitely in control.

"We also need to speak with Chef Mike's next-of-kin. We'll be doing that in the next hour. Until that's done, no one can talk about what's happened here." Bob gave Mathew a pointed look.

"You know we have to be able to speak with our sponsors about what is happening and the same with our crew." Mathew almost spat the words out at Bob.

Detective Morris' carefully sculpted brows dropped, and her black eyes narrowed. "What part of what Detective McLean just told you didn't you understand? This is a police investigation. Under no circumstances are you to inform anyone about the identity of the victim or the cause of death."

Tim spoke up before Mathew had a chance to respond. "Detective, can we tell the crew and sponsors that today's taping will need to be rescheduled due to a police matter?"

Detective Morris checked with Bob, and he nodded. "Yes, and that's all you can say until the Public Affairs Officer makes a statement. Are we clear?"

"Perfectly," Tim said. He pulled out his smartphone and tapped some keys. Tim looked at Brenna. "I'm sending a message to the crew, chefs, and sponsors that the studio is closed for today and that you will be the contact for any questions. I've included your contact information in the email. Do you have any concerns about that, Brenna?"

"Well, there isn't a lot of information I can share with them. You heard the police. We can't say anything about Chef Mike until his next-of-kin has been notified."

"That's true, but you can provide them with reassurances that we will continue with the show. I think a lot of them will be worried about their employment in the next few days. Besides, the news is going to break on Chef Mike very soon. His family lives here in town, and the police will be able to notify them immediately." Tim rubbed his face, pushing his glasses off to the side.

"Fine. I'll deal with the questions as diplomatically as possible. I'll tell them the show will resume taping as soon as the studio is cleared, that they will be questioned by the police simply because they work for the show, and that we'll notify them by email when we have access to the studio."

Mathew gathered his messenger bag. "Brenna, where are you going to be?"

"I'm going home. Anything I need to do can be done from there."

"Right. We're going to have to adjust our schedule and find a new chef." Tim picked up his backpack.

There was a noise from the area the reporters were confined in. Brenna turned around and saw they were watching the front of the building.

Coming out of the doors, the ME was directing her staff to move the stretcher carrying Chef Mike to the van to transport him to the morgue. Brenna sat back on the bench to watch.

Mathew looked up from his phone at her. "Are you going to be okay?"

"I guess so."

"Still, it has to be upsetting finding him like you did."

"I still can't believe this has happened. I hope the police solve this soon."

Emily stood. "I take it we're done for now?"

Mathew put his phone in his pocket. "Yes. Tim and I will meet with the PR agency shortly."

Emily linked her arm through Brenna's and walked to Brenna's Jeep. "Perfect. Got your keys? 'Cause you aren't driving."

Brennan searched her bag for the keys, pulled them out, and gave them to Emily. "Thanks, Em. I'm so glad you were here."

CHAPTER SIX

As Emily drove to Brenna's apartment, Brenna thought back to the events of the morning. She slumped in the passenger seat and leaned her head back on the headrest. She closed her eyes until the car came to a stop.

Emily shook Brenna's arm. "Brenna, come on. We're home. Let's go in so I can get you some coffee."

Familiar with Brenna's apartment, Emily headed straight for the Keurig. Brenna took off her tool belt and jacket, dropping them on the chair in the living room. She turned on the television, curious to see what, if anything, was being reported about the murder.

The local station had a special news bulletin. The on-air reporters were rehashing the same news. A body had been found on the set. They didn't know who it was. They suddenly cut away to the scene, and Brenna saw a woman on the screen and noticed Tim and Mathew standing behind her. "Oh, for Pete's sake! I don't believe this."

Emily asked. "What's happening?"

"Just listen."

"Good morning. My name is Margaret Shaw. I'm going to make a brief statement, and there will be no questions answered. This morning, at approximately six-fifteen, a studio employee entered the building and found someone believed to be dead. Police were notified and are on the scene. Studio One is cooperating fully with the police. Production on

Bayview Cooks! will continue once the studio is released. We will provide more information when we are able."

Margaret's voice was steady and strong throughout her speech. Brenna wondered if she knew who had been killed.

The reporters shouted questions at her. "Who was found in the studio?" "Is it murder?" "What are the police saying?" "Who was the studio employee who found the body?"

Margaret walked away from the reporters. Mathew and Tim followed her quickly.

Brenna's landline and cell phone started ringing. She answered her cell.

"This is Detective Morris. Who was that speaking with reporters?" Detective Morris' voice cracked.

"I believe that was the spokesperson for the PR agency the studio is working with. Her name is Margaret Shaw."

"Right. I'll be in touch with Tim Harris directly. Please send me his number. What part of not speaking to anyone did they not understand? Talking to the media?" Detective Morris made a rude sound. "We haven't even made a statement."

"Detective, I voiced my concern to Tim and Mathew, but my voice didn't carry a lot of weight."

"I'll be following up with Mr. Harris right away. I'll be in touch with you shortly. Please send me his number."

Brenna hung up and texted Tim's number to Detective Morris.

Another call came through on Brenna's cell.

"Brenna, thank goodness you're okay." Her mom's voice sounded relieved.

"Hi, Mom. I'm fine. I can't talk about what's happened at the studio. The police were there, and they were pretty clear on what they expect from everyone." Brenna's voice broke.

"Oh no! Are you at home? Do you want me to come over?"

"I'm home now. And no, Mom. I'll be okay. Emily's here. She came to the studio when she heard what happened. We're going to have coffee, and then I have a few things I need to get done for work."

"Work! What do you mean?"

"I have some things I need to deal with. We're shut down until the police release the set. And Tim and Mathew have a few things that I need to get done right away."

"Brenna, I'm worried about you. You sound shaky."

Brenna sighed. "I am. And Mathew and Tim are behaving like jerks. All they're thinking about is the bottom line."

"Why don't you come here for lunch? By then, you'll have some of the work out of the way and you can relax a bit."

"Sounds like a plan. I'll send you a text when I head over."

"Don't bother. Just come by when you're ready. I'm home all day."

Emily handed Brenna a cup of coffee with cream and sugar, just the way she liked it after she set down her cell. "I take it that was your mom?"

"Yes. She saw the reports on the news. And the first caller, well that was Detective Morris. Not at all happy, I have to say."

"Well, you can't blame her, but you are in no way responsible for Tim and Mathew's actions with the PR agency."

"I know. And she did say she was going to speak with me later. I'm not sure what else she needs."

Emily looked around the kitchen. "Do you have food here?"

Brenna took a sip of her coffee and nodded. "In the cupboard. There are some bagels and peanut butter."

Emily opened the pantry and pulled out the food. "Time to get some carbs in you. I bet you haven't eaten yet."

Brenna's phone pinged with a text.

> J: Are you alright?

"Who's texting you? Tim or Mathew?" Emily asked.

Brenna sighed, "It's Jackie Randall. I can't tell her a lot, but I'll let her know I'm okay."

> B: I'm fine. I can't talk about what happened, but I'm safe.
> J: Ok, let me know if I can help.

They ate a quick breakfast, and Emily left to get ready for work, but not before extracting a promise that Brenna would take care of herself.

"Not to worry. I'll deal with whatever comes up this morning. And I'm going to Mom's for lunch, so I'll get a break then."

"Good. I'll text you when I'm done in court later today. If you need anything from me, you know how to reach me."

Brenna opened the laptop from the studio. Her email was flooded with messages from the crew members. She took a few minutes to put together a standard answer that addressed most of the concerns and sent it out as an answer to the questions.

Margo called her cell phone. "Brenna, I just spoke with Tim, and he told me you're the person who found Chef Mike. Are you okay? That must have been a horrible experience . . ."

Brenna was taken aback. Tim shouldn't have told Margo who died and that Brenna had found him. "Um, well, I'm okay. I'm actually surprised Tim gave you all that information. The police were pretty clear no information was to be leaked out."

Margo's voice broke. "Well, I was pretty worried. I didn't know what happened and who it could have been. He didn't want to tell me, but he finally did. You've been connecting with the cast and crew. How are they reacting?"

Brenna walked to the Keurig and put in another pod. She was going to need more coffee to get through this morning. "I've had a lot of questions. I came up with a standard answer—the studio will reopen when the police release it—everyone will be expected to return to work as soon as the studio is released. I've had the 'who died?' question from just about everyone, but I'm not discussing it with them."

"I'm going to be meeting with Tim and Mathew later this morning. Have you been able to connect with John Simms, the director?"

"No, but John was part of the email list Tim sent the message to. I haven't heard from him directly. Why?"

"No particular reason. Tim needs John to attend the meeting, and he's not answering his phone."

"Has someone sent a text? He might be able to respond to that."

"Good point. I don't think anyone has tried. I'll send him a message. I'm sure everything is fine. I'll let you go. I wanted to touch base to make sure you were okay."

"Thanks for the call, Margo. I'm going to finish up here and grab some lunch with my mom. I'll talk to you later on."

Brenna worked steadily until close to noon. She had the television on for some background noise, and as she was closing her laptop, she noticed the police were on the news. She turned the volume up.

Detective Morris was standing in front of the studio. "Thank you for your patience. I'll make this brief. The victim found this morning at Studio One Productions was Chef Mike Jones. He was found by an employee of Studio One early this morning. Our investigation is ongoing. If anyone has any information on Chef Jones and his activities in the last week, please contact our office." She turned away from the microphone and walked away.

The Public Affairs Officer fielded several questions.

Brenna slumped back. *Well, they must have connected with his family and his fiancée to release his name.* Brenna was thankful her name hadn't been mentioned in the report. She didn't need that notoriety. Dealing with the fallout from her husband Dave's gambling and his death had been challenging enough. Brenna's head was spinning, and she needed a break.

Grabbing both her personal and work cell phones and her bag, Brenna headed out the door to have lunch with her mom.

She drove through the downtown core on her way to her parents' house. The city planners had worked hard on revitalizing the downtown area and had taken full advantage of the lake views. Many of the businesses had access to the boardwalk following the lakeshore. The boardwalk led to a couple of parks where picnic facilities were available. In the summer, several food trucks set up shop along the boardwalk. The boardwalk went as far as the marina and then looped back to the downtown area.

Her parents lived in one of the older subdivisions. Her grandfather had purchased several properties close together and had deeded them to his children. Brenna's father, his brother, and his sister lived within a block of each other. Brenna's family home was on a hill overlooking the bay. The marina was on the left-hand side of the bay, and in the summer, sailboats dotted the water. Brenna and her brothers and cousins had spent a lot of time on the water. To the right of the bay was Pebble Island, so named because of the pebbles that formed the beach. The island had a large resort on it, and no motorized vehicles were permitted on the island, except for emergency and delivery vehicles.

Brenna pulled into her parents' circular driveway and realized her mom had company. Her phone pinged with a text from Emily letting her know court was finished for the day. Brenna hopped out of her car and hurried to the back door.

"Mom, are you here?" Brenna opened the door.

"Brenna, is that you? We're in the kitchen. Come in." Brenna's mom, Cecile Flynn, was in her mid-fifties and had recently retired from being a high school teacher. Cecile walked around the corner and pulled Brenna into a hug.

Brenna allowed herself to sink into her mom's arms. She felt safe and secure.

"Who's here?" Brenna murmured against her mom's shoulder.

"Rita and Jackie Randall." Cecile gave Brenna a quick kiss on the cheek. "When Rita heard there had been a murder at the studio, she called to check on you. And then she insisted on coming when I told her you'd be here at lunchtime. Jackie called me this morning really worried about you. I told her you'd be here at lunch, and she asked if she could be here."

Brenna sighed. "It's fine. I don't mind Aunt Rita being here. She's family. It's been a crazy morning. And Jackie is almost family; she's been part of our lives for as long as I can remember."

Cecile walked Brenna into the kitchen. Rita got up from her chair and scurried over to wrap her arms around Brenna. Rita held onto Brenna and gently rubbed her back. "How are you holding up?"

Brenna's eyes filled with tears. She shook her head and disengaged from her aunt's embrace. "I'm doing the best I can. It's been a shock."

Jackie stood for a hug as well. "I was so worried about you. I wouldn't be able to forgive myself if anything happened to you."

"Not your fault, Jackie. The studio is as safe as anywhere else in town. It was just my luck I found Chef Mike."

"Still, let me see if there's something else that's come up for work." Jackie's face wore a frown.

Brenna shook her head. "I'd like to stay at the studio and see what happens. There hasn't been a lot of work available."

Jackie sighed. "Fine, but I'll keep my eyes open in case something comes up."

Cecile busied herself, making Brenna a cup of coffee. "What are the police saying?"

"Not a lot. Apparently, everyone at the studio's under suspicion simply because we work there." Brenna accepted the coffee from her mother and took a drink. Sweet and creamy, just the way she liked it. "Bob's new partner, Detective Morris, is in charge. Because we're related, he can't be the lead in the investigation. He and Detective Morris had a lot of questions for all of us, especially me. We don't know how the killer got in or how Chef Mike got in. Chef Mike told me the chefs didn't have a key to the building. Someone from the studio must have let him in." Brenna took another sip of coffee. "You need a key to unlock the door, and you also need to know the alarm code. We each have an individual code." She put her coffee cup down. "I don't know why someone would want to kill Chef Mike. From what I understand, he was one of the nice guys. He was always willing to help someone out, and some of the work he did with the restaurant went to help the less fortunate in Bayview."

Rita gave an unladylike snort. "Well, yes, now that he's dead, he's going to be made into a saint. You can be sure he had some secrets or he wouldn't have been killed."

Brenna considered what her aunt was saying. "How well did you know him? You were a reporter on the city paper for years. Did you cover him in any of your stories?"

Rita took a sip of coffee. "I remember when he first started out. He had just come back from working all over the country. He didn't have a lot of savings and couldn't get a start-up loan. Your uncle Ian and I loaned him the down payment for his restaurant. The restaurant took off quickly, and he made money hand over fist. He repaid the loan in just over a year. He was a rare mix of a really good cook and a good business head."

Brenna said, "I sense a 'but' in there somewhere."

Her mom brought her a thick sandwich and a bowl of soup. "Yes, there is. A short while after he got started, there was some talk about a problem at the culinary school where he had studied. Nothing definite came out, but it seemed as if he, Chef Rosa, and Chef Aaron had all gone to the same school and there had been some issues with another student. Rita, do you remember that?"

Rita nodded. "Yes. It was just as Chef Rosa was getting her restaurant under way. Someone wrote a letter to the paper and made a reference to a scandal back in their cooking school days. I couldn't believe the editor allowed the letter to go in, but he did. Guess he was looking to sell papers. I also remember there was a big increase in the interest in their restaurants, and they all did well from then on. It was as if they had something to prove."

"Any idea what the scandal was? I mean, what could it be at a cooking school? It isn't like you can cheat on your finals." Brenna was making notes on her phone.

"I asked Chef Mike what it was all about. He told me, in confidence, that a former classmate had come looking for work with the three of them because he had lost his job at a restaurant in Ann Arbor. None of them wanted to hire him because he had accused them of bullying him at school. They almost got kicked out of school because of his accusations. The profs at the school spoke up on their behalf."

Jackie put her coffee down. "I vaguely remember someone coming in to see me a few years ago. He was a chef, had studied at the same school as the three you're working with. But his references weren't good. I'll take a look in my files when I get back to the office."

Brenna nodded. "If you find any information, could you tell me? I'd like to know more about this person."

"Why do you want to know more about him? You are not to get involved with this. It's a police matter." Her mom appeared less than pleased.

"Cecile, you know Brenna has a way with people. They tell her all sorts of things they wouldn't think of telling anyone else." Rita tried to smooth things over.

"Mom, I'm just going to check on a few facts and talk to some people. I had some tough questions to answer this morning. Some of the crew wanted answers, and I didn't have any. We knew Chef Mike. He spent a lot of time here with Brady and Jim when they were in high school. He was likely killed by someone he knew, probably someone we know too. I don't know why he would have been at the studio last night or how he got in, and I'm going to check it out."

"Well, it sounds as if you've made up your mind. But I'm warning you; you best be very careful. I'll know if you get too involved." Cecile pointed her finger at Brenna. "Come on, let's eat some of this soup."

Brenna's phone rang.

"Brenna, Detective Morris here. I'm going to need you to come into the station to go over your statement, and I have some additional questions. When can you come in?"

"I can be there at two."

"Fine. Come to the station and ask the desk sergeant for me."

Brenna disconnected and noticed Jackie, Rita, and Cecile watching her closely.

"It was Detective Morris. She needs me to go in and go over my statement with her. I'll go as soon as I have lunch with you."

"Well, you aren't going in alone; that's for certain," Cecile said. "You either take me with you, or you get Emily to go with you. If she can't, she'll know another lawyer who can help you with this."

Rita agreed. "She's right, Brenna. You don't want to talk to the police without someone there to make sure your rights are protected. Make the call."

Jackie nodded in agreement.

"Let me touch base with Em. She had to go to court this morning with some clients, but I think her calendar is free this afternoon." Brenna connected with Emily and filled her in.

"Of course I'll go with you. Text me when you leave your mom's, and I'll meet you at the station. Do not go in without me. Got it?"

"I understand. I don't think the police would do anything to trip me up, but it's probably a good thing to have you with me."

CHAPTER SEVEN

Brenna texted Emily as she was getting ready to leave her mom's house. Emily was waiting outside the police station when Brenna arrived.

"Thanks for meeting me, Em. Mom and Aunt Rita wouldn't let me leave without having a lawyer with me. Mom threatened to come as well. That would have been a disaster. And Jackie Randall was at lunch too. She's told me she's looking for different work for me."

"No worries. I'm pretty sure this is just standard procedure, but it doesn't hurt to have someone who's familiar with the law with you. I'll make sure Detective Morris sticks to what she needs to. But first, do you have a dollar?"

Brenna raised her eyebrows. "A dollar? Why?"

"Because that's my retainer. Hand it over." Emily held out her hand.

Brenna reached for her wallet and gave Emily the dollar.

"Perfect. Now, I'm your attorney of record. Anything you say to me is privileged information." Emily slipped the dollar bill into her purse. "Has anything happened since you and I talked this morning?"

Brenna said, "No, I dealt with questions from the crew most of the morning and then lunch with mom, Jackie, and Aunt Rita."

Emily nodded. "Good. Let's go meet with Detective Morris."

They entered the police station and went up to the desk sergeant.

"Hi, I'm Brenna Flynn. Detective Morris asked me to come in to go over my statement from this morning."

"Right. Just one second." The sergeant made a call. "Someone will be out to get you in a few minutes. Have a seat in the waiting area."

A few minutes later, one of the uniformed officers came around and motioned for them to follow him. They went through a secured doorway and walked down a hallway. Brenna opened her mouth to say something, and Emily shook her head and shushed her. The uniformed officer escorted them to an interview room and asked them to have a seat.

Brenna asked Emily, "Is this how it normally works?"

Emily nodded. "I don't think you're considered a person of interest or a suspect. You haven't done anything wrong. Don't worry. This is a formality."

Detective Morris walked in as Emily finished speaking. She cleared her throat. "Brenna, thanks for coming in. And I'm sorry, I didn't catch your name this morning."

"Detective Morris, Emily Connors. She's my attorney."

"Good to meet you, Detective."

Detective Morris nodded. "Thanks. I do have a few more questions to ask Brenna."

Brenna leaned forward, put her elbows on the table, and waited for the questions.

Detective Morris took one of the chairs and opened her notebook. "You indicated this morning that the doors were locked and the alarm was activated. Is that correct?"

"Yes. I remember it was locked because I was worried about entering the code in correctly. I didn't want the alarm to go off. Last night, Chef Mike was with me when I looked it up on my phone, and he waited to walk me to my car in the parking lot. But I wasn't the last person out of the building."

"We'll get to that in a minute. Who has the alarm code?" Detective Morris asked.

"Anyone who has a key. Each key holder has their own personal code. There isn't a general code for everyone."

"Do you know anything about this Frank Simons? The man you replaced?"

"No. I thought the person I was replacing had moved to a different job."

"And where were you last night?"

"I was out for dinner with Emily and Kate. I got home after nine and went to bed by ten. My morning started pretty early today. I was supposed to get to the market to pick up supplies for the taping."

"And were you alone from nine until this morning?"

"Yes. I live alone."

"You didn't speak with anyone or see anyone?"

Brenna looked at Emily. Were these routine questions? They didn't sound like it.

Emily asked, "Detective, what are you getting at?"

Detective Morris sat back. "Brenna's code was the only one used to open the doors last night after everyone was gone, and it was used at midnight. So, Brenna, again, you're positive you didn't leave your place after you got home?"

"No, I didn't leave my apartment until five-thirty this morning when I went out for my run."

"Detective, is Brenna a suspect?" Emily put her hand on Brenna's arm.

"Given that her code was the one used last night and her fingerprints were found on the door, light switches, and counters, she's a person of interest."

Brenna gasped. "Am I under arrest?"

Detective Morris narrowed her eyes. "At this time, we don't have sufficient evidence to arrest anyone."

"This is nuts! I didn't kill Chef Mike. My fingerprints are on the door because I opened it this morning. And yeah, I turned on the lights, and I put my hands on the counters. I told you all of this earlier today." Brenna's voice rose as she spoke with the detective.

Emily squeezed Brenna's arm. "Brenna, that's enough. Detective, if she isn't under arrest, we're leaving."

"Em, this isn't right. I haven't done anything wrong."

Detective Morris interrupted. "Thank you for coming in. Unless you have anything to add, I'm going to strongly recommend you don't leave town."

Emily pulled on Brenna's arm. "Come on, Brenna. Let's go."

"Oh, before you leave, one more thing."

Brenna glared at the detective. "What?"

"You can let Mr. Harris know the CSU team cleared the offices and the conference rooms. You'll have access to those rooms tomorrow morning. The set, however, is still closed."

"Right. I'll let him know." Brenna rubbed her face.

They walked out of the police station, and Emily marched them both to her car.

Brenna sagged against Emily's car. Her shoulders slumped, and her head bowed. Emily stood next to her, quiet for a few minutes.

"I didn't kill Chef Mike." Brenna's voice was so low Emily leaned in closer.

"I know you didn't. And I'm surprised Bob let Detective Morris question you like that."

"He isn't allowed to talk to me because we're family."

"I know that. And how do the police have your fingerprints?"

Brenna looked at Emily. "When I worked for the city, I had to be fingerprinted. They must still be on file."

"Look, I think you need to hire a criminal lawyer. Someone with experience in this field. My specialty is family law, and I don't have the knowledge you need."

Brenna's eyes filled with tears. "You can't be serious! I don't need a criminal lawyer. I'm innocent. And dammit, I'm going to prove it."

"You need someone to look out for you. Someone who practices criminal law and is good at it. And what do you mean, you're going to prove it?"

"Someone killed Chef Mike, and it wasn't me. I'm going to figure out who did and give the police the information."

Emily groaned and pulled at her hair. "Oh my god! That isn't a good plan."

"What? You think I'm just going to sit back and be railroaded for something I didn't do? Not on your life. I've had a pretty crappy year, and I'm done with it!" Brenna pushed herself away from the car and stood with her feet shoulder-width apart and her hands on her hips. "I'm tired of having stuff happen to me. I am done. Just done! I'm taking control again, and things are going to change from now on."

"Brenna, come on. Let's go home and figure out a plan."

"Thanks, but right now I think I just need to be alone for a while. I promise I'm not going to do anything rash. I have to get in touch with Tim and Mathew and let them know we have access to the offices."

"Call me later tonight. I'm going to be worried if I don't hear from you."

Brenna sighed. "I've had to deal with a lot this year, but I'll get through this too. You aren't going to say anything to my mom, are you?"

"No. I couldn't even if I wanted to. Remember, client privilege?"

"That's right. K. I'm going home. And yes, I'll be in touch with you tonight. I promise."

Brenna drove home on autopilot. The day had been a long one, and her brain was still processing everything that had happened. She checked her mailbox in the lobby. Nothing but flyers. That was a relief. She put her jacket and purse away and placed a call to Tim.

"Tim Harris."

"Hi, it's Brenna Flynn. I spoke with the police, and they're releasing the offices in the morning."

"Excellent. We'll be able to work there. Can you send an email to everyone as an update? And then send an email to John, Margo, Mathew, and me. In that email, set up a meeting at eight tomorrow morning for us. And I'll need you to be there as well."

"Sure. Anything else?"

"No. That's all." Tim disconnected the call.

She drafted the emails and sent them out as per his instructions. That done, she ordered a pizza online from her favorite pizza place and had it delivered. She had thirty minutes before it arrived and planned to use that time well.

Her brain wouldn't stop going over what had happened during the day. After a quick shower, she dressed in a comfortable pair of sweats and an oversized sweatshirt and poured a generous glass of Shiraz. She grabbed a notepad and pen from her office. Settling on her couch, she wrote everything she could remember from her day, including what Rita and Jackie had told her about Mike. She was so absorbed that she lost track of time and was startled when her bell rang with the pizza delivery.

She turned on the television and watched the local news while eating dinner.

Chef Mike's murder was the top story. The reporter had been busy. Bob and Detective Morris had been interviewed, although they gave very little information. Vicky Samson, Chef Mike's fiancée, and his sous chef, Tina Patterson, were also interviewed. Vicky looked to be in her mid-thirties. She had long, dark hair, and although her grief was evident, she was a beautiful woman. She was well-spoken in the interview and had a slight British accent. Even though the reporter was sympathetic, Brenna could see both Vicky and Tina were upset. The interview closed with a shot of Chef Mike's restaurant.

"This is Lindsay Christie reporting for *Bayview City News*. Mike's Place will be closed for the week, and a memorial service will be held at his restaurant later this week. Police are investigating Chef Mike's murder, and *Bayview Cooks!,* the reality cooking show being filmed here in Bayview City, has suspended the taping of the show. Producers are currently waiting to hear from the police with regards as to when they can resume production."

The shot ended with a still of the show's billboard on top of the studio.

Brenna's landline rang, and she checked the caller ID before answering. It was her aunt Rita.

"Hi, Brenna. I'm just calling to see how things went at the police station. I saw the news report tonight. This is a pretty big story."

"Thanks for calling. I should've touched base with you when I got back." Brenna quickly filled Rita in on what had happened at the police station.

"It sounds pretty standard, and yes, you would be a person of interest simply because you work there and you found the body. Detective Morris has to be the lead investigator on this. It protects both you and Bob from any question of impropriety."

They chatted for a few minutes and then hung up.

A few minutes later, her cell phone rang. She answered cautiously.

"Hi Brenna, it's Jackie. Just checking to see how things went at the police station."

Brenna smiled despite the day she'd had. "Thanks, Jackie. I'm okay. But I'm a person of interest in Chef Mike's murder."

Jackie drew in a sharp breath. "You're kidding, right?"

"Afraid not. I found the body, and I work at the studio. I'm going to see what I can learn about Chef Mike. Maybe he was at the wrong place at the wrong time. I don't know, but I'm going to figure this out. Do you have any information on that person who came looking for work a few years ago?"

"I don't get a lot of chefs working with me. This one I remember because no one would hire him. The references he had from the previous restaurant weren't good. He had worked at a restaurant, and some of the customers had been poisoned with their meal."

"Food Poisoning? Whoa. That's big. I don't suppose you remember his name?" Brenna asked.

"I'd have to look it up in the system. I do remember his name was different than what I normally see around here. It may take me some time to find it. I didn't have time this afternoon. I had a meeting with the mayor. Why do you want to know?"

"It might help the police in their investigation. He may still be in the area."

"You need to be careful. I don't think you should be getting involved in a police investigation."

"Too late. The police think I may have done this. I'd better let you go. Let me know when you find this guy's name. We'll talk again soon." Brenna disconnected the call.

If there had been a scandal at the culinary school, there should be some kind of write-up about it. If not in the area newspaper archives, then at the school newspaper. The culinary school was part of the local community college. It might be possible that this person came back for revenge and he killed Chef Mike.

She did a search, found the school's website, and located the year the three chefs graduated. It had been a small class, only twelve graduates that year. Brenna followed this with a search of newspaper archives to see if anything popped regarding a poisoning at a restaurant in the region. There were several articles about a story dating back three years ago. The same reporter, Mary Gilles, had written all the articles.

Gilles had reported one of the boutique restaurants in Ann Arbor had been involved in a case of food poisoning. One of the line chefs had been let go for using produce brought into the restaurant from someone other than their normal supplier. The patrons had been compensated for their illness, and the restaurant appeared to have recovered in recent years. This line chef was named in one of the later articles. His name was Charles Mathews.

Brenna recognized his name. He had graduated with the three chefs. She did a search for his name and found an obituary, dated a year and a half ago. Charles Mathews had been killed in a shooting. He had been living in Ann Arbor at the time. His family included an older brother, and his mother and father.

Brenna sat back. Well, that eliminated him as a suspect. She'd have to look further for information. She still had some questions about this Charles. Was there any way she could confirm Charles was the chef who had come to Bayview City looking for work? And if she did, what would it prove? And did any of this have to do with Chef Mike's murder?

Jackie should be able to tell her if Charles Mathews was the person who had contacted her looking for work. She sent Jackie a text.

> B: Could the person looking for work have been Charles Mathews
> J: Could be. Will check my records tomorrow

Brenna stretched. Time to turn in. It had been a pretty stressful day. She hoped sleep would come easily.

CHAPTER EIGHT

Brenna woke up after a restless night. Turning off her brain had proven to be difficult; she kept reliving the events of the day. Every time she closed her eyes, she saw Chef Mike on the studio floor. The old house's creaks and groans had kept her awake as well. She sighed and decided to pass on her morning run. Rolling out of bed, she went straight to her shower. A long, hot shower would help clear the cobwebs. She took her time and then stepped out of the shower and pulled on her robe. She wrapped her hair in a towel and made her way to the kitchen.

Coffee and cereal might help her brain start to work again. Leaning against her kitchen counter, she ate the cereal while waiting for the coffee. She took her mug into the bathroom and finished doing her hair and makeup.

She went back to the kitchen for more coffee and glanced down her hallway. With a start, she noticed a white envelope on the floor. It hadn't been there last night when she came in. Her name was on the envelope, but there was no postmark on it. Opening it, she pulled out the single piece of paper. There was a photo of the cast and crew of the show. Chef Mike's likeness had a red X through it. Under the photo was the caption "Who's next?"

She dropped the paper, grabbed her cell phone, and called Detective Morris. It took several rings before she picked up, and when she did, her voice was groggy.

"Detective, it's Brenna Flynn. Sorry to call so early, but I was just getting ready to go to work, and I found an envelope addressed to me in my hallway, in my apartment. I opened it, and there's a picture of the cast and crew from the show with a red X through Chef Mike. Under the photo is a caption saying, 'Who's next?' I don't like this."

"You found this at home?"

"Yes. It must have been slipped under my door sometime last night. I know it wasn't there when I came in."

"Okay, just stay put. I'll be there in a few minutes. I need your address, and then I'm going to call Bob and ask him to meet me at your place. Don't open the door until you hear one of us out there. Got it?"

"I'm at forty-five Superior Road, apartment five, the top floor."

Brenna picked up the paper by the corner and placed it on her counter. Brenna paced back and forth in her kitchen. Who could have done this? And how did they know where she lived? The building was fairly secure, but she knew she'd have to let her father know. He'd take steps to beef up the security.

Detective Morris and Bob arrived in less than ten minutes. Brenna let them in. "I put it on the counter and tried not to handle it too much."

Bob leaned over to look at the message. "And you're certain it wasn't here when you got in last night?"

"Yes, I'm sure. This morning, it was in the middle of my hallway. In front of the side table. There's no way I could have missed it."

"Do you recognize the picture?" Bob asked.

"It looks like a copy of the one that's in the reception area. It may have been taken at the first show."

"Who has access to the photos?" Detective Morris asked.

"I don't know. I'm not even sure who took the picture. It might even be on the show's social media pages. Maybe the Facebook page. If that's the case, anyone can print it out."

"Okay, we'll take this with us. We'll run it for prints. We'll do the envelope as well," Detective Morris said.

"Any idea who could have done this? I'm not exactly happy this person knows where I live."

Bob shook his head. "As Detective Morris said, we'll check this out. I don't know what we'll find. We're going to have to look into the chefs' history a bit more. Don't mention this to anyone."

"Did you know about the scandal involving one of the students who graduated with the three chefs? He worked in one of the boutique restaurants in Ann Arbor," Brenna asked.

Detective Morris glanced at Bob. "No, we didn't hear about that. What scandal are you talking about?"

Brenna filled them in on what she had found online.

"How would the scandal impact the chefs on the show?" Detective Morris asked.

"Aunt Rita told me he had come looking for work with the three chefs. It was around the time when they were opening their restaurants. Chef Mike was just getting started, Chef Rosa was in the process of opening, and Chef Aaron had just opened his restaurant. None of the chefs wanted to hire him. Apparently, he accused them of bullying at school. They almost all got expelled."

"And why are we just hearing about this now?" Bob asked.

"Because I didn't know anything about it. I did some checking online last night and learned that one of the graduates in the chefs' class was killed in a shooting about a year and a half ago. The obituary made a reference to him being a chef. Jackie Randall may have worked with him; she's going to check her records today. The newspaper reports indicated he had been a person of interest in a poisoning at the restaurant he worked at in Ann Arbor. But the police couldn't prove he had been responsible. The restaurant let him go. He wasn't able to find work in the area after that. And then the three chefs here wouldn't hire him. His family declined to comment for the article."

Bob ran his hand through his hair. "Okay, Bren, is there something else you haven't told us? About anything related to this case, to Chef Mike, or to the show?"

Brenna thought for a moment. "No, I don't think so."

"Right. If you do remember anything else, you need to let us know immediately. I need you to be extra careful at work and keep your eyes and ears open. If you hear or see anything that doesn't sound right, get in touch with us right away. Are you going to work now?" Bob asked.

"Yes, I am. And I'll make sure to let you know if anything seems off."

"Come on then; we'll walk you out." Bob opened her door and waited while she locked her door before he and Detective Morris followed her down the stairs. When they reached their cars, Bob said, "Don't forget to let your dad know that someone made their way into the building. You know he won't be happy if he hears it from me."

Brenna sighed. "I know. I'm not looking forward to that call. But I'll make it. Thanks." She made the call to her father while she sat in her car in front of the building. "Morning, Dad. I need to let you know that someone got into the building last night."

"What! Are you alright? Is anyone hurt?"

"Hmm, no one was hurt that I know of. But someone slipped a note under my door. I called the police, and Bob and Detective Morris came by. Bob suggested I call you and let you know. I don't know how they would have come in."

"Don't worry. I'll be over first thing this morning and check the house. I'll change the lock to the main door and put the keys in everyone's mailbox. I'll email an explanation about the new keys."

"Thanks, Dad."

"Glad you're okay. I'll talk to you later."

Brenna shook her head. That was one issue solved for today. Her father must be rattled. He hadn't asked what the note said. She started her Jeep and drove to work.

Tim and Mathew were in their offices when Brenna arrived at work. A quick glance down the hall toward the studio and she saw the police barrier tape, preventing people from going any farther.

Brenna popped her head in Tim's office. "Good morning. I just wanted to let you know I'm here. Is there anything you need me to deal with this morning?"

"We're just getting ready to review our calendars. We're going to need to get a new script ready. Margo will be working on it with us. Last night, I spoke with sous chef Tina Patterson. She's agreed to take Chef Mike's place and will find a sous chef to work with her."

"Is there anything from the public relations agency we need to distribute this morning?" Brenna asked.

Mathew said, "Yes. They've got a press release going out to all media this morning, and it should be on the noon news with the local station. I'll make sure you get a copy of it. Please send it to all staff."

Tim cleared his throat. "We'd better get a few things straight. As soon as the police tell us we have access to the studio, we'll need to get production moving. We have contracts that have to be honored with the sponsors and the crew. Once the set is released, it'll have to be cleaned before we can get to work. Brenna, do you have a contact?"

"Yes. One of the officers gave me business cards from local companies that do this type of cleanup."

Mathew asked, "Did the police give you any indication who their suspect might be?"

Brenna wasn't about to say the police were looking at her. She shook her head. "Right now, everyone associated with the show is a possible suspect."

"That's crazy. Just because we work here, we're suspects." Mathew threw his pen on the desk.

Tim shook his head. "They must be grasping at straws." He took off his glasses and pinched the bridge of his nose. "Anyway, we've taken steps for additional security. I've spoken with the firm providing the security system for the building. There will be some changes, beginning with a physical presence in the form of security guards throughout the building. The president of the firm will be coming in this morning around ten for a quick meeting with our team and will provide information on how security is going to work."

Brenna asked, "Is everyone aware they have to be here for the meeting? And should the chefs and judges be here as well?"

Tim tapped his pen on the desk. "The crew will have to be told about the meeting. I have an email you can send out to them. It needs to go out right away. The judges and the chefs don't need to be here for the meeting, but we'll need to make sure they're informed. Brenna, can you meet with Chef Aaron and Chef Rosa later today and go over the changes? Margo will be in touch with the judges this morning."

"I'll contact the chefs shortly and set something up for this afternoon."

"And one more thing before you start your day. I've heard from Vicky, Chef Mike's fiancée. The family will be doing a memorial service on Saturday afternoon at the restaurant. We've decided to have a moment of silence out of respect for Chef Mike during our next taping. We thought about having Chef Mike's photo above his kitchen during the show. It'll seem as if he's watching over his team."

Brenna took a step back when she heard the latest development. "You're not serious. I don't think that's in good taste." She was shocked Tim would think this was an appropriate idea.

Tim glared back at her. "Well, it was Mathew's idea, and I thought it was a good one. You don't agree?"

Mathew frowned at Brenna, but she plowed ahead. "I think the moment of silence is a good idea. While that's happening, you could have a photo collage highlighting his career."

Tim folded his arms across his chest. "You're probably right. I didn't think it through. I certainly don't want to offend anyone, especially Chef Mike's family."

"I like that idea. Can you take the lead on it? Get some photos together and get it ready for the next taping?" Mathew asked.

"I'll see what I can put together. Do you know if there are any photos we could use from the PR agency?"

"I'll give you their number, and you can follow up with them." Mathew scrolled his phone. "Here you go, sent in a text."

Brenna confirmed the number and then headed for the room she used as an office. She had plans to connect with the PR agency and to touch base with Chef Aaron and Chef Rosa. She heard someone calling her name, turned around, and saw Margo coming down the hallway.

"Hey there, Brenna."

"Hi. How are you this morning?"

"I'm fine, but I was worried about you. Did you get any sleep last night?"

"I did, but it wasn't great. I still haven't heard back from the police about releasing the set. I'm not sure when we'll be able to get in there to get it cleaned up."

"I wouldn't worry about that now. That's out of your control. Besides, Tim, Mathew, and I met most of yesterday afternoon, and we have plans in place to keep the production on schedule. If we have to, we'll move the taping to another location or tape two shows in one day. It's not ideal, but we'll make it work. Did they talk to you about the new security system and the meeting this morning?"

"They mentioned changes to the system. And they want me to meet with Chefs Rosa and Aaron to check in with them. I'm also to let them know about the beefed-up security. I thought I would ask if they have any photos of Chef Mike I could use in a photo collage for the next taping."

"Sounds like you have your work for the morning. I'll catch you later." Margo walked off to Tim's office.

Brenna went into the room she used as an office and made her call to the PR agency. When she was done, she saw she had a voice mail. She checked it and found a message from Detective Morris telling her they would have access to the studio by noon today. Brenna was surprised the studio would be released this quickly and took a few moments to call the detective.

"Detective Morris, it's Brenna Flynn. I just got your message and want to make sure I understood correctly. We can have access to the studio today at noon, right?"

"That's right. The crime techs have finished processing the scene, and there isn't anything else we need."

"Great, I'll let Tim and Mathew know."

"We'll be in touch if we need anything else from you."

Brenna hung up and sent a text to Tim and Mathew with the news. Tim replied immediately.

> T: Let's get the show back on track

Brenna mumbled to herself, "I need to contact the cleaning companies to get the studio in order. My day just got a lot busier. Not sure there are enough hours in today."

She heard the jingle of keys on a key chain and walked to the door to see who was there. A tall, muscular man with short, cropped gray hair dressed as a security guard was walking in her direction.

"Hi there, you must be with the security company."

The man stopped in front of the door. "I'm Joe Adams. I work with Malone Security."

"I'm Brenna Flynn, production assistant for the show." Brenna shook his hand and took a good look at him. He appeared to be in his early fifties with a strong build and an intelligent face. "How long have you been doing security?"

"I retired from the police department about a year ago and was starting to go a little stir crazy. My wife could only handle me being retired for a few months, and she's the one who suggested I might like to try this. The job suits me. It's easier on the body than police work was." He looked down the hall toward the studio and shook his head. "Hard to believe someone would want to kill him."

Brenna asked, "Did you know him well?"

"Not that well, but my wife and I had dinner at his restaurant fairly often. We liked him. He seemed to be a pretty good guy."

"I found him," Brenna said.

"Now that can't have been a good situation. How're you doing?"

"It was pretty unnerving. I've tried to process it as best as I can, but it doesn't make sense to me. I don't know why he came back or how he got into the studio. He didn't have keys to the building or an access code for the alarm. Someone had to have let him in. He'd come in the evening before looking for his tablet, and I helped him search for it, but it wasn't around."

"The police will get to the bottom of it," Joe said.

"My cousin, Bob McLean, is one of the detectives. He and his partner, Clare Morris, were here yesterday."

"Bob's a good officer. Detective Morris was just coming on the force when I retired. I've heard good things about her. Well, I'm going to head back to the front. If you need anything, you can reach me on channel four on the radio."

"Thanks, Joe. It was good to meet you."

"I'm here until seven tonight, and then my replacement comes in. There will be someone here around the clock."

"What's going to happen with the back entrance?" Brenna asked.

"The back entrance is a problem as far as maintaining a secure building. Unless we bring another person in to work the back, we're recommending it stays locked."

"Good luck with that. The crew goes out there for smoke breaks during the day. They leave the door propped open while they go to the smoking area," Brenna told him.

"Good to know. I'll make sure to advise my supervisor. He'll deal with it." Joe headed down the hall to continue his rounds.

Brenna pulled the desk chair away from the desk. She had a lot to get done in a short amount of time. She sent the email out to the crew from Tim and Mathew.

That done, Brenna turned her attention to getting a cleaning company to come in that afternoon. Pulling one of the business cards out, Brenna made a call to QuickClean. She was preparing to leave a message when someone picked up the phone.

"QuickClean, Marnie speaking. How can I help you?"

"Hi, this is Brenna Flynn with Studio One Productions. We had an incident here yesterday, and the police have released the scene. One of the officers gave me your business card and said you might be able to deal with the cleanup."

"Yes, that's the type of work we do. Can you give me more information? Are we dealing with gunshots, drug overdose, or a stabbing?"

Brenna was taken aback by the matter-of-fact way Marnie asked the questions. "It was a stabbing, and it happened in the studio itself. There's a fairly large area that needs to be cleaned."

"And when can we have access?"

"I've been told the scene will be released at noon today."

"Let me check the schedule."

There was the sound of papers being flipped. "We can be there at one this afternoon. Will you be there to give us access to the space?"

"Yes. Thanks for fitting us in today."

"No problem. I need the address and a contact phone number for you."

Brenna provided her with the information and hung up. It was just past eight. She couldn't call Chef Aaron or Chef Rosa. It was too early since they both worked late hours. She sent them a short text message asking to meet with them later that morning.

"I may as well see about getting photos from the studio for the moment of silence."

She opened the show's website and found several photos that would be suitable. His restaurant's website also had a few she could use. One, in particular, was very good. Chef Mike was standing at his counter with a dish in front of him. He had a big smile, and his eyes were looking straight into the camera. He looked alive and full of energy.

Her phone pinged with a text from Jackie Randall.

J: Found the resume on the chef looking for work in town. His name was Charles Mathews

B: Thanks!

She heard people walking down the hall. Checking her watch, she saw it was almost time for the meeting with the security company. She copied the photos and saved them to a file for the moment of silence. Her phone pinged with a couple of texts from Chef Aaron and Chef Rosa. Both agreed to meet with her just after eleven. She hoped the meeting didn't take too long.

CHAPTER NINE

The conference room was half-filled with members of the crew. Brenna went to the back and made herself a coffee before finding a seat. Tim, Mathew, and John walked into the conference room a few moments before the meeting was scheduled to begin. Mathew and John moved to the side of the room. Brenna noticed a tall, well-built man at the back of the room. He was wearing a distressed black leather jacket, dark jeans, and a white dress shirt. He looked vaguely familiar, but she couldn't place him.

Tim stood at the front of the room. His eyes were shadowed, and his face was pale. He adjusted his glasses and took a drink of water. "Thanks for coming in this morning. I'm going to answer some of your questions about what happened and the security in the building and on the set. Then I'll let you know how we're going to move forward with the show."

Tim briefed everyone on what had been done regarding the murder investigation. Brenna noticed no one spoke while he spoke. People were looking at their coworkers with sidelong glances.

Tim looked around the room. "The two detectives in charge of the case will be joining us shortly. They'll provide you with additional information. If you have anything you think should be shared with them, please make certain you connect with them. Your safety and that of our chefs, judges, and the studio audience is of paramount importance to this production company." He paused a moment. "You may have noticed some changes in the security of the building. With that in mind, I'd like to introduce you to Mr. Connor Malone of Malone Security."

The man from the back of the room walked to stand next to Tim. He cleared his throat and waited a moment for the room to be quiet.

"Good morning. I'm Connor Malone. First, I want to assure you I will do everything I can to make certain the studio and this building are as safe and secure as they can be. To do that, I'll need your cooperation. You will all be required to wear an ID card with your name and photo on it. When you come in, you'll be asked to swipe the card at the front. When you leave, you'll have to swipe the card to show you are out of the building. My team and I will have the camera set up in one of the offices down the hall to take your photo. Once we're through here, please make your way to the office. And yes, we do have everyone's name, so we won't miss anyone. Questions?"

He paused for a moment, looking around the room. His eyes rested on Brenna for a moment too long, and he frowned. She wondered what that was about.

"No questions, great. Next, several people come in and out of the building who don't work here. For those individuals, we'll need to have them sign in and be accounted for by someone at the studio. We have security personnel at the front desk. They will be monitoring everyone who comes in and out of the building. And that includes deliveries or visitors. Questions?"

Brenna raised her hand, and Mr. Malone looked in her direction. "Yes, go ahead."

"How are you going to deal with the studio audience? You can't expect them to be signed in and vouched for. We don't know who is going to come in."

"Great question. We'll have two personnel working the front desk when the show is taping. Anyone who is coming to watch the show and is carrying a bag will have to put the bag through a security screening device similar to what is used at an airport. We've discussed other options with the producers, and they believe this is the most cost-effective and time-efficient method to use."

One of the lighting guys raised his hand.

Mr. Malone pointed to him. "You have a question."

"Yeah, are we still going to be able to get out the back door for our smoke breaks?"

"That can pose some security issues, but we aren't here to make life difficult. The back door can be used, but we're going to add a security camera and a sensor. That way, we'll know if the door is left ajar. So yes, you'll still be able to get out to smoke, but the door will need to be closed as you go out."

The lighting guy and several others nodded their heads.

There were a few more logistical questions from the crew. By the time these were answered, the detectives had arrived.

Brenna noticed Detective Morris had changed into a black suit with blue pinstripes and had coordinated her shirt to match. Her long black hair was pulled back in a braid. Gold ball earrings were the only jewelry Brenna could see.

Before he left, Mr. Malone reminded them to have their photos done for their ID cards. On his way out, he shook hands with Bob and exchanged a few words.

Tim introduced the detectives to the crew, and Detective Morris took over.

"My partner and I want to make sure you understand, if you have any information you think might be of importance, you need to contact us right away. Don't try to decide if it's worth calling us; just make the call. We'll determine if the information is valuable to our investigation." Detective Morris then answered a few questions from members of the crew.

Bob spoke up. "You'll be seeing a lot of Detective Morris and me in the next few days. This is an ongoing investigation, and we'll be coming in if we have additional questions for any of you. We'll leave our business cards on the table in the back if anyone needs to contact us. Don't hesitate to do so."

They left the meeting room.

John stood at the front of the room. "All right, I just need a few minutes of your time. I want to make sure everyone understands what is going to happen production-wise in the next couple of days. The studio will be released at noon today. We're bringing in a professional cleaning crew. They'll make sure everything is cleaned up properly. Tomorrow morning is rehearsal. We've been able to get a replacement for Chef Mike, and we want to make certain the chefs are comfortable proceeding. Taping will take place tomorrow afternoon. I need everyone on their best game and keeping the show moving forward. We'll be including a moment of silence in respect to Chef Mike just before the show gets underway. Brenna is responsible for putting together a photo collage. If any of you have photos she could use, please let her know."

Tim said, "We'll be issuing a press release about the taping, and we'll also do a social media blast. And one more thing before you all head out, I want to let you know Vicky Samson, Chef Mike's fiancée, has been in touch with me. She and Chef Mike's family will be putting together a memorial service on Saturday afternoon at his restaurant. If any of you want to attend, please let Sally at the front know."

Tim paused and took a deep breath.

After a moment, he continued. "That's all, everyone. Have a good one. Don't forget to have your IDs done. You'll need them to leave today and to get into work tomorrow."

As the crew left the room, Margo approached Brenna. "Brenna, do you have a minute?"

"Sure. What's up?"

"Why don't we go out for a bit of fresh air?" Margo motioned toward the patio.

Margo led the way to a bench under one of the trees.

Margo stuck her hands in her pockets and frowned. "You know the detective who's investigating, don't you?"

"Well, Bob's my cousin. I just met Detective Morris. What's this about?"

Margo paced for a few moments. "I'm not sure. I overheard something, and now I don't know what I should do about it."

Brenna waited patiently.

"You know, it's at times like this, I wish I smoked. It would fill the gap." Margo smiled ruefully.

"Take your time. You don't have to rush, and you don't have to say anything to me at all if you don't feel comfortable."

"No, I need to tell you what I heard. I was putting some things away in my locker. I don't think anyone knew I was there, but I heard someone walking by, speaking on a phone, at least I think it was on a phone. Anyhow, the person was asking about where they could get some China

White, which apparently is a street name for fentanyl. I don't know who it was. Whoever was talking moved to the backstage area quickly. I do know it was a man, but I can't place the voice. And I know it's someone from the production company."

Brenna rubbed her forehead. "When was this?"

"It was late Friday afternoon."

"So, what do you want to do with this?" Brenna asked.

"I'm not sure. From what I overheard, it seemed like this person was looking for a street drug. I know he was someone involved with the show. What if this person made arrangements to have the drugs dropped off here at the studio?"

"Well, do you think that's a possibility? When would that happen?"

"Up until now, security has been pretty slack. It would have been easy for someone to use the studio as a drop-off point. Any of the deliveries we've had could have included drugs. Until you got here, things weren't organized. No one person was responsible for signing or accepting deliveries. What if this guy was looking for fentanyl and he had arranged to have it dropped off here when other items were being delivered? And somehow, Chef Mike came to the studio for something on the same night and he got caught up in the middle." Margo's voice dropped to a whisper.

"Well, I guess anything is possible. But, Chef Mike was found in the kitchen. And the big mystery is how he got in. He didn't have a key or an alarm code, so he would have had to come in with someone who did."

"That's up to the police to figure out. I'm not sure if I should bring this information to them or not." Margo played with her wedding ring.

"I think you need to bring this up to Bob and Detective Morris. At the very least, they need to be made aware of it, and they can decide what to do with the information."

"I don't want to talk to them here, though. I don't want anyone to know I overheard that conversation."

"You could always call them."

Margo bit her lip. "Fine. But, can you call? I left my phone in the conference room."

Brenna called Detective Morris and explained what Margo had just told her. Detective Morris asked to speak with Margo, and Brenna handed her the phone.

Margo took the phone and provided Detective Morris with the information. She answered a few questions and then handed the phone back to Brenna.

"Thanks for the call. We'll look into this. I also want to let you know the only prints we found on the envelope and the message were yours. I strongly recommend you be cautious at work and at home."

"Thanks. I will."

Brenna disconnected the call. She looked around the patio. It was clean and well maintained. There were still members of the crew sitting in the conference room.

She lowered her voice. "Do you think someone working here has a drug problem? Wouldn't we be able to tell?"

Margo eyed the windows in the conference room. "I'd like to think we would be able to tell if someone were using, but unless the signs are obvious, I don't think we could." She played with the leather bracelet on her wrist. "It would be nice to believe everyone on this crew is happy and healthy, but you never know with people. I heard a rumor about Frank Simons, the PA who was fired last week. The person you were hired to replace." She pushed her hair back from her face. "Apparently, the police received an anonymous tip. They checked his apartment and his backpack. They found drugs with a street value of over two hundred fifty thousand dollars. He was arrested for possession. And he's the last person I would have thought was into drugs. He was a fitness nut, doing all kinds of training for marathons. I guess you never know."

"No, I don't think you can. Do you think he was the person you overheard?"

"I don't think so."

"We'd better go back and get to work. Otherwise, people will wonder what we're doing out here." Brenna picked up her tablet and started to walk back to the entrance.

"Thanks. I appreciate you helping me out."

"Anytime."

"We'd better get those IDs done. What do you think of this Malone guy? Do you know him?" Margo tucked her hair behind her ear.

"He looks familiar. I just can't place him. He could have been in high school with my brothers. I hope his company is good. I thought it was a bit strange we didn't have an on-site security."

"There wasn't a need for any, at least that's what Tim said. He didn't want to push the budget too much. Now, this is going to put a dent in the funds we have for sure. Twenty-four hours a day of security, you better believe that's going to cost."

Brenna shook her head. "No one's life is worth being sacrificed for a budget."

"I wonder if Chef Mike's family is going to sue the production company?"

They had made their way to the smaller conference room, and there were just a few other people ahead of them.

Connor Malone was off to the side talking with Tim.

Brenna shushed Margo. "Don't let Tim hear you say that. I bet he's worried about it."

"Didn't think he'd be here. Oh well, I'm sure he's thought about it and has a plan in place. He always thinks ahead."

They had their IDs done and were just heading out the door when Mr. Malone called out to Brenna. "Excuse me, are you Brenna Flynn?"

Brenna turned around. "Yes. Can I help you with anything?"

He took a couple of steps toward her and smiled. "You don't recognize me, do you?"

"Hmm, no, I don't. You do look familiar, but I don't know from where."

"I was one of Dave's groomsmen for your wedding. I had just returned from serving overseas. I don't quite look the same as I did then."

Brenna grinned. "Oh, now I remember. You were so quiet. You showed up for the rehearsal and the wedding. We didn't get a chance to talk much. And your hair was a lot shorter then."

"I heard about Dave. I'm sorry you've been going through a tough time."

"Thanks. I came home to Bayview City for a fresh start. My family still lives here." Brenna's phone pinged with an alarm. "Sorry. I have a meeting I have to get to. It was nice touching base with you." Brenna held out her hand.

Connor shook her hand, and a tingle ran through Brenna as the solid feel of his hand enveloped hers. "Not a problem. I'm sure we'll be running into each other over the next few days. I'll be keeping an eye on things here."

Brenna left the conference room smiling.

CHAPTER TEN

A glance at her watch showed Brenna she was cutting it close to meet with Chef Aaron and Chef Rosa. She hurried down the hallway and back to her small office. She grabbed her jacket and power walked her way to the front door.

The security guard, Joe, looked up as she arrived in the lobby. "You're in a hurry."

"I have to get across town to meet with the chefs. Oh, and I should let you know, QuickClean will be coming in at one."

"And who are they reporting to?" Joe asked.

"Oh. Hmm, I suppose me. I'll make sure I'm back before then."

"Sounds good. You'll need to sign them in."

"Right." Brenna swiped her ID card through the reader, signed herself out, and left the building.

On the drive to Chef Aaron's apartment, Brenna thought back to her wedding day. Connor had been a groomsman, but she didn't remember much about him. Dave had asked him to be part of the wedding when they had started planning the event. He had been surprised when Connor had said yes. She knew Dave and Connor had been good friends at university, playing for the hockey team, but they had gone their separate ways afterward.

She pulled up to Chef Aaron's apartment building. He lived in the downtown area, close to his restaurant. Brenna remembered when his building had been built. There was an uproar from some of the historical society because it was ultra-modern in design. Lots of angles, concrete, wood cladding, and large windows. The building and the architect had won numerous awards. The front of the building had conformed to the historical society's demands, but the back of the building, facing the water, was a wall of windows.

Brenna parked in one of the visitor parking spots. Entering the lobby, there was a large desk manned by two concierges. One of them was on the phone, and the other was watching the door.

"Can I help you?" she asked Brenna.

"Brenna Flynn to see Aaron White."

The concierge made a quick call. "You can go right up. Take the red elevator to the fourth floor and then turn right. The apartment number is four ten."

Brenna thanked her and walked to the elevators. "The restaurant business must be doing well for Chef Aaron to have an apartment here. It's pretty pricey," she mumbled to herself.

She walked out of the elevator and turned right. She saw Chef Aaron standing in his doorway. "Brenna, thanks for taking the time to come and see me. Can I get you a cup of coffee?" Chef Aaron led her to the kitchen in his open floor plan apartment.

"Coffee would be great. Tim asked if I'd come by and see how you were doing. I also need to bring you up to speed on the changes in security at the studio."

Chef Aaron poured a coffee for her, spilling some on the counter, and growled, "I've been like this ever since I heard about Mike. Who would do this to him and why? He never hurt anyone in his life. He was one of the good guys." He wiped the counter as he spoke.

Brenna added cream and sugar to her coffee and then picked up her cup. "I don't understand what he was doing at the studio after hours or how he got in."

Chef Aaron shook his head. "I don't either. The rehearsal went well. We worked out some of the timing issues. The three of us got together for a drink afterward, and we all felt great about the show. We thought it was going to be a terrific opportunity to help promote the restaurants." He pointed Brenna in the direction of his living room. "We weren't competitors in any sense of the word. We just thought this was going to be fun. The first show was a piece of cake, and we had already heard some good things from people who watched the show."

He sat on the couch facing the lakefront. His long legs reached under the coffee table.

Brenna sat in one of the chairs next to the couch. "He didn't give any indication he would be going back to the studio?"

"No. He did get a text while we were having a drink. I don't know who it was. He seemed annoyed by it and said he'd have to go out later in the evening. I thought it might have been his fiancée, Vicky, but I guess not. It could have been someone from his restaurant. He did say one of the line chefs was giving him a hard time."

"Could it have been someone arranging to meet with him at the studio?"

"Well, who would it have been? It isn't like the judges would need to speak with him, and besides, the studio would have been locked up." Chef Aaron sighed and stroked his goatee. "None of us have keys or a security code to get in. We don't need them. Only the people working for the studio have those. I can't think why anyone from the studio would need to meet with him there. And especially at night."

Brenna was quiet for a minute. She didn't want to alarm him. She doubted the text was from someone at the restaurant. Anything urgent, they would have called him. Who could it have been? The police would have the resources to check his phone records, and she wondered if they had checked them yet.

She shook her head. "Definitely a puzzle. Anyway, let me fill you in on the changes to the security." She brought him up to speed on the changes.

"Do you think the screening process will put people off from coming to watch the show?"

"I don't think so. Unfortunately, this type of screening is becoming more commonplace. I think the security company is doing as much as they can to make sure we all feel safe at work."

"I never thought we'd be in danger filming a reality show." Chef Aaron took a sip of coffee.

"You also need to know we'll be having a moment of silence at the beginning of the show in respect for Chef Mike. And we'll be showing photos of him in his career. I wondered if you have pictures I can use?"

Chef Aaron put his coffee cup on the table and walked to the bookcase on the far wall. He took a photo album down and returned to Brenna. "This album is from our time at the culinary school. I took pictures almost every day. There should be some in here you can use. Just return the album to me when you're done."

"Wow. Thanks. I didn't expect a full album. I'll return it to you as soon as possible." Brenna stood. "I should go. I have to meet with Chef Rosa next. If you have any questions or concerns, don't hesitate to contact me." She picked up her bag. "Oh, one more thing. Did you receive the email from Tim about the short rehearsal tomorrow morning at ten?"

"Yes. Tim's message made it pretty clear it would be business as usual. I'll make sure to tell my sous chef Jamie about the security changes."

"Anything else?"

Chef Aaron stroked his goatee. "I'm missing one of my knives. I haven't been able to find it since we left the studio. I know I put it in my knife roll, and now, it isn't there. I've looked everywhere for it, my restaurant, here, and even in my car."

"Which knife is it?" Brenna remembered exactly what the knife in Chef Mike's chest had looked like.

"It's my chef's knife. I use it every day."

"And your sous chef Jamie doesn't have it?"

"No."

"Have you notified the police?"

He shook his head.

"Well, they need to know about this. It could have a bearing on the investigation."

Brenna pulled out her phone and made the call to Detective Morris. She got the detective's voice mail and left a detailed message about Chef Aaron missing his knife. She also mentioned the text message Chef Mike had received.

"There's nothing else we can do now. I'm sure Detective Morris will get in touch with you. If you do find it, let her know."

"I probably should have called her myself. But I kept thinking it would turn up."

"All right. I'll see you tomorrow at the studio. And you do realize we're doing both the rehearsal and the taping tomorrow?"

"Yes, Tim's email was very clear."

The drive to Rosa's house took Brenna through some of the prettiest residential streets in Bayview City. The streets were lined with tall oak and maple trees that still had the full green color. Those trees would be changing to bold reds in the next few weeks. The houses were stately Victorians, many of them over a hundred years old. They had majestic views of Lake Superior and most had a widow's walk on the rooftop. Bayview City had been built around the shipbuilding and sailing industry.

Brenna puzzled about Chef Aaron's missing knife as she navigated the streets. Why hadn't he called the police? And how did he lose it? She thought back to the knife found in Chef Mike's chest. It was certainly large enough to be a chef's knife, but she couldn't be sure.

Ha, if I knew what a chef's knife was, I'd probably do more cooking. She shook her head and murmured, "I need to stay focused so I get back to the studio on time." Brenna pulled up to Chef Rosa's house. It was a large, detached Victorian. "Wow, this place looks great. I wonder who did the restoration work?" Brenna mused. She parked her Jeep and started up the walk. She heard voices in the backyard and remembered Chef Rosa had told her she'd be out on her deck. She walked around to the back of the house and called out, "Chef Rosa, are you back here?"

Chef Rosa answered. "Is that you, Brenna? Come on back. We're just relaxing a bit before we have to get to work."

Brenna walked toward the deck, and Chef Rosa waved her to a deck chair.

"Come and join me. Abby's working in the garden. I just made some fresh lemonade. We won't be able to drink this for much longer. Before we know it, winter will be here." Chef Rosa raised the pitcher in Brenna's direction, her bare arms showing their muscle tone. "Abby, come meet Brenna," Chef Rosa called out to Abby.

Abby made her way to the deck. She pulled off her gardening gloves and held out her hand. "Hi, Brenna. It's good to meet you."

Brenna shook her hand. "Hi. Your garden looks great."

Abby smiled and took a seat. "Thanks. I grow the herbs Rosa uses in the restaurant."

Chef Rosa filled their glasses with ice and then poured the lemonade over them. She added a sprig of mint and pushed a plate of cookies toward Brenna. "Eat. It's good for the soul."

Brenna reached over and took one of the black and white cookies. "Thanks for seeing me. I wanted to check in with you and make sure you are okay. I know you and Chef Mike were close."

Abby put her hand on Rosa's, and Brenna saw the compassion in her eyes.

Chef Rosa's eyes were red-rimmed. "Mike, Aaron, and I go back a long way. The three of us were always together. If one of us didn't understand something at school, one of the other two would make sure to help out. We spent a lot of time with each other. It seemed strange when we started out that we weren't working together, but we each had our own vision for our restaurant."

"You guys were still friends, even though you were in the same business?" Brenna took a bite of the cookie and groaned. "Oh, my these are good."

"Thanks." Rosa smiled. "We were close friends. We did go our separate ways after school, but that was because we wanted to grow in our careers."

"How did you all wind up here in Bayview City?"

Rosa reached out for one of the cookies. She broke it in half. "Well, that was a coincidence. We hadn't planned that. I had spent time in Italy working with a few chefs in Tuscany. Aaron was in France, learning at the Cordon Bleu school. And Mike, well, he traveled across our country. He was on a quest to learn as much as he could about American cuisine. Mike and I have different menus in our restaurants. Mine is Italian, and his is definitely what I would call American style. Aaron was always more into French cuisine, and it's served him well."

"How long were you all away?" Brenna asked.

"We were gone for a full year. I looked at that year as an apprenticeship. I worked hard to learn the techniques I'm using now. It was one of the toughest years I had. I was away from my family, and that was difficult. Aaron contacted me at about ten months into the year and asked what my plans were. I told him I would be coming back to Bayview City. He had touched base with Mike, and Mike had said the same thing. We did a Skype call one night and made plans to meet up at the end of the year back here."

"And when you came back?"

"It was as if we'd never been apart. We looked at the opportunities here and realized there was room for the three of us to work here. Our restaurants are quite different, and there's enough diversity in Bayview to support the three cuisines. Plus, there's the tourist trade up until Christmas that's a big influx as well."

"Did you see each other socially?" Brenna took a drink of her lemonade.

"Oh, yes, we did. The three of us got together as often as we could. Lots of times we met up at one of our homes for a meal and to discuss business. Aaron's quite close with my family. He spends most of the holidays with us. And I fixed up Mike and Vicky. I thought they'd be a great couple."

"Chef Aaron told me the three of you were together after the rehearsal and everything seemed normal. Is that how you remember it?"

"Yes. We talked about the show. We wondered how it would all play out. I remember asking if they thought we would have to stage disagreements with each other to spice things up."

"Did Chef Mike get a text or a phone call while you were there?"

"He did. It was just before we got ready to go back to our restaurants. He didn't seem happy with the text. He said he hadn't expected to hear from him again."

Brenna's eyes opened wide at Chef Rosa's words. "Did he say who it was?"

"No, but I thought it might have been someone from his restaurant. He had just let one of the line chefs go. The guy had been coming in late, and Mike had given him plenty of warnings. He tried to help his cook staff as much as possible, but this one wasn't working out. It happens, you know. Someone isn't suited for the work. And Mike hated confrontations."

"Did he say if he was going to meet with this person?"

"No, he didn't mention it. Are you thinking it was the killer who contacted him?"

"I don't know. I'm trying to figure out how he got into the studio and why he went back."

"Mike said he was going to his restaurant. We all had to get back to work for the evening."

"Do you know if anyone had a grudge against Chef Mike? Would he have any enemies?" Brenna asked.

"Enemy is a strong word. I can't believe someone would have wanted to harm him."

"Well, someone did. I don't mean to be insensitive, but he's dead because someone killed him."

Chef Rosa shook her head. Some of her dark, curly hair came out of her bun. "He wasn't the kind of man who hurt other people. He was always helpful and pretty charitable. He had his Food for the Hungry charity. He hated the thought of people going without nutritious food. And, as for getting into the studio, maybe the back door was unlocked. You know the crew uses that to go out to smoke, and they might not have closed it securely."

Brenna thought back to when she left the studio. She was certain the back door had been locked, but Tim and Mathew had still been at work, so they might have left through the back. There was a possibility Chef Mike had gained access to the building that way. But why would he go back? Was there someone who worked there he knew from somewhere in his travels?

"Do you know if he knew someone at the studio from anywhere else?"

Chef Rosa's forehead wrinkled. "No, I don't think he did. And he would have said something to Aaron and me if he had known anyone."

Brenna sensed Chef Rosa was starting to wonder why Brenna was asking so many questions. She knew she had to turn the conversation around. "Well, the reason behind my visit this morning is to make sure you're okay with coming in tomorrow morning for the rehearsal. Did you get Tim's email?"

"I did. I'm not looking forward to this, but we'll get through it. Mike was one of the good guys. Do you know who's going to replace him?"

"Tim spoke with Chef Mike's sous chef Tina Patterson. Tim, Mathew, and John thought she would be a good choice. She's agreed and is bringing someone in from the restaurant as her sous chef, Carol Alcott."

Chef Rosa smiled. "Tina's a great choice. And Carol will be a good addition. She's new to the cooking industry and has a bubbly personality that will work well on the show."

They sat on the deck for a few more minutes discussing the show and the people who worked at the studio. Just before she left, Brenna told Chef Rosa about the additional security and possibly needing a few more minutes to get through. She also mentioned the moment of silence and the photo collage.

Chef Rosa smiled. "I'm glad there's going to be something on the show to honor Mike."

Before she left to go back to work, Brenna placed a call to Detective Morris to let her know what she had learned from Chef Rosa. The call went directly to voice mail, and she left a message asking the detective to call her when she had a moment.

CHAPTER ELEVEN

Brenna's stomach growled. Breakfast had been hours ago, and she needed food. The cookies Chef Rosa had given her had been good, but not enough for lunch. Driving through the downtown area, she pulled into one of the sandwich shops that had popped up while she had been living in Wayhaven. Her brothers had raved about the food and service. She knew exactly what she wanted. The Italian spices permeated the air in the sub shop and had her salivating. She placed her order for a twelve-inch Italian meatball sub with lots of sauce, a can of Diet Coke, and a bag of chips. Her order was done up quickly, and she was out the door in a few minutes.

It was just past twelve-thirty when she arrived at the studio. The studio parking lot was half full, and she knew there would be a lot more work waiting for her when she got in. She made certain she had her photo ID on the lanyard and headed to security.

Joe was manning the desk. "Afternoon, Brenna."

"Hi, Joe." Brenna swiped her ID. "When QuickClean arrives, how are you going to get in touch with me?"

"I'll call you on the radio. That seems to be the easiest way to reach everyone."

"Great. I better go eat before they show up."

"Oh, the police were in earlier and took down the crime scene tape. They've given access to the studio. I checked things out there with them. It looks pretty messy."

"I was told it would be. I'll check it out and make sure I get the lights turned on before QuickClean arrives."

Brenna walked toward the room she used as her office. She was going to eat first and then deal with the rest of her day. She would eventually have to go to the studio again but wasn't sure what to expect.

Just before one, Margo popped her head in the doorway. "Hey there. Have you heard anything from the cleaning company?"

Brenna looked up from her tablet. "Not yet. I expect them anytime now. I guess I should go turn the lights on in the studio."

Brenna walked down the hall to the studio. Margo followed. Brenna snapped the lights on. Brenna stopped in the doorway and surveyed the scene before her. There was dark dust everywhere and a chalk outline where Chef Mike's body had been found. Brenna grabbed the doorframe.

"Are you okay?"

Brenna drew in a deep breath and let it out slowly. "It feels like it's been a week since I've been here. But it was just yesterday. He was there, where the outline is, and I couldn't do anything for him." Brenna sighed. "I wasn't scared. I just felt helpless."

They walked into the kitchen, taking care not to step in the dust or on the chalk outline. They checked the pantry. The entire area had been taken apart and was also covered in black dust.

"What is that stuff?" Margo asked.

"Bob told me it was fingerprint powder and it would be all over everything. I'm surprised to find it in here. The cleaning crew will deal with it. In the meantime, it looks as if everything will need to be replaced."

Margo shook her head. "What a mess."

Brenna pulled out her phone and started taking photos. "I'm going to take as many pictures as I can. I want to catalog this. I have a list of supplies on the back wall. Would you mind taking it down, and I'll work from that list?"

Margo walked around the debris on the floor and pulled the list off the corkboard. "This looks pretty thorough. When did you make it up?"

"I put it together after the last rehearsal. I pulled the supply list from a master list I found in the files. I'll use this list to replenish the shelves. The chefs were complaining the pantry was a mess for the first show, so I asked them if there was a specific way it should be organized. They came up with a diagram. I printed it out and laminated it. This should make it easier to find the items they need."

Brenna's radio squawked. Both Margo and Brenna jumped at the sound.

"Brenna, just letting you know QuickClean arrived." Joe's voice boomed in the small pantry.

Brenna chuckled. "I guess we're a bit jumpy." She pressed down on the speaker button. "Thanks, Joe. I'll be right there."

Margo said, "I'll wait here until you get back."

Brenna made her way to the security area. Five people wearing dark-blue QuickClean uniforms stood by the desk.

"Hi there, are you Brenna?" the woman in the front called.

"Yes. I take it you're our crew from QuickClean?"

"We are. I'm Marnie." The woman held out her hand to Brenna. She was Brenna's height, around five-two, but carried a bit more weight than Brenna did. Marnie's graying hair was pulled back in a ponytail.

Brenna shook her hand. "Let me just sign you in, and we'll go to the studio."

Marnie looked around. "Where can we bring our push carts in?"

Joe asked, "How big are they?"

"The size of custodian carts. And we each have one."

"It would be easier if you came in through the back door. Brenna, you okay with that?" Joe didn't seem overly concerned.

"That would work. If you'll follow me, I'll take you through the studio and to the back door. Are you parked in the back lot?"

"Yes. It's a big truck."

Brenna led them to the studio.

Marnie gave the studio area a quick once-over. "We can easily get this cleaned up by four today."

"That's a relief! We have a rehearsal scheduled for tomorrow."

"Not to worry."

Marnie and her team hustled out the back door and started bringing in their carts and cleaning supplies.

Margo watched as they set up. Marnie directed her crew to different areas of the studio. Brenna introduced Marnie to Margo.

"We'll get started. We each have our own section. Are you going to be in the area while we work?" Marnie looked around the studio.

Brenna nodded her head. "Yes. I have some work I can do while I'm here. Um, how are you going to deal with the area where Chef Mike was found?"

"We'll assess the entire space. Then we'll work our magic. By the time we're done, you won't be able to tell anything happened here. We use eco-friendly products. There won't be a lingering antiseptic smell in the room."

Brenna took a seat in the studio audience and started checking the list of supplies.

Margo joined her. "How did things go with the chefs?"

"They're both pretty shaken up by Chef Mike's death, but they understand the commitment they made to the show. They'll be here in the morning for rehearsal. How did things go here after I left?"

Margo shrugged. "Tim, Mathew, and I made some significant changes to the script. John came in as well. Tim contacted Sean to let him know about the replacement chef. He's going to need some background information on her and her sous chef. I sort of expect Sean to show up this afternoon looking for some information."

"Is it my responsibility to do the research for Sean? I don't remember Tim going over that when we were going over my duties."

"Yes, Tim should have mentioned that. Although, he probably didn't think we'd be replacing a chef."

"Fine, I'll see what I can find online. It should be relatively easy to get some information." Brenna added a note to her growing to-do list.

"What about the photo collage for the show tomorrow?"

"Oh, Chef Aaron gave me a photo album of the three of them when they were in culinary school. I haven't had much of an opportunity to look at it yet."

"Did you want to do that while the cleaning crew is here?" Margo asked.

"Sure. I'll go get the album. I'll be right back."

Brenna hurried to the small office.

When she returned, they spent some time going through the album. Brenna noted there were photos with other students in them. "I don't know if we can use these photos with the 'unknown' students. We might be infringing on privacy laws by doing so."

Margo agreed. "There are a lot of photos with just the three of them.

And if you wanted to use other students, you could always blur out their faces."

"I need to keep the number of photos down. I think Tim said there would be a minute for the moment of silence."

"Well, you won't get additional time from John. He keeps a pretty tight watch on the schedule, and anything extra winds up being left on the editing table. Can you narrow the photos down to fifteen?"

"I'll put the presentation together tonight. It won't take long. But cutting down the number of photos to fifteen will take some time. There are a lot of good photos here."

"Are you going to run this by Tim and Mathew before the taping?"

"Yes. They'll need to see it for final approval."

Marnie called out to Brenna and Margo. "Excuse me, could you come here please?"

"What's up?" Brenna asked as they made their way to the set.

"One of the team found this button lodged between the cupboard and the floor. Do either of you recognize it?"

Brenna took a close look at the gold-colored button. It was a shank button with some fancy scrollwork on it, and there was a bit of dark-blue thread still attached to the shank. She pulled out her phone and snapped a photo of the button, paying close attention to the scrollwork. "I don't remember anyone wearing clothing with this type of button. Margo, do you?"

"No. It might be from a jacket. What do we do with it?"

Marnie placed the button on the counter. "I've got a plastic bag and I'll put it in there. It may be evidence. If that's the case, we'll need to give it to the police. Usually, the crime scene techs are pretty good, but they may have missed this since it was stuck under the cupboard."

"I'd better call Detective Morris and tell her about this." Brenna called the detective. This time, she reached her.

Once she told Detective Morris what had been found, the detective indicated she and Bob would be at the studio shortly. They were all to stay where they were and hold onto the button.

"Marnie, she wants you to stay here until they arrive in order for you to show them exactly where the button was found. They'll probably take it back with them."

"No problem. We'll keep working the other areas. I'll make sure Lauren is close by since she's the one who found it."

A short time later, the two detectives were back in the studio. Detective Morris took the button, placed it in an evidence bag she had, and labeled it accordingly.

Bob took Marnie and Lauren aside and spoke quietly to them. He took out his notebook and jotted down something. He returned to stand next to Detective Morris, and Marnie and Lauren went back to work.

"It's unusual for our team to miss anything like this, but mistakes do happen. We'll bring this in, and we've noted where it was found. I take it neither of you recognizes the button?" Bob asked.

Margo shook her head. "Most of the people at the studio don't wear clothes that have those types of buttons. Almost everyone wears T-shirts or sweatshirts. Sean and the judges are the only ones I've seen in a suit, and that's only when we're taping."

"Brenna, could I speak with you, please?" Detective Morris asked.

"Sure."

Margo moved aside. "I'm going to check with Tim on a couple of things."

Detective Morris waited until Margo was out of earshot. "Thanks for the messages this morning. We brought Chef Aaron in for questioning."

Brenna winced. "Well, I don't think he killed Chef Mike. Those two were good friends."

Bob looked at Detective Morris, and she nodded. "Bren, I'm telling you this in confidence. The knife that was used to kill Chef Mike was Chef Aaron's. He identified it as part of his equipment. It doesn't look good for Aaron."

"Well, darn. I like him. I don't think he did it. And I know I didn't do it either. What would be Chef Aaron's motive? You guys have to keep looking." Brenna's voice dropped to a loud stage whisper.

"Apparently, Mike and Aaron had an argument a few weeks ago about doing this show. Mike wanted the three of them to do it, and Aaron felt it wouldn't be a good idea—that it would take too much time away from their restaurants," Bob said.

Brenna's eyebrows rose. "That's the first I've heard of this. No one here has mentioned it. And Chef Rosa didn't say anything about it when I talked to her this morning."

Bob crossed his arms. "Do you really think anyone would bring it up?"

"Probably not. But surely that couldn't be motive. The show's done well for all three of them. And friends can have disagreements."

"You're right on both counts. But the fact remains, the murder weapon belongs to Chef Aaron—and he didn't report it missing. *You* did." Detective Morris's voice held an edge.

"Well, the fact he told me about it should prove he had nothing to do with it. And what about the texts Chef Mike got last night?"

Bob nodded. "The techs were able to pull the texts off his phone. We're looking into where they originated from, but it will take some time."

"We need to get back to the station. Please don't share this information with anyone. It hasn't been made public yet. We'll be releasing the information about the weapon later today," Detective Morris said.

"I won't repeat anything you've told me. I'm having trouble processing it all right now. Am I still a suspect?"

Detective Morris paused. "At this time, yes. Both you and Chef Aaron warrant further investigation."

Brenna crossed her arms. "I told you I had nothing to do with this."

Bob put his hand on her arm. "Let us get to work. We'll see where this goes. Remember, if you hear anything that's off, let us know as soon as possible."

"I will."

The detectives left with the button.

Brenna's phone pinged with a text from Tim asking to see her as soon as possible. "Marnie, I have to meet with someone. I'll be back in a couple of minutes."

"Not a problem. We should be done here in about an hour."

Brenna hurried to Tim's office. "You needed to see me?"

"Yes. How did things go this morning with the two chefs? Are they okay to come in tomorrow morning?"

Brenna sat down in the chair facing Tim's desk. "They both seem unsettled and upset, but they understand their obligations to the show. I made sure they know about the new security measures, and that seemed to put them a bit more at ease. It may be difficult for them to come in tomorrow, but they'll show up."

"Did the cleaning company come in?"

"Yes. They're still here. I think they'll be done in an hour." Brenna paused. Should she tell Tim what the cleaning crew had found? Bob and Detective Morris hadn't said she couldn't.

"Anything else?" Tim asked.

"The cleaning company found a button under one of the cupboards. I called Detective Morris. The police came in and took it into evidence. I have a picture of it on my phone." Brenna opened the phone's photo app. "Here it is. I don't recognize it, and Margo didn't either. Do you?"

Tim glanced at the photo. "No, I don't. Margo had mentioned it to me. I wonder who it belongs to."

Brenna looked at the photo again. "It looks as if it should be on a suit jacket or a coat." She put her phone away. "Do you have the new script ready for me to send out?"

"We have a few more changes to make. I'm heading home to finish them up, and I'll send the script out to you when it's finished. And how are the photos coming along for the moment of silence?"

"I have thirty photos. Margo suggested trimming the number down to fifteen so we don't overwhelm the audience. What do you think?"

"Fifteen will be better. You do know there's only going to be one minute for this, don't you?"

"Yes, and I've been told John is really tight with time." Brenna smiled as she remembered how adamant Margo had been.

"He is. Are all the photos of Chef Mike during his cooking career?"

"There are a few of him at his restaurant and some at culinary school. I have a couple with him doing work with his charity. I'd like to include those as well."

As Tim looked up from his computer, his eyes narrowed. "You'll need to ensure the only people in the photos are the three chefs in the competition. No one else."

Brenna was taken aback by his tone of voice. He didn't sound happy about something. "Ah, yes. I had already checked with Margo on that, and the photos will be of Chef Mike. There's only one with the three chefs together."

"Okay, that's fine. It sounds like you have a handle on what's happening there. Mathew and I will need to see the final presentation before tomorrow morning. And what's happening with the supplies for tomorrow's show?"

"I've put a list together, but I still need to contact the suppliers."

"We need those supplies for tomorrow afternoon, or we won't be able to tape. Is it going to be a problem to get them?"

"No. I know the suppliers on the list. I'm going to call them shortly and arrange to meet with them in the morning at the market. They'll be able to bring everything we need there. I think that's easier than trying to arrange for items to be delivered. I'm going to stop at the warehouse store to pick up the dry goods we'll need for the taping."

"Great. I'm going to head home to finish the script changes. I'll see you early tomorrow morning." Tim closed down his computer and got up from his desk.

"Right. If I have any questions, I'll be in touch." Brenna walked back to the studio.

Brenna had just finished the supplies list for tomorrow's taping when Marnie stopped in front of her. "Excuse me. I wanted to let you know we're done here."

Brenna looked around the studio. It was cleaned and gleaming. The kitchen countertops shone under the lights. There was no sign that anything had happened in the studio. "Wow, this place looks great. You do excellent work."

"Thanks. Do you have an address for the invoice?" Marnie asked.

"Yes." Brenna pulled out a business card with the information Marnie required. "Thanks for coming in. If you send the invoice to this address, Sally will see that it gets taken care of."

"Will do. Ladies, we're off now."

Brenna contacted Joe on the radio. "Joe, I'll be letting the cleaning team out through the back. I'll be up front in a couple of minutes to sign them out."

"Roger that."

Once she had signed out the cleaning team, Brenna connected with the merchants from the farmers' market. She contacted them directly at their offices and put through the requests for supplies. It was too late to arrange for a delivery, so Brenna arranged to pick up the supplies at the market in the morning between six and six-thirty.

Brenna took the time to go through emails Tim had sent out and did a walk through the kitchen as well.

CHAPTER TWELVE

Brenna checked her watch. It was well after six. No wonder she was tired. She grabbed her jacket and backpack and made her way to the front.

Joe was still working at the security desk.

She swiped her ID card. "Bye, Joe. I'll see you tomorrow. Are you here tonight as well?"

"No, my replacement should be here soon. We work twelve-hour shifts. I've been told when the show is being taped, there'll be two of us at the front to make sure the audience gets through security."

"Sounds great. I'm going to head home. It's been a long day."

"Have a good night."

Brenna stopped at the warehouse store on her way home. A half-hour later, she had all the supplies the chefs would need for the taping. She'd deal with putting them in order in the morning.

Once Brenna got home, she unlocked her apartment door and peered down the hallway. No envelopes on the floor. She sighed. That was a good thing. She put her gear on the table. Now, to think about dinner, and then she'd finish up the photo collage.

Her phone rang. Glancing at the caller ID, she saw it was Emily. "Hi, Em. I just got home, and I'm trying to figure out what to have for dinner."

"That's why I'm calling. I just got off the phone with Kate, and we're bringing in some pizza. I've just called it in, and Kate is going to pick it up, along with a couple of bottles of wine. You okay with that?"

Brenna rolled her shoulders. "You bet. And thanks. It's been a long day."

"We'll be there in thirty minutes."

Brenna picked up her bag and jacket and hung them up. "I have time to finish up the collage before they arrive," she said to herself. Opening the laptop she had brought from work, she quickly sorted through the photos. After carefully culling the photos, she had what she thought would be a good presentation. "I need to get this out to Tim and Mathew now." She composed an email and attached the presentation. "Hope they approve it."

Her house line rang. It was Emily and Kate at the door. She buzzed open the door to the building and then put the laptop away. A quick check around and the apartment looked fine.

There was a knock at the door, and Brenna opened it for her friends.

"Hey there! We've brought dinner!" Kate pulled Brenna into a hug as she walked through the doorway. "Brenna, why didn't you call and let me know what happened? I'm so sorry I didn't know and wasn't there for you. I was going to phone you last night, but Emily told me you were probably sleeping."

"Sorry. Yesterday was insane. And I did go to sleep pretty early last night. I should have connected with you, though."

"Not to worry. We're glad you slept." Emily slipped out of her heels and walked into the kitchen. The open plan of the space allowed the conversation to flow easily. She opened the cupboards and pulled out plates for the pizza. "Kate, can you grab some wine glasses?"

Emily set the pizza on the coffee table, and Kate poured generous servings of wine. They sat on the couch and love seat and took a deep breath.

"So, you're okay? You were back at work today?" Emily picked up a plate and started dishing out the pizza.

Brenna took a gulp of wine. "Yes, we were back at work. I had quite a few things to do, and the police released the studio as well. That meant bringing in a cleaning company. I had to meet with Chef Aaron and Chef Rosa too."

Kate dabbed her lips with a napkin. "Why did you have to meet with them?"

"Tim wanted me to make sure they're okay with coming back to work. We have a rehearsal tomorrow morning, and then we're taping the show in the afternoon."

"And are they okay?" Emily asked.

"They seem to be. Honestly, I don't think they have much of a choice. They signed a contract, and if they don't appear, the production company could sue them."

"Well, that sounds crappy. Chef Mike was their friend, wasn't he?" Kate frowned as she put down her plate.

Brenna swallowed. "Yeah, he was. But, guys, there's all kinds of stuff I'm learning about the chefs and their time at the culinary school. Promise you won't repeat any of this stuff."

Both Kate and Emily promised, and Brenna filled them in on what she had learned about the chefs and their former classmate.

Emily frowned. "What does he have to do with this?"

"I don't know. Probably nothing, but there's something about him that doesn't feel right. And none of the chefs would hire him. There has to be a reason for that."

"Uh, yeah. He lost his other job because patrons were poisoned at the restaurant when he was working. That would be the reason." Kate shook her head.

"I know that. But look, here's a photo of him." Brenna grabbed her laptop and opened the photo file. "It's from the newspaper article I found online. I've looked for photos of him in Chef Aaron's photo album. I've found someone who looks like him, but I'm not sure if it's the same person."

Kate looked at the photo. "He's quite attractive. Do you think you've seen him somewhere else?"

"He reminds me of someone. Around the eyes and the nose. I just can't place him," Brenna said.

Emily leaned over and glanced at the photo. "He does have the kind of face you think you've seen before. That could be it."

Kate asked, "Did you ask Chef Aaron or Chef Rosa about him?"

"No. They were pretty upset about Chef Mike, and honestly, I didn't even think about it. I should have, though." Brenna looked at the photo again before closing her laptop.

"So, Brenna, fill me in. Are there any hot guys at the studio?"

"Really, Kate! Only you could make me laugh right now." Brenna chuckled. "That feels good. Hmm, hot guys at the studio. There are a couple of guys you might find the right type. The host of the show is pretty good-looking, and the executive producer isn't too bad either. But neither of them would be my choice."

Kate sighed. "Details, please."

Brenna rolled her eyes. "The host's name is Sean Jamieson, and he thinks a lot of himself. He's attractive and has blue eyes and dark hair. He's about six feet and kinda lean, but he has some muscle definition. And, you know, he looks great in a suit. I guess he has to have a lot of self-confidence to be on television. At the rehearsal on Monday, he pretty well carried the show."

"And the executive producer?" Kate prodded.

"He's hot in a nerdy kind of way. You know, he wears these cute tortoiseshell glasses, and his hair flops over to the side. He's tall too, but really skinny."

"So, a brainy look?" Emily asked.

"Yeah, I guess so." Brenna reached for another piece of pizza.

"Did you say you're going to be taping tomorrow afternoon?" Kate was looking at her phone.

"Yes. We're going to start around three. Are you thinking of coming in?"

"I might. I don't have to go in to work until seven tomorrow night."

"That would be awesome."

They spent the next hour or so eating and drinking wine.

Brenna looked at her clock. "Guys, this has been great, but I have a couple of things I need to finish up before I can get to bed tonight. So, I'm kicking you out."

"What time is it anyway?" Emily asked.

Kate sighed. "It's almost nine. Let's go, Emily."

They picked up the dishes and the empty pizza box and made their way out the door.

"Thanks so much for coming over. You guys are the best." Brenna wrapped them in a hug before they headed out.

Brenna got ready for bed and brought her laptop in with her. She wanted to see if she could find out more about Charles Mathews. She thought back to the articles she had read about him online. Maybe the reporter could give her some more information.

Pulling her laptop toward her, she composed her message to Mary Gilles, the reporter. It was brief, explaining what had happened at the studio and asking if she would be willing to speak with Brenna. She added the photo from Chef Aaron's album of the student who looked similar to the person in the newspaper article and asked if he was Charles Mathews.

That finished, Brenna turned her attention to finding out as much as she could about the new sous chef, Carol Alcott. There were a lot of good resources online, and Brenna was able to pull together some information that would help Sean tomorrow.

BRENNA'S ALARM got her up at five-thirty the next morning. A hot shower and a strong cup of coffee helped her wake up. She pulled on the clothes she had laid out the night before, black jeans and a green button-down shirt, and then grabbed her tool belt, backpack, and jacket. A cup of coffee in her travel mug and a muffin and she was on her way to the market by six.

Located downtown, by the waterfront, the market was a bustling hive of activity in the summer with people in the area for summer holidays. In the fall, the activity fell off during the week but picked up on the weekends, with people coming to their cottages. There were several islands just outside the harbor where cottages had been built, and the only access to the cottages was by boat.

The market had a wide variety of foodstuffs, including fresh meat, poultry, game, fish, fruits, and vegetables. There were also several stands selling baked goods, breads, and preserves. On Saturday mornings, craftspeople had displays from paintings to pottery. Large, colorful canopies provided protection from the elements. Some vendors had sandwich boards advertising their products; others had banners across the top of their booths with information. In the summer, there was live music on the weekends from noon to four. In winter, the market moved indoors to a large warehouse on the waterfront.

The first vendor on her list was the farm where the studio purchased produce, Hastings Farm. Brenna walked up to the stand.

"Hi. I'm Brenna Flynn with Studio One Productions. I ordered supplies yesterday to be picked up this morning."

The woman sitting behind the counter stood. "Hi, Brenna! I guess you don't recognize me."

Brenna took a good look at the woman. She appeared to be the same age as Brenna and was sporting a large baby bump. The woman's eyes crinkled in a smile, and Brenna gasped. "Lori, is that you?"

"Yes, it is. How long since we've seen each other?"

"It has to be at least four years. I left Bayview and moved to Wayhaven, just outside of Chicago. I'm back home now. I didn't realize you were with Hastings Farms."

"Ken Hastings and I got married a few years ago. We took over his dad's farm when he retired last year. I have to tell you, Brenna, being one of the suppliers for the cooking show is a big deal for us. Ken's been working hard to ensure the crops we grow are organic, and we think it makes a big difference in the quality of the food prepared. Our logo shows up on the credits, and we've seen a jump in shoppers showing up here because of it. Shoppers are actually telling us they've seen our logo."

"I'm glad to hear that. The chefs were pleased with the produce they've been working with. Do you have the studio's order ready?"

"I do. It's in the back. Do you have other vendors you need to pick up items from?"

"Yes."

"Where did you park your car?"

"It's in the side parking lot. Why?"

"There's a laneway behind the stalls that you can use to pick up your orders. If you drive across the square to Front Street and then take the first left, that's the laneway. You'll be able to see each individual vendor because we have signage in the back."

"Thanks, Lori. That's great. I should be back here in about twenty or thirty minutes."

Brenna hurried back to her Jeep and followed Lori's instructions. She had never known about the laneway and was happy to see it made life easier. The vendors had the studio's orders ready for her, and she made certain they had the correct address for the invoice. Her final stop was at the Hastings Farm stall.

She got out of the Jeep, opened the tailgate, and moved some of the bags around, as the back of the Jeep was starting to get full. Then she knocked on the side of the stall.

"Lori, is it ok if I pick up the order now?"

"Ah, there you are. Yes. Everything is ready. We put them in two separate bags for you."

"And you have the information for the invoice?"

"I do. I have a copy here for you." Lori was at her table and picked up the invoice for Brenna's signature. "I just need you to sign for the goods."

Brenna picked up a pen and signed the invoice.

"Awful what happened with Chef Mike, isn't it? Do the police have any leads?" Lori looked at Brenna.

"All I know is they're looking at everyone who worked with him or knew him. They released the studio yesterday afternoon. That means we can get back to taping today. It's been a pretty stressful start to a new job."

"When did you start working there?"

"On Monday. I haven't been able to get work with any of the school boards. Everyone has been hit with budget cuts. I've been working with Jackie Randall over at Randall Temp Agency to see if I can find anything. This position at the studio came up, and I lucked into it." Brenna bit her lip.

"Chef Mike used to come here early every morning to pick up the freshest produce. I really liked him. He built a good life for himself. But I do remember hearing him argue with someone on his phone a few weeks ago. I think it was someone from his restaurant. I heard the other guy yelling at him about money owed to him. Mike didn't seem too happy with the call."

"Do you remember what day it was?" Brenna asked.

"Not really. Like I said, he came here every day."

"Thanks, Lori. It was good to see you again. You take care." Brenna picked up the bags and the small crate of mushrooms and put them in the back of the Jeep. As she drove back to the studio, Brenna couldn't help but think about what Lori had said about the argument she had overheard. That was twice someone had mentioned Mike had been arguing with another person. She wondered if the police were aware of it.

She drove into the studio parking lot and checked her watch. It was already seven.

Brenna carried several of the bags into the building and stopped at the front desk. The security guard was at the front desk, along with Connor Malone.

"Here, Brenna, let me help you with those," Connor said. "Do you have more to bring in?"

"Thanks, and yes I do."

"I'll give you a hand." Connor followed Brenna out and helped with the bags.

Brenna went back for her backpack and her travel coffee cup.

Joe had the sign-in book ready for her to sign. "Don't forget to sign in."

"Thanks. I'd better get these to the kitchens."

Connor grabbed one of the carts and placed the bags on it. "If you tell me where you want these, I'll take them for you."

"Great. I need them in the kitchens in the studio. Just about everything needs to go in the fridges, and the meats need to go in the walk-in fridge."

Connor led the way to the studio. Once there, they placed the bags on the counter.

"Thanks for your help. I'm fine. I can put this away." Brenna started pulling items out of the bags and placing them on the counters.

"No problem." Connor looked around the studio. "The cleaning company did a good job. How are you doing? It must have been difficult to find the body."

Brenna was sorting the dry goods on the counter. "I think I'm doing all right. But there are moments when I can't believe it happened. He was there, on the floor." Brenna pointed to her right.

"Well, there wasn't anything you could have done for him. From what I understand, he had been dead for several hours."

"How do you know that?"

"I spoke to Bob yesterday. I wanted to know what the police had found and what to expect as far as dealing with the security. Bob and I were in high school together. And yes, I knew Mike too."

"Is that where you met Dave?"

"Yes. Dave and I went to the same university after high school and played hockey on the varsity team."

Brenna continued sorting the food she had picked up. "I do remember you from the wedding party. But I didn't get much of an opportunity to talk to you. That day flew by."

"And I went back out on assignment shortly after the wedding. You guys had already left for Wayhaven when I got back." He paused for a moment. "I'm sorry about what happened to Dave. I was surprised to hear he had died—and about the issues surrounding his death."

"Yeah, well, there was a lot I didn't know about. It was a shock to learn what he'd been up to." Brenna's posture stiffened. She stopped what she was doing and let a deep breath out.

"If there's anything I can do to help, let me know. Is there still an investigation surrounding his death?"

"No. His death was accidental. He was driving way too fast, and there was ice on the road. He lost control of his car. The trucker he passed saw everything. It was actually recorded on his dashcam. The only ongoing investigation is the one regarding the drugs." Brenna paused for a moment, closing her eyes.

Connor waited for a beat. "What about the drugs?"

"You know he was working as a pharmaceutical rep for one of the larger companies, right?" Brenna looked at Connor.

He nodded in agreement.

"It appears he developed a gambling problem and started to sell some of the drugs the company was producing on the side to a syndicate. The syndicate was also involved with the gambling. It's a big mess. The DEA, FBI, and State Police are trying to figure it all out. It took a lot of talking to convince them I knew nothing about what he had been up to. They finally have a trail leading them away from me. That was one thing Dave did well. He left a trail with his email and Internet searches. Once they searched my phone and computer, they realized I didn't have a clue what he was doing." Brenna shook her head. "I haven't talked to anyone about this. Well, except my parents and Emily. They know, and they've been great."

Connor put his hand over hers. "Well, the offer is there. If you need anything, let me know."

"Thanks. I may take you up on that in the future, but for now, I'm doing the best I can. I better get this put away and make sure these kitchens are clean. It's going to be a busy day."

Connor smiled. "Yes, it will be busy. I'll let you get to work."

CHAPTER THIRTEEN

Brenna finished putting the produce and meats away. She took a moment and looked around the set.

Everything appeared to be the same as it had been when she left last night. Clean and organized. She kept walking to the back and put her jacket in a crew locker. She heard something fall. Closing the door of the locker, Brenna called out, "Is anyone there?"

No one answered. A scuffling sound came from behind the set. Brenna made sure her radio was secure and walked quietly back to the set. She couldn't see anyone there. She made her way to the makeup room. Just outside the door, she saw a chair on the floor. It looked as if it had been knocked down.

"Well, this is dumb. No one's around, and chairs are falling. I don't have time for this." Brenna picked up the chair and set it right. "And I need some coffee."

She found her backpack and pulled out her travel mug that she had put in there earlier. She walked into the small office and looked around for a coffeepot. None in sight.

"Maybe they have one in Tim and Mathew's offices." Opening the door to their offices, she was startled to see Mathew setting up his laptop. "Mathew, I didn't realize you were here already."

Mathew looked up. "Um, yes. I just came in. I must have missed you. I wanted to come in a bit earlier than normal. With everything we're doing today, I thought it would be a good idea to get a jump on things."

"Were you able to get a press release out about the show moving forward?"

"We've worked with our PR agency to get a release out with the information on Chef Tina replacing Chef Mike and how we're proceeding with the show. The release should be in this morning's paper and on the morning news shows. Is there anything I can help you with?"

Brenna held up her empty travel mug. "Is there coffee around here? I really need another cup this morning."

"There's a full coffee and tea service in the larger conference room. It's a Keurig system so no one's responsible for having to brew it."

"Thanks. I'll get out of your hair and get on with my day."

Brenna found the coffee maker and sighed. Thank goodness, more coffee. A glance at her watch had her moving a bit faster. The crew was expected in about a half hour for a meeting, and she wanted to check the kitchen cupboards and drawers. Everything had to be organized for the rehearsal later that morning. And she needed to double-check on the items in the walk-in fridge and pantry.

The pantry was starting to come together. Dry goods had been placed on the shelves, labels had been attached, and the space looked organized and well-stocked.

Now, to check on the meats. She walked in and shivered. The temperature was set just above freezing. Nothing froze, but the meat was kept at the ideal temperature. *Not so ideal for people.* Moving quickly, she verified the packages were correctly labeled and made certain they were displayed properly.

That task completed, she hurried out of the freezer and ran into Sean Jamieson. "Argh! What? Who . . ." Brenna pushed at him with both hands.

Sean Jamieson backed away and raised his hands. "Hey, hey! It's me, Sean. I didn't mean to frighten you."

Brenna put a hand to her throat. "Well, you scared me. I wasn't expecting anyone around here. You're lucky I didn't scream my head off and punch you in the stomach."

Sean rolled his eyes. "Sorry. I didn't realize you were still jumpy."

Brenna closed her eyes for a moment and drew a deep breath. "I'm not 'still jumpy.' I am jumpy. It was unnerving to find Chef Mike. It sure would help if people around here made a bit of noise when they walked around."

"Hmm. Maybe we should all wear bells so you can hear us."

Brenna smiled, despite herself. "Really funny. Okay, I guess maybe it would be a bit extreme. Did you need something from me?"

"Actually, I do. I came in to find out what was happening with Chef Mike's replacement. Tim told me you might have some information on Chef Tina and the new sous chef. He told me about the photo collage you're putting together for the moment of silence. You and I should probably talk about how it's going to roll out."

"Sure. I can give you the information I have on both of the chefs. The new sous chef is Carol Alcott. I have a bio on each of them, more on Chef Tina, since what I had earlier was a bit sparse."

"Unbelievable. You have additional info? That would be great. How much do you have?"

Brenna crossed to the red kitchen's island where her tablet was. She pulled up a file. "I have six pages of information on the two of them. Chef Tina has been working in the industry for a while. There's more on her education and her experience around the area. She started with Chef Mike two years ago. Carol Alcott is fairly new to the industry, and she's a bit older than one would expect. Let me send you what I have in an email, and you can read it through. It should help for when you sit down to talk to them."

"That's great! I'll take a look at it now. I have some time before the rehearsal gets underway."

"Done. Now, about the photo collage. I have fifteen pictures of Chef Mike. Some were pulled from the show's website, others from Chef Aaron's personal collection, and I have some from the restaurant's website. We only have a minute to display the photos, and there will be a moment of silence while the photos are being shown. The studio audience will need to be told when we're doing this."

"I don't have a problem making sure people know about it. I'll check with Tim and Mathew on the timing. And where are the photos going to be shown?"

"Tim has agreed to have the photos off to the side of the kitchens. Everyone will be able to see them, but the photos won't be over his kitchen." Brenna was glad Tim had agreed with her choice of where to show the photos.

"We'll see how the chefs react to the photos at the rehearsal this morning. I'm going to take some time to speak with Chef Tina and make certain she's okay with what's happening. I don't want her surprised by anything this morning." Sean was checking his phone as he spoke.

"I know Tim and Mathew met with her yesterday, but I'm not sure what they spoke about."

"Thanks for your help, Brenna. This information is invaluable. I'll review it and be well prepped. Everyone should be here in an hour or so."

Brenna watched as Sean walked to the studio audience area to sit down. She assumed he was reading through the material she had sent him. She turned around as Margo came in.

"Hi. Just checking to see if you're on target to be ready for this morning's rehearsal?"

"Thanks. I'm a bit behind. The kitchen cupboards and drawers need to be checked over once more. I want to make sure nothing's been moved around since last night."

"I'll give you a hand. There's no one else available."

They found a few items had been moved from one cupboard to another. It was annoying but not something that would have been dangerous. They were able to get the kitchens in order.

Margo gave the area one last look. "We're meeting in the conference room in fifteen minutes. Tim wants to go over everything one last time before the rehearsal."

"Oh, that reminds me. I need to get the script to Sally so she can upload it to the teleprompter. I better get this done right away or I'll be late." Brenna grabbed her tablet.

"I'll see you in the conference room." Margo left as Brenna hurried to the front desk to speak with Sally.

Brenna made it to the conference room just as Tim was getting started. She slipped into a chair and drew a breath. The morning had been busier than she expected. All the crew appeared to be present for the pre-production meeting.

"Alright, everyone. Let's get the show moving again. I just have a few things to share with you all. First, you need to know everything is set to roll for this afternoon's taping. The rehearsal this morning will be slightly abbreviated, but we think it's important for the chefs to get back to the set and do a run-through. We'll spend most of the rehearsal working on the blocking, and Sean is going to do his best to get the judges and chefs to relax. Brenna, did you get the script to Sally?"

"Yes. She's setting it up now."

"Sean, any questions?"

"No, I'm good. I spoke with Brenna and have some information on Tina Patterson and the new sous chef, Carol Alcott. I'll make sure to connect with both of them when they arrive."

Brenna felt someone come into the room. She turned around and saw Connor Malone standing at the back. He looked at her and smiled. She nodded and then focused her attention on Tim.

"We heard from the police. They have a few 'persons of interest' in Chef Mike's murder, but they aren't divulging any information. Both of the detectives will be stopping in this morning and will be attending the taping this afternoon."

John stood at the front of the room. "We're cooperating fully with the police. I don't want any of you to be alarmed when you see them here. We also have Connor Malone with us today. He'll be watching how we operate during the rehearsal and the taping. I'm hoping he can pinpoint some areas where we can improve the security of the set."

Margo spoke up. "How is it going to work for the studio audience today? I want to make sure people can get in quickly and be seated. It's going to be tough enough on the chefs to be here without waiting too long."

"Connor, if you could address this?" Tim asked.

Connor moved to the front of the room. "Good morning. We'll have two security guards in the front lobby working with the members of the studio audience. As I mentioned yesterday, anyone who has a bag will need to have it scanned through our machine. Anyone who objects will be turned away. There will be signs posted in the lobby before people get to the front desk. We'll also have a third guard at the door, ensuring everyone coming in is there for the show or has business in the studio."

Tim nodded. "That will work. We aren't doing a live show. We can be flexible with our start time. I don't want us to go much past the scheduled time, though."

"Understood. But our priority is the safety of everyone in the building, and we won't skimp on the screening." Connor's voice rang with authority.

"Right. Okay, everyone, let's get ready for the rehearsal. Brenna, if I could see you for a minute please?" Tim looked at her.

Brenna made her way to the front of the room.

"Mathew and I are going to meet with the judges and chefs in the smaller conference room in about twenty minutes. Can you run out and pick up some muffins and coffee?"

"Sure. Do you have a preference, or can I get whatever is available?"

"Anything available is fine. I'm trying to put them at ease before we start today. Mathew and I will go over the security information and let them know what's been happening so far."

"No problem. Is Mr. Malone joining you?"

"That's not a bad idea. I'll see if he's available. Thanks." Tim left the room.

Brenna shook her head. Another thing added to her list on an already busy morning.

She hurried out of the building and ran across to the coffee shop on the corner. Fortunately, a fresh batch of muffins had just come out of the oven. She had to wait while they brewed a couple of extra pots of coffee and poured them into the thermos carafes.

Getting to the studio, she went directly to the conference room to set things up. She texted Tim once that was complete.

T: Please stay for the meeting in case something comes up

Brenna groaned. Really? She didn't respond to Tim's text. Instead, she sat down and waited a few minutes before everyone showed up.

CHAPTER FOURTEEN

Brenna stood to greet the chefs and judges as they quietly entered the conference room. "Good morning. Tim will be here shortly. Please help yourself to coffee and muffins." Brenna led them to the coffee service.

They nodded their thanks. Brenna poured coffee and handed them each a napkin for their muffin.

Chef Tina introduced sous chef Carol to the other chefs and judges.

Chef Rosa leaned in to give Chef Tina a hug. "How are you doing today?"

"It still seems surreal. I can't believe he's really gone and not coming back. Vicky and I got together last night. We had a good talk, well, we did after we stopped crying. We've decided to keep the restaurant closed for a week, and then we'll see about reopening."

Chef Aaron stood next to her. "You know, anything you need you just have to call. We're here to help. Mike was like a brother to me."

Chef Tina sniffled, and her eyes filled with tears.

Carol cleared her throat. "The restaurant staff is devastated. Chef Mike was a great guy to work for, always willing to show you new techniques and to give you a chance to prove yourself."

Tim walked into the conference room and grabbed a cup of coffee. Brenna stood back as he filled the room with his presence. She took her tablet and sat down, prepared to take notes if needed.

"Thank you all for coming in a bit early today. I wanted to make sure you're all aware we're doing everything we can to cooperate with the police." He took a sip of coffee. "We want Chef Mike's killer caught as much as anyone else. We've had the police here several times, and we've turned the studio over to them as needed. Moving forward, we've upped the security and made significant changes about tracking who's entering the building. I've also been advised the police will be here for the taping this afternoon."

Ms. Keene, one of the judges, asked, "Do they have any idea who did this?"

Tim said, "I don't think they have any answers yet. It's still early in their investigation."

Mr. Fitzgerald said, "We've all been questioned as well but haven't been given any answers. I can tell you, as mayor, my office has advised the chief of police we will authorize additional manpower if needed."

Tim nodded. "Do you have any questions for me at this time?"

Connor arrived just as Tim asked the question.

Tim said, "Connor, perfect timing. Ladies and gentlemen, Connor Malone of Malone Security. He's been working with us to ensure everyone's safety. Connor, I'll turn this over to you."

Connor took a few minutes to explain to the judges and chefs the changes that had been made in the security for the studio. He reiterated the steps that would be taken with the studio audience and reminded everyone about the new procedure anyone else needed to go through to get into the studio.

Tim then took charge again. "I suggest we get in the studio and start the rehearsal. Carol, welcome to the team. Don't worry about making any mistakes. This morning is a rehearsal and where we work out the bugs."

Brenna followed the group and found a seat in the studio audience. Margo sat next to her, and they watched as the chefs and judges made their way on stage.

John welcomed the chefs and judges to the rehearsal. He made sure they understood the rehearsal would focus on blocking, placement, and Sean walking through the script.

Detective Morris and Bob were sitting in the studio audience watching the rehearsal carefully. Bob went to Connor and spoke with him briefly and then returned to his seat.

The rehearsal went better than Brenna had thought it would. There were some hiccups and dead air, but Sean was able to ad-lib through these moments. Sean kept the show on track. John made sure to run through the different segments of the show several times. It was important the chefs and judges relaxed and became comfortable being on the set again. At the end of the rehearsal, everyone was ready for the taping later that afternoon.

Tim walked to the kitchen area. "Thanks, everyone, for your hard work this morning. I know it wasn't easy coming in, but we've taken a huge step forward. This afternoon's taping is scheduled for three. We'll need everyone in makeup no later than two. The postproduction team will meet in my office for a short debrief in a few minutes. Sean, I'll need you to attend as well."

Detective Morris and Bob got up to leave.

As they walked by Brenna, Bob stopped. "We'll be back for the taping. Is there somewhere we'll be able to stand where we won't be in anyone's way?" he asked.

"You don't want to be in the audience section?"

"No, we'd prefer to be a bit more anonymous."

"There are a few seats around the corner, where the sponsor booth is. You can sit there."

"Thanks, that'll work. See you this afternoon."

Brenna walked into the conference room, and Mathew was already talking to Sean about some of his concerns. "You have to be careful with the ad-libbing. The judges seemed to have a hard time following when you deviate from the script."

Sean frowned. "I don't think the ad-libbing is giving them any difficulties. I stick as much to the script as I can. The chefs and judges are going to have to be able to roll with it. And I'm going to bring in some audience questions like I've done before. John, Tim, do either of you think it's an issue?"

John said, "I don't think it is. The studio audience questions keep the show fresh, and that segment needs to stay in the show."

Tim said, "The chefs will be fine. They should be able to answer the basic questions. I'm confident the judges will be able to work with anything that comes their way. All three of the judges can think quickly on their feet."

Mathew threw his hands up in the air and scowled. "Fine. I just want to make certain my comments about the flow of the show are heard. If you're all good with the way things worked, I have nothing further to say."

Brenna wondered what Mathew was so upset about. She thought the rehearsal had gone well.

John said, "Our editors do a great job of cleaning up the show and making it work."

They wrapped up the meeting after another half hour. Mathew was conspicuously silent for the remainder of the meeting.

Brenna planned to grab a quick lunch from the food truck down the street from the studio and take a few minutes to herself before the craziness of the afternoon started up.

Sean walked up to Brenna. "What are you doing for lunch? And please don't tell me you survive on coffee alone."

"I was just going to head to the food truck down the street. Apparently, it has great sandwiches."

"Do you mind if I join you?"

"No, but we'll need to be quick. I have a few things to deal with before this afternoon's taping."

They signed out of the building and walked down the street toward the food truck. It was just past one, and most of the lunch crowd was gone.

They placed their orders and sat on a nearby bench to wait.

"How are you enjoying the work?" Sean asked.

"I've never done anything like this before. I'm still learning and trying to figure out what's coming next. I hadn't planned on being involved in a murder investigation, though."

"Yeah, I hadn't planned on that either. Do the police have any leads?"

"All I know is they're still looking into alibis and doing some digging into Chef Mike's life. Apparently, stats show most people are killed by someone they know."

"Well, no one on the show knew him well—except for the other chefs and maybe Mr. Harlow, the restaurant critic." Sean got up to grab their sandwiches and walked to a picnic table with Brenna.

"Thanks." Brenna unwrapped her sandwich. "I think the police will be looking at everyone involved in his life. I had to go back to the police station and go over my statement and provide them with my alibi. Not a lot of fun."

Sean put his steak and cheese panini down. "They can't suspect you. Why would you have killed him?"

"Well, they were looking at me because I found him. And apparently, we're all suspects. Just because we work here. The police are going over everything they've found carefully. None of us are in the clear. I have to tell you, it's given me a few bad moments. I'm looking at people here, and I realized I don't know them at all. How many people working on this show do you know?"

Sean chewed his panini. "I've worked with John, Tim, and a few other people on the crew before. But know them well? I can't say that I do. We've gone out after the show for a meal or drinks, but no one is a close friend. I would think the police would be looking at the people in Chef Mike's life, his family, employees at the restaurant, or his friends."

"I'm sure the police know what they're doing. So, how long have you been working in television?" Brenna was desperate to change the focus of the conversation. She didn't want to give anyone information she shouldn't. Detective Morris and Bob wouldn't be pleased.

"About five years. It hasn't been steady work, but I've been building a following as a host. I've done a few other reality shows and some game shows too. This is my first cooking show."

"Is this show different from the other shows you've worked on?"

"Yes. The chefs are fascinating people, and the fact their restaurants are successful here in town makes people want to learn more about them. And their personalities are so different and so is their style of cooking and preparing food. Chef Mike and sous chef Tina were always talking in the kitchen. Chef Rosa speaks very softly to her sous chef Frankie. Honestly, those two seem to communicate by just looking at each other. And Chef Aaron's Cordon Blue training really comes out in his technique. And that's why I like bringing in the audience questions. You never know what they're going to ask, even though we pre-screen them. They've been a key factor in keeping things interesting."

Brenna nodded. "I can see where the personalities play a big role in the show. What about the judges?"

"They're harder to get involved, so what I've been doing with them is making sure they get a chance to speak up when they're finished with the scoring."

Brenna finished her turkey bacon wrap and glanced at her watch. "I need to get back to the studio. I want to check on everything before we tape. We've been running into some problems with supplies being moved around on the set."

She and Sean walked back to the studio. As they signed in at security, they noticed the chefs and judges going through to the makeup department.

When they got to the set, she said, "Thanks for coming with me to lunch. It was great chatting with you."

"I enjoyed our talk. I hope this murder hasn't put you off the television industry."

"No. I don't think this has anything to do with television. We'll see what the police can find out. Hopefully, this is resolved soon."

"I'd better head to makeup. Will you be able to do some pre-screening of audience members who might want to ask questions?"

"I think so. I'll check with Margo to see what she needs done."

"If the two of you can talk to some people who'd be interested, put a few names together. Then I'll talk to them and make the final decision. You'll need to let the makeup people know, and they'll make sure the audience members look good."

"Sounds like a plan."

The crew was busy making sure the lighting, cameras, and booms were all in place for the show. Brenna took one more look at the pantry and large walk-in fridge. Everything looked fine. She decided to check the kitchen cupboards and found items had been moved since the last time she tidied up.

"I can't believe this. Who on earth is doing this?" she muttered.

She began to rearrange the kitchen cupboards in Chef Rosa's kitchen and then took a look into the other two kitchens. Sure enough, those were a big mess as well. "I can't do this on my own before the chefs get back here."

She pulled out her phone and sent a text to Margo.

    B: In the kitchens need help
    M: Coming

Margo came running around the corner and called out, "Brenna are you okay?"

Brenna stood up from behind the counter, where she had been sorting the pots and pans. "Yes. But I need help with these kitchens. Someone's been in and changed everything around again."

"You've got to be kidding. We just got them done before rehearsal, and the chefs didn't touch anything in here." Margo hurried around the counter and opened one of the cupboards in Chef Aaron's kitchen. Trays came tumbling out when she pulled the cupboard door open.

"Here's a picture of what they're supposed to look like. If we work quickly, we can have them in order before the studio audience starts coming in." Brenna showed Margo a photo on her phone.

Margo and Brenna reorganized the cupboards and drawers in record time.

When they were done, Margo said, "You know, Tim and Mathew are going to have to be told about this. They may need to look at putting security in here too."

"I know, but what a waste of manpower. I hate to think this is a prank or, even worse, sabotage."

"Well, who would gain from the show being sabotaged?" Margo asked.

"I'm not sure. Maybe Tim and Mathew will have a better idea." Brenna looked at Margo thoughtfully. "And although I do agree we need to talk to Tim and Mathew, it might be best to wait until this afternoon's taping is finished."

"You're right. Did you check the pantry?"

"I did. Both the pantry and the walk-in fridge are fine."

They were just leaving the kitchen when Brenna's headset chirped. "Brenna, Joe here. We have people showing up for this afternoon's taping. I seem to recall being told we can't let them in until a half-hour before the show starts."

Brenna spoke into her headset. "Let me talk to John and Tim and see what they want. I think it's too early to have anyone come in yet."

"What's happening?" Margo asked.

Brenna filled her in as they walked toward Tim's office.

Margo shook her head. "It'll be Tim and John's call, but I think it's way too early to bring the audience in."

"What's up?" Tim asked as they entered his office.

Brenna provided Tim with the information security had given her.

"It's too early. I'll contact security and let them know we can't have people in the audience until thirty minutes before we're scheduled to start taping. It's a safety issue. Anything else?" Tim's voice held an edge.

Margo looked at Brenna and nodded.

Brenna sighed. "I was going to wait until after the taping, but I may as well tell you now. Someone seems to be pulling pranks in the kitchens. Every time I look, the cupboards have items that have been moved around. I don't know who's doing it or why, but it's unsettling and potentially disruptive to the show. If I hadn't checked the cupboards and drawers after coming in from lunch, today's taping would have been a mess. The chefs wouldn't have found any of their utensils or pots and pans. It would have interrupted the flow of the show."

Tim threw down his pen. "You don't know who's doing this?"

"No. I don't know why anyone would do this. Do you?" Brenna put her hands on her hips.

Tim pushed his chair away from his desk and stood. He paced behind the desk. "One of the benefits of working in a small town is we don't have any competition for the show. I don't know anyone in this town who could have it in for me or for the sponsors."

"What about Mathew or John? Do they know anyone here or would anyone have a reason to try to make them or the show look bad?" Brenna asked.

"I can't think of one. John has been in the business for a long time, and he's well regarded by his peers. Mathew is just starting out, but he hasn't had time to rub anyone the wrong way."

Margo asked, "What about Sean?"

Tim stopped pacing. "You mean Sean doing this or someone out to get Sean?"

"I guess either one. Most of his work has been in the Southwest. He isn't well-known out here. Is it possible someone has a grudge against him? Was there someone he beat out for this job?" Margo asked.

"I don't see it. If someone were targeting Sean, they would likely use another method to get to him. So, what do you want to do about this?" Tim folded his arms across his chest.

"I'm going to talk to the detectives. No one's been hurt or put in danger by this, but it's annoying. Bob was quite clear with me when he said to alert them about anything that isn't normal, and I don't think this is normal."

"Right. Let me know what they say and keep me informed about what's happening. We may need to start having security monitor the set." Tim sat in his chair and returned to his work.

Margo and Brenna headed out, dismissed.

CHAPTER FIFTEEN

Brenna and Margo were walking to the set when Brenna's headset crackled.

"Brenna here." She slowed down. She put out her hand to Margo and motioned for her to wait. "I'll talk to Margo and see what she recommends. I'll get right back to you."

Margo's forehead puckered. "Now what?"

"Joe, at the front desk. He says there are at least seventy-five people lined up to be part of the studio audience. He asked how many people we can seat and if we have additional seating if needed."

"There's seating for fifty people in the studio audience. We can set up additional chairs if they're needed. I'll go talk to Tim and see what he recommends. He and John have the final decision on numbers for the audience."

"I'll go to the front and check on what's happening." Brenna hurried to the front. "Hi, Joe, how are things?"

The lineup of people waiting to get in was well past the front door and onto the sidewalk. It was still too early for the studio audience to be let in. Brenna was thankful the chefs and judges were already in makeup and wouldn't have to make their way through the gauntlet of audience members.

"Everyone's behaving. We're just wondering how many people can be seated."

"Margo's checking with Tim right now. He and John will make the final decision. There's seating for fifty, but we can add more chairs. We'll just have to hustle to make it work for today's taping."

"We're still going with the schedule we had set up, right? No one in until thirty minutes before taping?" Joe asked Brenna.

"That's right. Who do you have working with you this afternoon?"

"Doris will be here in a few minutes. She's used to working with larger groups of people, so this group won't be a problem. And we thought maybe having a woman working the crowd would be good, seeing as most the audience members are women."

"Good thinking. I'll go check with Margo and see what's happening. I'll call you once I have an answer."

Brenna hurried down the hall and almost ran into Sean.

"Hey, what's your hurry?" he asked.

"We have a large group waiting to come in for today's taping. I'm not certain we're going to be able to accommodate everyone. I need to touch base with Margo. She's talking to Tim."

"How many extra people are there?"

"Close to twenty-five. And right now, we don't have room for all of them."

"Hmm. Maybe I should go take a look at the front."

"You may find you're pulled into answering questions by some of the fans there."

"I don't have a problem talking with fans. They keep us going. I'll see if I can scout out some people who are willing to ask questions on-air." Sean walked to the front of the building.

Brenna saw Margo going toward the back of the studio. "Margo, what's happening?" Brenna hurried to Margo's side.

"We're scrambling to find extra chairs. The crew's getting them from other parts of the building. We've been able to come up with twenty-five chairs. If you can help set them up, we'll be ready for the taping."

While Brenna had been speaking with Margo, three men were piling chairs on a dolly to take to the studio audience section.

One of them walked by Margo. "We've got this. Finally found the extra chairs, and we'll set them up. Same setup as the others, right?"

Margo said, "Yes please, Ed."

Ed marched back to his coworkers, and they got to work setting the chairs up.

"Right. I'll let Joe know the cap is seventy-five." Brenna connected with Joe on the headset.

Brenna made her way to the makeup and wardrobe section to make sure the judges and chefs were getting ready.

The chefs were getting their makeup done. The sous chefs had their makeup done and were chatting quietly. Brenna overheard sous chef Carol asking them if they'd had nerves for the first show. Brenna smiled. Everyone seemed to be in a good frame of mind for the show.

The judges were dressed for the taping. They didn't have to use wardrobe but had been told what to wear and could select from their personal wardrobe. Ms. Keene was wearing a navy dress with a red blazer. Mr. Harlow had a black suit with a white shirt and blue tie. Mr. Fitzgerald wore a black suit with a blue shirt and a red tie. They still needed to have their hair and makeup done before the show got underway.

Brenna checked the time and saw they had forty-five minutes before the show got underway. Plenty of time.

Sean returned from chatting with the fans. He walked to the wardrobe department. He was wearing a blue-striped shirt with a solid navy tie. His trousers were dark blue. He pulled down a dark blue jacket from the wardrobe rack. It matched his trousers perfectly. When he raised his right arm to smooth back his hair, Brenna noticed his jacket was missing a button on the right sleeve. *That'll have to be fixed*, she thought. She looked around for someone from wardrobe and saw a woman helping Chef Tina with her jacket.

"Excuse me, could you see about Sean's missing button please?" Brenna asked.

The wardrobe mistress looked at Brenna. "He's missing a button? I didn't notice. Good thing you did. Let me see what I have here."

"Sean, can you come here please?" Brenna asked.

"What's up?" He strolled over.

"Ah, you're right. There is a button missing. Come on, take that jacket off while I find one to replace it with."

"Theresa, do you have time to do this?" Sean asked.

"Not a problem. It'll take five minutes. Go, I'll call you when it's ready." Theresa waved him away.

Theresa searched through her box of buttons. She found a gold shank button that would work on Sean's jacket.

Meanwhile, Sean made his way to sous chef Carol. Brenna overheard their conversation.

"How are you doing this afternoon?" Sean asked.

"I'm okay. A bit nervous about the cameras, but hopefully it's going to be painless." Carol smiled.

"Don't worry about a thing. Once the show gets started, you guys will be busy. Can you tell me a bit about how you started in the business?"

"Well, you can tell I'm not as young as some of the other chefs. I started this career later in life. I had always entertained for my husband's company, organizing business dinners. A few years ago, we got divorced, and I found myself having to go back to work. I decided to try my hand at cooking for a living. I went back to school and learned some skills. I was lucky. I did a placement at Chef Mike's, and he liked what he saw. He told me when I graduated, I'd have work in his restaurant. I've learned a lot from working with him and Chef Tina in the last year. I love it and know I haven't made a mistake in this career."

"Is it okay if I share this with the viewers? This is the kind of information that will make people root for you."

Sous chef Carol asked Chef Tina, "How do you feel about it?"

Chef Tina said, "I don't have a problem with any of it. It's up to you. I think it shows what kind of person Chef Mike was."

"Sure, it's fine. And yes, Chef Mike was always willing to take a chance on someone. Just don't call this a mid-life crisis. It was more of a mid-life awakening."

Sean chuckled, showing his perfect white teeth. "No problem, much more positive than a crisis."

Brenna smiled to herself. Maybe today's taping would work out better than they had all thought it would.

"Sean, here's your jacket. All fixed and ready to go." Theresa handed Sean the jacket. "Thanks, Brenna, for noticing that. I should have picked up on that."

Brenna smiled at the older woman. "You're welcome. I'm just glad I didn't have to fix it. We'd still be waiting." Brenna raised her voice to be heard by all in the area. "I thought you should know, we're going to have a full house today. The audience will be coming in shortly, and we're going to have close to seventy-five people in there."

Chef Aaron shifted in his chair. "Wow, what a great turnout! A lot better than the first show. Are we staying with the same format? The studio audience asking questions?"

Sean said, "For the most part, yes. I've found a couple of people from the studio audience who are willing to ask some questions. Brenna, when they come in, we'll need to have someone from makeup work with them."

"I'll make sure someone goes out. You'll need to point them out to me, though."

"Actually, I asked them to identify themselves to you. I told them you were the gorgeous redhead wearing a green shirt."

Brenna blushed. "Gee thanks, I think."

Mr. Harlow, one of the judges, asked, "Brenna, the studio audience questions will be screened, right?"

Sean said, "Yes. And, Brenna, you'll have to get them to sign a release from the studio."

"Where do I find one of those?"

"Check with Margo or Mathew. They should have some on hand."

On her way to find Margo, she did a fast walk through the kitchens and gave all the counters a quick wipe down. She hurried into the pantry and noticed some of the produce items had been moved around. She placed them in the correct bins and left. She glanced toward the audience section. It was filling up quickly. Most of the audience appeared to be women between the ages of thirty and sixty.

Brenna spotted Margo speaking with one of the lighting guys.

"Margo, apparently I need to get release forms for the studio members who are asking questions today. Do you know where I can find them?"

Margo opened her clipboard and pulled out some sheets. "Here you go. And for future reference, they're located in the filing cabinet in the small conference room. Filed under Forms- Release."

"Thanks. I'll get these signed off."

Sean was speaking with a few women, and he waved Brenna over. When she got closer, she saw Kate was with him.

"Kate, you made it. Great to see you." Brenna's face split into a large smile.

"I'm pretty excited. And my mom and your aunt Rita are here too. Sean asked if I'd be willing to ask the chefs some questions. I couldn't say no."

"I didn't know the two of you knew each other." Sean looked at the two of them. "I'm guessing good friends, right?"

Kate laughed. "We've known each other since kindergarten. We won't discuss how many years ago that was."

Brenna checked the large countdown clock on the wall. "I'd love to chat, but I need you ladies to each sign a release form. And then we need to get someone from makeup to do a few touchups."

The forms signed, Brenna hurried to the makeup department. The makeup woman was putting her equipment away, and the judges were getting out of the makeup chairs. She looked up as Brenna approached her.

"Can you go out and take care of the three audience members who are going to ask some questions?" Brenna asked.

"It would be easier if they came here. I have the correct lighting and the chairs."

"Of course. That makes sense. I'll go get them."

Brenna found Kate and the two other women and brought them to the makeup department.

"There you are, ladies. You're in good hands. Can you make your way back to your seats?"

"Yes. Thanks, Brenna," Kate said as the other two ladies nodded.

Brenna walked back to the set and glanced around to make sure everything was ready.

Mathew stopped in front of her. "Brenna, there you are. I completely forgot to get some coffee, water, and treats of some kind for the sponsors. Is there any way you can get that organized?"

Brenna nodded. "How many people are we talking about?"

"There are four people and well, myself."

"How about if I bring the coffee machine from the conference room and an assortment of pods? And we have some bottled water in the back. I can call the coffee shop and have an assortment of sweets delivered. Does that work?"

"Oh, that would be great. I'm sorry. I should have mentioned it earlier." Mathew glanced at his watch.

"No problem. I'll make sure I add it to my pre-show checklist."

Brenna called the coffee shop, and they assured her they would get the sweets delivered in the next ten minutes. She then radioed security to let them know.

Joe said, "You'll have to come to the front to pick up the order. I'll let you know when they show up."

"Thanks. I did tell them not to wait in line but to go straight to the front."

"We'll keep an eye out. The crowd is almost all in anyway."

She got the coffee and water service set up in the booth where the sponsors were sitting. The four people included Lori from Hastings Farms and two of the reps from the appliance stores. Brenna didn't recognize the fourth person.

"Hi, Brenna!" Lori said.

"How are you?"

"I'm doing well. I'm looking forward to seeing the show being taped. I wasn't able to come in for the first show. I did watch it, though. I'm pretty excited about being here."

Brenna grinned. "I know. I can't believe I'm here either."

Brenna's radio chirped, and Joe's voice came through. "Brenna, the delivery is here."

"I better run. I'll be back shortly. You all enjoy the taping."

She hurried out of the sponsors' booth and ran into Connor. He held out a box from the coffee shop. "I told Joe I'd bring this in for you."

"Ah, thanks for that. Saving me steps on a busy day like today is awesome. I'll just set these up inside."

That done, Brenna leaned against the wall of the booth. She went through her mental checklist. Script on the teleprompter, photo collage ready for the moment of silence, audience members to ask questions, their makeup taken care of, the button on Sean's jacket replaced.

She gasped. *The button on his jacket.* She pulled up the photo she had taken of the button found by the cleaning crew. It appeared to be similar to the one missing from Sean's jacket.

"Brenna, are you okay?" Connor was by her side.

Brenna looked up. She had forgotten he was close by. "Yes. I was just running through my list. Could you look at something for me?"

"Sure."

"This is a photo of the button the cleaning crew found. Sean's jacket was missing a button, and I had wardrobe replace it. Can you look at the photo and then look at the buttons on Sean's jacket to see if they're the same?"

Connor took her phone and enlarged the photo. Then he looked at Sean's jacket. "It's hard to tell from here if it's the same button. Tell you what. He isn't going anywhere for the next hour or so. I'll keep watching, and if I can't determine if the button matches, I'll make some kind of excuse to look at his jacket closely. Is it okay if I send this photo to myself?"

"Yes, of course."

That done, Connor gave Brenna her phone back.

"I didn't realize you'd be at the taping as well," Brenna said.

"I heard from Joe. When he called and told me how many people were coming in, I thought I'd better come by and make sure things worked smoothly. I spoke with Tim and Mathew. They both seem happy with the security changes. And well, you were in the meeting with the judges and the chefs."

"I thought you handled that well."

Connor asked, "Have you heard anything else from the police?"

Brenna sighed. "Well, did you know I'm a person of interest?"

Connor's left eyebrow raised. "Why? Because you found him?"

Brenna shook her head. "Not just that. My fingerprints are everywhere on the set, and the code used to disarm the system was mine. The codes are specific to each individual. I knew my code was unique, but I didn't know someone else could access it."

Connor gave a low whistle. "Not good. So, if you didn't kill him, it must be someone associated with the show."

"I've thought of that. But I can't think who would have had it in for Chef Mike. Although Margo overheard someone talking about drugs late Friday afternoon. She wasn't sure who it was. It could be that Chef Mike got tangled up in a mess somehow."

"It could happen. But the chefs don't have a key or access code. What about the production assistant who was let go? What happened with his keys and access code?"

Brenna frowned. "Well, shouldn't you know? Isn't it your company that takes care of this?"

Connor shook his head. "No, that's being done with another company, one based in Detroit. We don't have anything to do with that. I've tried to get Tim and Mathew to change it, but, so far, they aren't taking steps to change that."

"Well, from what I've been told, my access code is unique to me. Even if he hadn't returned his set of keys, he shouldn't have the same code as mine."

Connor pulled out his phone. "I'll do some follow-up on this. It's not acceptable that additional keys are floating around and we don't know what the access code for this guy was. You do know he was arrested for drug possession, right?"

"I heard that."

The floor director came out to warm up the audience in preparation for the show. Margo was walking around making sure the audience members were seated and ready to watch the show.

Brenna sighed. "We'll have to be quiet while the taping is happening, and I have to take notes. Bob and Detective Morris are supposed to be here as well, but I didn't see them come in."

Connor nodded to his right. "They're standing behind the studio audience. I spoke with Bob when he came in."

Brenna watched as Sean stepped out onto the stage, and the lights blazed as the show's theme music started to play. From her position, she could see the entire stage, the studio audience, and the backstage as well. She settled in to watch the show and make notes.

CHAPTER SIXTEEN

"Welcome, Ladies and Gentlemen, to our second episode of *Bayview Cooks!* Tonight, we have our chefs preparing a three-course meal. Our judges will be watching them carefully to ensure they use at least fifty percent of the items on the list. The judges have copies of the list of ingredients the chefs can use."

Sean moved to center stage.

"As many of you are aware, we lost a member of our *Bayview Cooks!* family a few days ago. I'd like to direct your attention to stage right, where you'll be able to see photos of Chef Mike. At this time, we'll observe a moment of silence."

The photo collage started playing. The studio audience maintained a respectful silence. Brenna could see most of the audience was riveted to the screen. She glanced at the judges and saw they were watching the collage as well. There wasn't a sound in the studio. Brenna saw Chef Tina and Chef Rosa wipe their eyes toward the end.

"Thank you all. And now we'll get this show underway. Let's meet our judges and our chefs." Sean moved smoothly to the judges' table. "Our first judge is the well-known, *Bayview City Times* food critic, Sam Harlow. Seated next to him, Lois Keene is president of Bayview College. And next to Ms. Keene is Malcolm Fitzgerald, mayor of Bayview City."

The judges stood as they were introduced, smiled, and waved to the audience. The audience clapped for each of the judges.

Sean crossed his arms over his chest. "Now, we aren't going to have a tie tonight, are we?"

The three judges and studio audience laughed, and Sam Harlow answered for the group. "Well, Sean, we came close last week. We'll work hard this episode to make sure we have a clear winner."

Sean moved into the kitchens, where the chefs were waiting at the counters. "I'll start with last week's winner and introduce you to Chef Rosa Cavalli. Tell me; what was your secret?"

"Our secret is a calm and efficient way of doing things. My sous chef, Frankie, has been working with me for a few years now, and we communicate very well. It's almost as if he can read my mind."

Sous chef Frankie smiled widely as the camera focused on him. "Chef Rosa and I do communicate very well. And as long as I remember who's in charge, we get along great. She's been bossing me around a kitchen for as long as I can remember."

The audience laughed at this. Brenna noted that Sean took advantage of their reaction and deviated from the script. "That's right, there's a family connection between the two of you. Chef Rosa, is it harder to work with someone who's family?"

Chef Rosa shook her head. "I've worked with a lot of different people, many who were great, but cooking with Frankie is like being with an extension of myself. He's able to anticipate what I'll need and what I'll do next without me telling him. That only comes from working together for a long time."

Sean moved to his right and smiled into the camera. "There you have it. The Red team's kitchen cooks smoothly because of a long history of working together. Being family has nothing to do with it."

He moved to Chef Aaron's kitchen, where he and his sous chef Jamie were taking knives out of Chef Aaron's knife roll and setting them on the counter.

"Chef Aaron, what are you and sous chef Jamie doing here?"

Brenna looked up from her notes. Again, Sean was deviating from the script. *What is he up to?*

"We're checking our equipment. Our knives are very important to us. We work with them every day, and they have to be in excellent condition."

"How do you take care of them?" Sean asked.

"I use a sharpening steel and stone to ensure they're always sharp. I never, ever drop my knives. To clean them, they're hand washed carefully with hot water and soap and then dried with a soft cloth. When they're not being used, I keep them in a specially designed knife roll that protects the blade and keeps them all in one location."

Sean turned and faced the audience. "Let's all remember that. Chef Aaron's knives are sharp!"

Brenna could see Sean's words had upset Chef Aaron. His mouth turned down, and his shoulders slumped.

Does Sean know Chef Aaron's knife was used to kill Chef Mike? Brenna didn't know how that would be possible.

Sean stood next to Chef Tina. "And finally, Chef Tina. How are you today?"

"I'm okay. Looking forward to today's challenge. Both Carol and I are ready for this. Chef Mike spent a lot of time working with us and training us. We're ready to honor him by winning today." Chef Tina smiled as she spoke.

"Great to hear that. And Carol, I understand you came to cooking later in life?"

Sous chef Carol grinned. "Yes. I call it my mid-life awakening. I went back to school to learn to be a chef. I loved cooking and entertaining and thought it was time to do something for myself. I was lucky. I had a placement with Chef Mike, and he nurtured me along. I've been quite happy since coming to his restaurant."

Sean walked back to his mark near the judges, and the music started playing again. "Ladies and gentlemen, you've met all the players in the show. We're ready to get the competition underway. Just a reminder to everyone. There are no recipes the chefs need to follow. Each kitchen has the same ingredients. It's up to the chefs how they use them. If you look at the monitors above the counters, you'll see the ingredients for tonight's competition. Chefs, please get started."

The monitors came to life with the list of ingredients. The chefs and their sous chefs huddled together, and then the sous chefs went into the pantry and to the refrigerators to gather what they would need to make the meal for this episode. The show clock had started its countdown.

Brenna paid close attention to the show and was busy making notes on what was working and questions she had to ask either Margo or Tim.

Sean said, "While our chefs get underway, we're going to take a break to bring you a message from our sponsors."

Despite Sean indicating there was a commercial break, Brenna noticed the activity on the set didn't stop. The chefs were issuing orders to the sous chefs and had started the food prep. The judges took the opportunity to stretch out a bit. Sean walked off stage to his cubby and took one of the water bottles for a long drink. The makeup lady was standing by to freshen him up.

Brenna noted when Sean was ready to start up again, the floor director called the judges back to their seats. Then, he asked Sean to go up in the studio audience, gave him a remote microphone, and then cued the cameras. She saw Bob and Detective Morris walk down the stairs, out of camera range, and closer to the sponsor's booth.

Sean was in the studio audience. "Welcome back. We're going to take some questions from our audience members." The two ladies asked their questions, and then Sean pointed the microphone at Kate. "Do you have a question for our participants?"

"Hi, yes, I do, and it's for Chef Rosa."

"Go ahead. I'm pretty sure Chef Rosa can cook and answer questions at the same time." Sean smiled at Kate.

"Chef Rosa, can you tell me how many of the recipes you have at the restaurant are family recipes?"

"That's a great question. For those of you who don't know, Chef Rosa's restaurant is called *Nonna's Place*. Is that in tribute to your grandmother?"

Chef Rosa looked up from the dish she was preparing. "Yes, Sean. My nonna played a large role in my cooking career. And in answer to your question about my recipes, most of my recipes are family recipes that were handed down from my nonna. I learned how to cook in her kitchen when I was a child. There are a lot of great memories with the recipes I use."

"That's great, Chef Rosa. A family connection is definitely important in your kitchen. And thank you, Kate, for your question."

Sean walked down to the judges' table.

"And now we'll chat with our judges. Tell me, what are you going to be looking for from our chefs?"

Mr. Harlow answered first. "Well, I'm going to be looking for well-cooked food with a lot of flavor."

Ms. Keene said, "I agree. I think flavor is really important."

Mr. Fitzgerald said, "I like to see a meal well presented. Honestly, if it doesn't look good or appealing, I'm just not going to eat it."

"Thank you, judges. And now let's see how the chefs are doing."

The chefs had completed their first course, a salad, and they prepared the plates to serve the judges.

The judges sampled the salads.

"Judges, what is your opinion?" Sean asked.

Mr. Harlow pursed his lips. "Overall, the salads were well executed. Chef Aaron incorporated cheese and nuts in his salad, a touch heavy for an appetizer. Chef Tina had a variety of greens and a lovely vinaigrette dressing. Chef Rosa had an ingredient that had a pronounced bitter aftertaste. We can't determine which ingredient that would be."

Ms. Keene nodded her head. "Yes, I think Chef Tina gets this round. A delightful, light appetizer, and the dressing was very flavorful."

Mr. Fitzgerald added, "Chef Rosa, what exactly did you use in the salad? There's a definite bitter aftertaste. I'm afraid that's not up to your standard offering."

Chef Rosa frowned. "Thank you for the comments. I used the ingredients available in the fridge and pantry. I'll check with my sous chef to see if anything was unusual. We did include arugula, which can have a slightly bitter taste."

Sean said, "Well, there you have it. Our judges are looking for the chefs to maintain their high standards in all aspects of this competition. Well done, Chef Tina. You win this round."

The studio audience clapped for Chef Tina, who smiled her thanks at the judges.

Meanwhile, the sous chefs were busy preparing the entrées. All of the chefs had selected a beef dish.

Brenna watched as Chef Rosa exchanged words with sous chef Frankie. He shook his head and pointed to the ingredients on the counter that had been used in the salad. Chef Rosa shrugged, and they went back to preparing the next dish.

Connor leaned closer to her and whispered, "Do you know if the judges were that picky last week?"

Brenna replied in hushed tones, "I don't know. Maybe they've decided to be more vocal. I know at one of the meetings this week there was talk about the judges not being involved in the discussion enough. Sean may have said something to them."

The chefs were working hard on the entrées. The studio audience was calling out encouragement to the chefs.

Sean stood at center stage. "Ladies and gentlemen, we're going to take a short commercial break while the chefs continue to battle it out here. When we return, the judges will sample the entrées. We'll be right back."

Sean waited until the assistant director had counted them off the air and walked back to his cubby.

"Could I have some water please?" Mr. Harlow's voice was shaking.

Brenna moved quickly to the judges' table. "Mr. Harlow, are you feeling okay?"

He was pale, and there was a sheen of sweat on his forehead. "I'm not sure what's wrong. I have some pretty bad stomach pains, and I'm really dizzy."

Quickly assessing the situation, Brenna hurried backstage to Sean's cubby. "Do you have some bottled water?"

"Sure. I always have a couple of bottles here."

Brenna grabbed one of the bottles and ran back to Mr. Harlow. She unscrewed the top and gave the bottle to him. His hand was shaking so hard, she had to help him hold the bottle for him to get the water down. Even with her help, he spilled some water on his jacket.

Brenna got a cloth and mopped up the water on his jacket. She had no doubt the water would dry quickly under the hot lights.

Brenna looked at Mr. Harlow carefully. His pupils appeared to be dilated. She wasn't sure if it was due to the excitement of the show or if it was because of any medication he might have taken.

"Mr. Harlow, are you taking any medication?" she asked.

Mr. Harlow nodded his head. "I'm on blood pressure medication, and I have nitroglycerin tablets to take when I need them."

John, the director, was standing nearby. "When did you last take the medication?"

"I took the blood pressure meds this morning, and the nitro, well, I had to take one of those just before we started. I was a bit stressed."

"And how are you feeling now? Brenna asked.

"I'm still dizzy, but the stomach pains have diminished somewhat. I'm okay to keep going. Really, I am."

"Sir, are you sure you're all right?" John asked.

"I think so. Let's just keep going with the show."

John turned to Brenna. "Could you let Tim know what's happening?"

Brenna raised Tim on the radio and brought him up to speed.

"So, is he well enough to continue taping, or do we stop?" Tim asked.

"He says he can finish the show. John wanted you to be made aware of what's happening."

"That's fine. We'll keep going. If, at any time, he feels like he has to stop, let him know we can."

Brenna looked at John and nodded. "Mr. Harlow, if you're certain you're good to go, we'll continue. But if you feel unwell at all, let us know immediately."

"I will. Thanks. Sorry for the delay." Mr. Harlow's face was flushed.

The sponsors were sitting in the booth, watching with interest. Mathew seemed to be doing his best to keep them occupied.

The show got underway with Sean in the chefs' kitchens.

"Welcome back. We're almost ready to have the judges sample the entrées. Our chefs have been busy, and they're just plating the entrées now."

The chefs were putting the final touches on their entrées.

Sean smiled at the chefs. "Chefs are you ready to present?"

The three chefs said in unison, "Yes, Sean."

The audience chuckled. The chefs brought the entrées to the judges one at a time. Chef Aaron went first, then Chef Rosa, and then Chef Tina.

The judges made notes on the individual entrées.

The sous chefs had the dessert dishes plated by the time the entrées were judged. Again, the chefs presented the desserts one at a time.

"Judges, do you need a moment to consult?" Sean asked.

Mr. Harlow said, "Yes, we'll take a few minutes."

The judges leaned forward and, in hushed tones, held a short discussion. A few minutes later, they leaned back in their chairs.

"Judges, do you have a decision?"

Ms. Keene looked at Sean. "Yes, we do. Tonight's winner is Chef Tina. The salad was light and flavorful, and the entrée was superb. The mushroom risotto blended perfectly with the grilled flank steak. And her dessert of apple blossom was an excellent choice."

There was much clapping and cheering from the studio audience.

Chef Tina and sous chef Carol high-fived each other, and then Chef Tina bowed to the audience and the judges. "Thank you, judges."

Sean walked up to her and faced the camera. "That wraps up tonight's show of *Bayview Cooks!* Tune in next week to see what the chefs will be up to then."

Brenna waited a few seconds for John to give the all-clear signal. "That's done. Now to do a cleanup."

Connor nodded. "It seemed to go well. I'm surprised at how long the taping took."

"Apparently, the editing team does a great job. They make it look seamless."

They were walking down to the kitchens when Brenna heard a crash, followed by a scream—and then someone swore.

CHAPTER SEVENTEEN

By the time Brenna and Connor reached the judges' table, Bob and Detective Morris were there and had taken charge. Brenna saw Mr. Harlow was on the floor and had been sick.

Bob had Mr. Harlow in a seated position and was undoing the top buttons of his shirt. Detective Morris was talking to someone on her phone.

Brenna and Connor walked to where Bob was with Mr. Harlow.

Brenna kneeled next to Bob. "How can I help?"

"I need some crowd control. Connor, can you make sure no one leaves the studio?"

"Not a problem." Connor walked to the stage and raised his voice. "Excuse me. I need everyone's attention."

The studio audience stopped where they were, and the studio employees turned to look at him.

"I need everyone to stay where they are. We've had a bit of a mishap, and to allow emergency personnel to get in quickly, we need you all to stay in your seats."

The audience sat back in their seats, and their voices sounded like bees buzzing. No doubt they were trying to figure out what was happening.

Bob looked at Brenna. "Can you make sure nothing leaves the kitchens? I don't know if what's happened with Mr. Harlow is an allergic reaction, the flu, or something related to Chef Mike's murder, but we need to make sure we have access to all the food stuffs used in the show in case we need it."

Brenna nodded. "I'll talk to the chefs and sous chefs."

Brenna reached the kitchens and saw that sous chef Frankie and sous chef Carol were getting ready to dispose of the meals that had been prepared. "Please don't touch anything in the kitchens. The police may need to test the food that was used."

Chef Rosa gasped. "They can't think any of us would poison the judges."

"I don't know what's going on. I think Detectives McLean and Morris are being extra cautious. I'd suggest you leave everything as is. The police will take care of this."

Detective Morris stood next to Brenna. "Thanks for your cooperation on this. Emergency personnel are arriving, and Mr. Harlow will be taken to the hospital. In the meantime, Chefs, I'd like to ask you some questions about the preparation of the food today. Brenna, I'll need to speak with you shortly."

Brenna walked back to the judges' table. She saw that Mr. Harlow seemed to be looking better. He was still pale, but he wasn't shaking anymore.

Bob turned around and saw her. "Brenna, could you sit with Mr. Harlow? I don't want him left alone until the paramedics get here. And I need to speak with the other two judges. Detective Morris has contacted the precinct, and officers will be coming to help us get the information we need from the audience. We just need their contact information."

Brenna nodded. "Sure, I'll stay with him."

Brenna sat next to Mr. Harlow. She smiled at him in what she hoped was a reassuring way. "Mr. Harlow, we'll have you looked at in no time at all."

Mr. Harlow grabbed at her arm. "Could you get in touch with my wife, please? This hasn't happened before, and I'd like her at the hospital."

"No problem. I have your contact information, and I'll give her a call as soon as the paramedics take you."

He smiled. "Thanks."

Joe radioed Brenna. "Ambulance has arrived. I'm sending them to the set."

Brenna relayed the information to Mr. Harlow.

The paramedics arrived and took over. Connor and Brenna stood off to the side, watching carefully as they prepared Mr. Harlow for transport.

The uniformed police officers had arrived and were at each of the two exits. Bob was talking to Ms. Keane and Mr. Fitzgerald.

Connor said, "Bob is smart to get this now in case this event is related to Chef Mike's murder."

Detective Morris was in the kitchen speaking with the sous chefs.

Bob was standing with Mr. Fitzgerald and Ms. Keene as the paramedics worked on Mr. Harlow. Brenna could hear him asking them questions.

"No, he didn't give any indication he wasn't well at the beginning of the show," Ms. Keene said to Bob.

"I knew he was on medication for his heart, but nothing else. He seemed fine. The trouble started when we took our first commercial break," Mr. Fitzgerald said.

"That's right. He had stomach pains and was dizzy. I thought it was nerves," Ms. Keene answered.

"Why would you think nerves?" Bob asked.

"We had been chatting before the show started taping. He mentioned he had some misgivings about returning to the show after Chef Mike had been killed. None of us were exactly happy about the situation, but we had committed to doing the show," Mr. Fitzgerald said.

Ms. Keened coughed. "And then the other matter was that he found one of the salads the chefs made particularly bitter. I couldn't discern anything wrong with it, but he kept repeating that one of the ingredients must be off."

"Whose salad was that?"

"It was Chef Rosa's," Ms. Keene said.

"Right. Thank you for your time and information. I'll be in touch if I need clarification on anything." Bob dismissed the judges.

Bob and Detective Morris met in the middle of the set. Detective Morris pointed at Brenna and motioned for her to come to them.

Brenna made her way to the set.

"What can you tell me about Mr. Harlow's episode with stomach pains?" Detective Morris asked.

Brenna repeated what she had heard and seen with Mr. Harlow.

"And no one else was bothered by the salad?" Detective Morris asked.

"No one. We thought it might be a reaction to a prescription he was taking; that's why we asked him if he was on medication."

"It's a good question and certainly one we'll follow up with the doctors at the ER."

"Well, the chefs had access to all the same ingredients. And most of those were picked up at the market this morning," Brenna said.

"And who picked up the items?" Bob asked.

Brenna winced. "That would be me."

"And everything came from the vendors at the market? Not anyplace else?" Detective Morris asked.

"The fresh produce and meats came from the market. All of the vendors were approved before the show started. I have the list and the invoices from this morning. And one of the vendors is here at the show. She's one of the sponsors. The dry goods, I picked up last night at the warehouse store."

"And you picked up the items this morning?" Detective Morris asked. "I just want to clarify again."

"Yes. And I'm the one who checked the order and put everything away."

"So, the vendors and yourself were the only ones who had access to the items used. Right?" Detective Morris looked at Brenna.

"Well, yes . . . but the pantry and kitchens are open. There aren't locks on anything. Anyone could have gone back there. And when I was doing a pre-show check before taping, I noticed the produce looked as if it had been disturbed."

"Disturbed, how?"

"I had asked the chefs for feedback on how the pantry items and refrigerated foods should be stored. They gave me specific locations on the shelves and in the walk-in fridge as to where the items should be placed. Each category is subdivided into fruits, vegetables, and greens. Even spices are sorted according to the chefs' requests." Brenna rubbed her forehead. "Anyway, I noticed some of the vegetables had been moved around. I took a few minutes and made sure everything was back in the correct bin. And that was just before the studio audience came in."

"Okay. And can you tell me if everyone connected with the show is still here?" Bob asked.

"I think so. Well, except Mr. Harlow."

"Fine. We'll need you to stick around. We're going to have questions for everyone." Detective Morris put her notebook away and raised her voice. "If I could have your attention, please." She paused as everyone stopped talking. "I'm Detective Morris of Bayview City PD. Members of the audience, we're going to ask you to file out the exits in an orderly fashion and provide the officers with your contact information. If you have anything you want to share with us about something you may have seen, please let the officer know, and we'll speak with you. We will do our best to get you all out as quickly as possible. Thanks." Detective Morris turned to Brenna. "Where can we question the crew?"

"What about the office area? There are two separate offices."

"That will work."

Meanwhile, the officers were setting up stations at the two exits. The studio audience waited until one of the officers motioned for them to form a line. The audience lined up at the two exits and were told to provide their name and contact information. Once that was completed, they were cleared to leave.

Brenna saw Connor speaking with Tim and Mathew. She walked to them to see what was happening.

Tim said, "Mathew, I need you to go to the hospital and keep me informed about what's happening with Mr. Harlow."

"What do I do about the sponsors? They're still here in the control room," Mathew asked.

"Mathew, this is a nightmare. I'm hoping we can get the sponsors out quietly. Have they noticed anything?"

Brenna gawked at Tim. What was he thinking? How could anyone not see what happened?

"Uh, well yes. The paramedics were here and so are the police. The sponsors aren't blind, you know." Mathew scratched his head. "Shouldn't we be doing something here?"

Connor said, "There isn't anything you can do right now. The police are here, and they'll be speaking with everyone connected with the show."

Tim said, "They can't possibly suspect what happened with Mr. Harlow has anything to do with the show or with Chef Mike's murder. You heard the man; he takes blood pressure medication and nitroglycerin. He was a heart attack waiting to happen."

Bob arrived just as Tim finished speaking. "At this time, the situation warrants us asking questions of everyone connected with the show. Do you have a problem with that?"

Tim raised his hands. "Well, I guess not."

Mathew put his hand on Tim's shoulder. "Detective, we'll cooperate and do what we can to help you and the department. What do you need from us?"

"We'll be speaking with everyone. Detective Morris is setting up two offices to interview the crew. Our officers are obtaining contact information from the studio audience and asking if they saw anything that could help."

"And what about the sponsors? Do you need to speak with them as well?" Tim asked.

Bob looked toward the control booth. "I'll have someone speak with them. It's unlikely they would be involved in this situation." Bob addressed the chefs in the kitchens. "I need all of you to come to the audience area. We're going to have to talk to each of you individually."

The chefs and sous chefs came down to the audience section.

The CSU team had arrived. Bob excused himself to go speak with them. As soon as he was finished speaking with them, they began working in the kitchen and where Mr. Harlow had been sick.

Bob called out to two of the uniformed officers. "Could you start splitting the cast and crew up? Take their names and contact information and start organizing them for the interviews?"

Detective Morris returned from checking on the offices. "We're good to go with the offices. The doors close, and there's room for one of us and whoever we're speaking to in each room."

"Great. Let's get this started. Brenna, could you go with Detective Morris? Mr. Harris, you're with me." Bob started walking down the hall to one of the offices.

Brenna followed Detective Morris into one of the offices. She wasn't sure what to expect.

The detective directed Brenna into one of the chairs and then closed the door. "Now, can you tell me if you noticed anything unusual today?"

"This is my first taping, so I'm not sure what normal should be. I can tell you what my impressions were. I've already told you about the produce being disturbed. We've had some problems in the kitchens as well. It seemed like a prank, but now, I'm not sure. It feels as if someone is trying to sabotage the show."

"What do you mean?"

"Before this morning's rehearsal, someone had moved pots and pans around. The kitchens need to be organized. The chefs like everything '*mis-en-place,*' which means at the ready. I guess last week the same thing happened, and it wasn't caught before the show started taping, and it caused problems for the chefs." Brenna's brow furrowed. "After the rehearsal, I made sure everything was organized the way it should be. Then just before we got underway, I checked the kitchens again. And everything had been moved around."

Detective Morris tapped her pen on her notebook. "Do you think it's more than a prank?"

Brenna shook her head. "I don't know. I know both Tim and Mathew were concerned about the sponsors pulling out from the show after Chef Mike was killed."

"Who stands to gain if the show shuts down?"

"No one associated with the show. We'd all lose our jobs. The sponsors would lose their visibility, and Tim and Mathew would each have a black mark on their records."

"Anything else you can add?"

Brenna thought for a moment. "I did hear something this morning about an argument Chef Mike had with someone last week."

"Go on."

"One of the vendors told me she overheard someone arguing with him on the phone about some money that he was owed. She didn't know who it was. She did say Chef Mike seemed to know the guy, and she thought it might be someone from his restaurant."

"Who was the vendor?"

"Lori Hastings, from Hastings Farms."

"I'll make a note of it, but people argue with other people all the time. It doesn't necessarily tie in with his murder." Detective Morris finished writing up her notes. "Right, thanks for the information. If I have any other questions, I'll be in touch."

Brenna went back to the studio, grabbed her tablet, and sat in the almost empty audience section. She watched as the CSU team went through the kitchens, collecting possible evidence.

Connor was speaking with one of the CSU officers. He glanced in her direction and wrapped up his conversation with the officer. He made his way to where Brenna was sitting. "How did the interview go?"

"Fine, I guess." Brenna's voice was flat, and she crossed her arms across her chest.

"Are you okay?"

Brenna frowned at him. "I'm not sure. I may be a suspect in this as well."

"What do you mean?"

"Well, I'm the one responsible for the foodstuffs used on the show. If Mr. Harlow was poisoned by something he ate, Detective Morris has me in her sights for this too." Brenna tugged at her hair.

"She didn't say that did she?"

"No, but she thinks I killed Chef Mike, so I guess she figures I'm dumb enough to stick around and kill more people. Why? I really don't know."

"Well, I'm sure you didn't kill Chef Mike. And the police have other suspects too. Chef Aaron is on the list as well."

"I know. I'm the one who told the police about the missing knife. How did you know about that?"

"Bob told me. He probably shouldn't have, but he knows I'm heading up the security here."

"I wonder if Chef Mike owed Chef Aaron any money? They could have been arguing on the phone, and that's who Lori could have overheard."

Connor raised an eyebrow at her.

"Right, let me fill you in on that." Brenna gave Connor the information she had given Detective Morris.

Connor shook his head. "That's kinda weak. If someone owes you money and you kill them, you won't get the money they owe you. I don't think Aaron would be the one arguing with Mike. Someone from his restaurant might work. Maybe the line cook he had to fire. I wonder if he felt Mike owed him something."

"Maybe. But then how would he know my security code for the alarm?"

"Good point. Who has the codes?"

"Sally and probably the IT people."

"That would be a few other people instead of you. And Sally probably has the codes on file somewhere. Something to look into." He took his phone and made a note.

Tim showed up. "Brenna, I'm going to need you to help me out here with damage control."

"What do you need?"

"A quick meeting with you, Margo, and John. Connor, if you could sit in, I'd appreciate it."

"Not a problem. Let me check with my people to see if the building is secured."

Connor stepped aside to make a call.

Tim and Brenna were joined by Margo.

"Where's John?" Tim asked.

"He's in with one of the detectives. He should be out soon." Margo sat down heavily in one of the chairs.

"As soon as he gets here, I want a brief meeting with the four of us and Connor. I've had some information from Mathew."

Connor returned. "My team is working closely with the police and we'll make certain the building is secured. The CSU team has all the foodstuffs used in today's show, and they'll be running tests."

John arrived as Connor was speaking.

Tim said, "Great, everyone's here. I'm going to call Mathew. He's at the hospital with Mr. Harlow. Let's go to one of the conference rooms." They settled in the chairs, and Tim placed the call to Mathew. "Mathew, go ahead. You're on speaker."

"I just heard from the doctor. They believe Mr. Harlow was poisoned with mushrooms. There were mushrooms used in the salad, in one of the risottos, and in the meat dish. They believe the mushrooms were Death Caps. They're found in the wild here, and they look very similar to the regular white mushrooms used in cooking. It doesn't take a lot to make some people quite sick. The police are going to be going through the foodstuffs to figure out if all the mushrooms were bad."

Brenna was stunned. The mushrooms had been picked up this morning with all the other food. They were loosely packaged in a cardboard crate. "Are they sure it was the mushrooms?"

"Yes, it would be the only thing they can see that would cause this kind of reaction. Why?"

"Because the mushrooms were fresh and from one of the local farmers. I saw the crate they came in."

"Well, maybe there were a few bad ones mixed in with the good ones," Tim said.

"I don't think so." Brenna's voice had an edge.

"Well, it will be up to the police to see what's happening. At least we know where this came from," Mathew said.

"What's happening with the other judges and the chefs? I know the chefs were tasting the food as they were preparing it," Brenna asked.

"The hospital contacted the police. They have the other two judges in to be checked, and they want the chefs in as well. Right now, no one else is showing any symptoms."

Everyone was quiet for a few moments.

"What are we going to do about security?" John asked.

Connor said, "I think we need to add security cameras throughout the building. We'll at least be able to keep an eye on all the areas. And we need to figure out a way to add a door to the pantry—one that can be locked."

"Agreed. Can you take care of that for us?" Tim asked.

"Yes. I'll get all of this done tonight. Just needed your go ahead."

"Mathew, any problems with the suggestion?"

"None. I think it's a good one."

"Mathew, have you spoken with our PR agency?" Tim opened his tablet.

"Not yet. I've been busy here at the hospital."

"Fine. Call the agency and see what they can put together to deal with possible media."

"Will do."

Tim said, "We're going to have to do a lot of damage control. We'll need to make sure everyone is on the same page. We can't let anyone except the PR agency talk to the media."

"I agree, but we're going to have to make sure the crew doesn't speak to anyone either. I'm not sure we're going to be able to deal with the studio audience, though. And, Tim, the sponsors were there when all this went down. Someone is going to have to deal with them as well. I hope the police were easy on them." Mathew's voice cracked.

"The crew signed a confidentiality agreement in their contract. They know they can't discuss anything that happens at the studio. If they do, they can be fired. We can't stop the studio audience from talking. But by getting a press release out quickly, we can minimize any damage. As for the sponsors, you and I need to meet with them and reassure them we're doing everything we can to ensure everyone's safety." Tim appeared to be in control with answers to Mathew's concerns.

"I need to check that Mrs. Harlow is comfortable and that Mr. Harlow is staying overnight at the hospital. I'll touch base with you about meeting with the sponsors." Mathew hung up.

"Thanks for taking the time, everyone. I guess we're done for now. I suggest you all go home and get some rest. Hopefully, we can get back to work in the morning."

Brenna left the conference room and headed to the crew lockers. The cleaning crew would be in tonight, and they would deal with the set. All she wanted to do was get home and put today behind her. She walked past the makeup room and noticed Sean standing in the doorway.

He had his back to her and didn't see her. His shoulders were slouched, and she wondered if he was okay. As she got closer to him, she realized he was speaking with someone on the phone.

"Yeah, I know what you've done." Sean paused. "I'll meet you at the bandstand tonight at eight. Have the money ready, and I won't say anything to anyone. If you're not there, I go straight to the police."

Brenna backed away quietly. She didn't want Sean to know she had eavesdropped on him. She kept walking to the lockers and grabbed her jacket. Who had Sean been speaking to? It sounded as if he was blackmailing someone. Could it be related to what had happened with Mr. Harlow?

CHAPTER EIGHTEEN

Brenna focused her attention on the road as she drove home. Her head ached, and her hands shook. She thought those were symptoms of a delayed reaction. Her day certainly had been eventful.

Pulling into the driveway of her apartment building, her body sagged in the seat. It was great to be home. She knew her father and uncle had worked hard to bring the building up to code, and the tenants were happy. The large, brick Victorian had originally been built for one of the lumber barons who settled in the area. Many of the other homes in the neighborhood were of the same design, but not as large as this one. The neighbors were a good mix of young families and older people.

She walked up to her apartment and dropped her toolbelt on the hall table. She put her jacket away and slipped out of her shoes. Her phone rang, and she glanced at the caller ID. Mom. *Great, I hope she hasn't heard about what happened at the studio.*

"Hi, Mom. What's up?"

"I just heard from Rita about Mr. Harlow being sick at the taping. What's going on with that place?"

Brenna grimaced. She had forgotten Aunt Rita had been in the studio audience. Brenna filled her mom in on what she could.

Cecile sighed. "I don't like you being there. Maybe it's time to go to work for your father's company."

"I'll be fine. And I appreciate Dad's offer. But I'm going to see this contract through. The work is different and keeps me busy."

Brenna's mom snorted. "Yes, when you're working. Right now, it seems as if you work a day and then are off for the next because of the problems the show has. Fine, I won't nag. You know the offer's there."

"I do, and I'm grateful for it. Look, Mom, I just got home, and I need to get a few things done here. I'll talk to you soon."

Brenna hung up and turned the TV on. She needed some noise. Unfortunately, it was a breaking news item on the latest developments on the show.

Mathew was at the hospital with a member of the PR agency. She was speaking with reporters. In the background, Brenna saw Ms. Keene and Mr. Fitzgerald walking out. The reporters called out to them, but they didn't respond.

Listening to the report made the day worse. Brenna opened the freezer compartment of the fridge and found a pint of Ben and Jerry's Chunky Monkey. Grabbing a spoon, she made her way to the couch and sank into it, the soft cushions enveloping her back like a hug. Ice cream could fix everything.

Her phone pinged with an email. Tim was sending a message to the cast and crew reminding them about the confidentiality clause in their contracts. His message was clear—anyone who spoke to the media or posted anything on social media about what was happening at the studio would lose their job.

Well, I hope everyone remembered that. His message is a bit late in the day.

She went back to her ice cream, the last few days' events running through her head. "It just doesn't make sense. Why would someone from the crew want to sabotage the show? Their jobs are all on the line. Maybe it's personal. Someone with a grudge, but against whom?" She looked at the ice cream and saw that she was halfway through the pint. "Time to put this away." She put the lid on and placed it back in the freezer.

She opened a drawer in her kitchen island and grabbed a notepad and pen. She returned to the couch and started writing down everything she could remember about what had been happening at the studio. She decided on a chronological timeline from her start date. She would add details to those events later.

At the end of twenty minutes, she had a fairly comprehensive list of events. Now she needed to see where someone could have introduced the poisonous mushrooms. Not for one minute did she believe Hastings Farms would have included Death Caps in the order. She saw the crate with the mushrooms in it. What if instead of substituting all the mushrooms, only a few had been added to the crate? That would have been easier to do, just tossing the mushrooms on the pile.

She checked the timeline and saw there had been several opportunities for someone to go in the pantry and do just that. She noted when she and Margo had been in the pantry and when they had been in the studio audience area. There had been people working backstage most of the day, people had been around for the rehearsal, and later, the taping had taken place. The only time the substitution could have been done was in the morning or over the lunch hour.

It would have to be someone who worked at the studio, who was familiar with the routine of the show, who knew where the foodstuffs were kept, and, most importantly, who was familiar with the ingredients they would be using. He or she, because a woman could have done this, would also need to know where to find the poisonous mushrooms.

Mathew had said the doctors told him the mushrooms were only available in wooded areas in the fall. They did resemble the regular white mushrooms the chefs used in today's taping.

She did a quick search online and learned the only visible difference was in the spores on the underside of the mushroom. No one would have thought they would have to verify the mushrooms were what they were supposed to be.

She made a list of all the people who were on the set that morning. There were about twenty people who were in and out of the area. Not all of them could have added the mushrooms. She knew the grips had been busy all morning working on making sure the lighting and audio were working properly. They wouldn't have had a reason to go in the pantry. Nor would the makeup people or wardrobe lady.

Security had passed through a few times, the director and assistant director had also been around, as had Tim and Mathew. She remembered

Sean had arrived early for the rehearsal and had wandered everywhere on the set just before the taping. He had told her he did this to put himself in the right frame of mind. She remembered seeing him on the set and had noticed him going into the pantry as well. At the time, she had wondered what he was doing.

Tim and Mathew had been everywhere. And, at the time, she had thought it was logical, given their positions. Now, she wondered if it was. The assistant director had been backstage and had been missing for about a half-hour. Brenna wasn't sure what he had been doing.

The judges had shown up about forty minutes or so before they were scheduled to start the taping, but they had all stayed backstage and in the makeup room. They weren't on her radar for this, and really, why would they eat something they could have poisoned?

At the end of an hour, she had six pages of notes, a lot of questions, and no definitive answers. She stretched her arms over her head and glanced at the time. It was seven-thirty.

Her thoughts went to the conversation she had overheard Sean having. She wondered who he was meeting and then guiltily remembered she hadn't told Detective Morris about overhearing his phone call.

Her phone rang.

"Hi, Bren. I just wanted to tell you I heard from Sean." Kate's voice was upbeat and cheerful.

"All ready? He must really be interested in getting to know you. I thought you were working tonight?" Brenna asked.

"Well, duh, you know I'm irresistible. He asked if I wanted to go out for dinner tomorrow night. I didn't think I'd hear from him at all. And I'm just grabbing a coffee. I'm at work. I actually had to come in early."

"So, where are you guys going for dinner?"

"He mentioned the new Thai restaurant, and we're going to meet there."

"Did he say anything about what he was doing tonight?"

"No. He called about fifteen minutes ago, and it sounded as if he was outside somewhere. I could hear kids playing."

Brenna made up her mind. "I have to go. I'll talk to you later."

Brenna disconnected the call and went into her bedroom. She quickly changed into a pair of dark jeans and a navy sweatshirt. She pulled her hair back in a ponytail and put on a dark baseball cap. She slid her feet into her sneakers and grabbed her wallet, keys, and phone and hurried out the door.

She got in her Jeep and headed toward the only bandstand she knew of in the city. It was located in the City Gardens, downtown. She drove across town, pushing the speed limit. She didn't want to be pulled over for speeding tonight, but she didn't have time to waste.

Brenna arrived downtown and circled the block around the Gardens. The only parking spot she could find was between two high-end cars—a BMW and a Mercedes. Groaning, she realized she'd have to parallel park. Not her favorite activity. Carefully maneuvering her Jeep, she managed to get in.

She checked her watch and saw it was a few minutes after eight. She needed to hurry to get to the bandstand to see what was happening.

She found the path leading to the bandstand and scooted down it. The low-lying lights on the path were starting to come on. She was turning the corner when she heard a muffled sound like a car backfiring. She stopped for a second and heard someone running in her direction. She ducked behind one of the large pine trees.

A man dressed in black and wearing a ski mask was running down the path toward the south exit of the Gardens. He was carrying a handgun in his left hand.

As soon as he was out of sight, Brenna raced in the direction of the bandstand. She didn't see anyone there and bounded up the stairs. Sean was lying on the floor of the bandstand, bleeding from his chest. She ran to him and dropped to her knees.

"Sean, Sean can you hear me?" she shouted. She found a pulse. It was faint and irregular. His chest was barely moving. "Sean, come on! Open your eyes! I'm calling for help, but you need to stay with me." She punched in 9-1-1.

As the operator responded, Sean opened his eyes.

Brenna said, "I'm at the City Gardens, in the bandstand. I've found someone, and I think he's been shot. He's just opened his eyes, but there's blood coming from his chest."

"Ma'am, I'm sending an ambulance, and the police are on their way. Do you know if the shooter is still in the area?"

"I don't think so. I saw someone leave the area, and he was carrying a gun."

Sean tried to speak but lost consciousness before he could say anything.

"Oh no! He's passed out. What do I do?"

"Make sure his airway is open. Then apply pressure on the wound, as hard as you can."

Brenna dropped her phone on the bandstand floor and made sure Sean was breathing. The blood pouring out of the wound slowed down as she applied pressure. Her hands grew sticky from the blood. The wait for the paramedics seemed to take hours.

"Sean, I don't know if you can hear me, but you need to stay with me. Help is coming. The paramedics are going to be here soon. Don't give up. Come on! I just spoke with Kate, and she's excited about your date. Dammit, Sean, open your eyes!"

"Okay, ma'am, we'll take over from here." One of the paramedics dropped next to Brenna.

Brenna stepped aside and realized her hands were covered in blood. She wiped her hands on her jeans but couldn't get all the blood off.

She picked up her cell phone from the floor of the bandstand. "The paramedics are here. I'm going to hang up."

Brenna disconnected the call and knew she had to let Detective Morris know what had happened. She made the call.

"Morris here."

"Detective, it's Brenna Flynn. I'm at the bandstand in the City Gardens. Sean Jamieson, the host of the show, has been shot. I think I saw the man who shot him run away from the scene. The paramedics are here. Sean's still alive."

"I'm going to call Bob, and one of us will be with you in ten minutes tops. I'll call the dispatcher and speak to the responding officer and let him know this may be tied to our case. Stay where you are. We'll be there as soon as we can."

Brenna hung up the phone, moved out of the bandstand, and stood off to one side. She was beating herself up inside because if she had been here earlier, maybe Sean wouldn't have been shot. Her stomach was in knots, and she had a massive headache. Why hadn't she talked to Detective Morris about this when she had gotten home?

She called Emily and told her what had happened.

Emily gasped. "Oh, my God! I'll be right there. Don't speak to the police until I get there. Do you understand?"

"Yes, but I've already called Detective Morris to tell her what happened. And now there are police everywhere." Brenna was doing her best not to lose her composure, but she was starting to get pretty shaky.

"I'm on my way. I'll be there in less than five minutes. Do not move, and do not speak to anyone." Emily's voice was very firm as she spoke to Brenna.

Brenna's legs wouldn't stop shaking. She dropped to the ground and put her head between her knees and started taking deep breaths. Her head was spinning and her stomach was queasy.

"Ma'am, are you okay?"

She lifted her head. One of the responding officers was standing over her.

"Yes. I'm not hurt. I found him."

"Are you sure you aren't injured? There's a lot of blood on your hands and clothes."

"It's his. I had to apply pressure to stop the bleeding, and his blood got on my hands, and then I wiped my hands on my jeans." Brenna's voice quavered.

"I'll be right back." The officer said.

Brenna watched as he walked to the ambulance and then he came back with a blanket.

"Here you go. Put this around your shoulders. We can't have you going into shock. You're Bob McLean's cousin, aren't you?"

"Yes. Do I know you?"

"No. We haven't met, but I just spoke with him. He'll be here shortly. My name is Peter Murphy. Bob and I have worked together for a while, and he asked me to keep an eye on you."

"Thanks, Officer. Appreciate it." Brenna closed her eyes for a minute, and when she opened them again, Emily was being held back by one of the officers setting up a perimeter, and Brenna could hear her arguing with the officer.

Officer Murphy raised an eyebrow. "Friend of yours?"

Brenna nodded her head. "I called her after I called Detective Morris. She's pretty upset with me, and she's my attorney."

Officer Murphy called out to the officer setting up the perimeter. "Let her through. She needs to talk to Ms. Flynn."

"Thanks," Brenna said.

"Oh, my God! Are you okay?" Emily ran up to Brenna. She dropped to her knees and grabbed Brenna, wrapping her in a huge hug.

"Yes. Really, I am. Just super pissed off and dirty. Emily, this is Officer Murphy. He's been sitting with me to make sure I'm okay, as per Bob's instructions."

Emily asked Officer Murphy, "Is she going to be held for anything?"

"We'll need to ask her some questions and probably do a field test for gunshot residue."

"Okay, fine. Brenna, you and I need to talk before you speak with Detective Morris and Bob." Emily said to the officer, "Could we have a few moments, please? I'm her lawyer."

"No problem. I'll get the field kit from my car."

Emily scowled at Brenna. "Okay, spill it. What happened?"

Brenna's face crumpled as she filled Emily in on what she had overheard at the studio and her decision to come to the Gardens to check on Sean. "I really didn't think Sean was in danger. If I had, I would have told Detective Morris what I overheard."

"You have nothing to be guilty about. It was Sean's decision to blackmail someone. There wasn't much you could do about any of this. Even if you had told Detective Morris what you overheard, Sean probably would have denied it. Do you really think he would have said, 'Uh, yes, I'm blackmailing someone.' Let's focus on what we can work on. A description of the person you saw running down the path might help." Emily wasn't going to let Brenna beat herself up on this.

The sound of car doors slamming had them both turning their heads. Bob and Detective Morris had arrived. Officer Murphy walked toward them and had a brief discussion with Bob. He nodded his head toward Brenna and held up his field kit.

Bob and Detective Morris walked to Brenna and Emily. Officer Murphy was with them. Bob stopped by one of the CSU techs and spoke quietly for a minute. Brenna could see him taking in the scene. Then he started moving toward Brenna.

Bob's jaw was clenched, and he scowled. Detective Morris' face was a blank mask. Brenna knew this wasn't going to be an easy conversation with them.

CHAPTER NINETEEN

Bob and Detective Morris stopped a few feet away from Brenna and Emily.

"Brenna. First thing. Are you okay? Not injured?" Bob asked.

Brenna shook her head. "I'm fine. I'm not hurt, I'm . . ."

"Just stop right there." Bob held out his hand. "Now, you're going to get tested for gunshot residue. Officer Murphy will take care of the field test. When he's done, you're going to tell us exactly what you were doing here at this time of night. And I don't believe you were here for the fresh air."

Brenna went on the offensive. She stood and threw the blanket off her shoulders. "You know what, Bob? Yes, I do know how close I came to getting hurt. I saw the shooter running away. He didn't see me, but I saw him. I heard the gunshot, I found Sean, and the whole time I was on the phone with nine-one-one, I kept hoping the shooter didn't come back. He could have, but he didn't. Yes, I do know how dangerous and stupid this was. I so don't need you to tell me that."

Emily stood next to Brenna and put her hand on her shoulder. "Brenna. Calm down. It's been a bad day and night all around. Everyone, take a step back, and let's start over. Bob?"

Bob put both hands on his head and then rubbed his face. "Em's right. It's been a bad day, and now I get this call. I'm pissed at you for putting yourself in harm's way. What don't you get? There are some bad people out there." Bob glared at Brenna. "Now, why don't you tell Detective Morris and me what brought you here?"

Brenna's eyes filled with tears. She raised her arm and rubbed her eyes with her jacket. "Right." She put her hands at her sides. "What do you want first? The field test or me explaining myself?"

Detective Morris pulled out a notebook. "Why don't we do both? Officer Murphy can do the test now, and you can tell us why you came out here tonight. And what happened."

Officer Murphy opened the field test. "This won't take long."

Brenna held out her left hand. "Okay, earlier today, I overheard a conversation Sean had with someone on his phone. It sounded as if he was blackmailing that person. He told whoever it was 'I know what you did' and to meet him here tonight at eight and to bring the money. I thought if I came early enough, I could prevent whatever was happening and maybe reason with Sean. But I got here too late." She then held out her right hand for Officer Murphy.

Bob shook his head. "The chances are you wouldn't have been able to stop him from doing whatever he had planned. You could have been caught in the crossfire. Now, how about you tell us exactly what happened from the time you to the Gardens?"

Brenna walked them through the events of the last thirty minutes.

When she was done, Detective Morris said, "We'll need to get some specifics from you about height, weight, and body type. The fact he was wearing a ski mask means he didn't want to take a chance on being recognized by anyone. We'll get you to work with one of our sketch artists. You might be able to provide information on the suspect you don't know you have."

Brenna nodded. "Do you know anything about how Sean is doing?"

Bob said, "He was just getting to the hospital when we pulled in here. We'll go to the hospital after we're done here and see when we can talk to him." Bob asked Emily, "Can you bring her to the station to work with the sketch artist?"

"Yes. But first, she's going home to shower and change."

"No problem. In the meantime, CSU will work the scene. We'll go to the hospital to see how Sean is doing and what we can learn from him."

Brenna glanced up as she was cleaning off her hands from the gunshot residue test. "He was talking to someone on his phone this afternoon. Isn't there something you can do to pull his phone records to get the information? It might tell you who he was meeting."

"Not to worry. We have it under control. You have to remember, this isn't television. It will take us more than an hour to solve this," Bob said.

Brenna and Emily headed to Emily's car. Brenna was in no condition to drive, and Emily was going with her to the police station.

"I have to let Tim and Mathew know about Sean. This is going to impact the show."

"You're right. Why don't you call them now?"

Brenna pulled out her phone and called Tim. The phone rang several times before he picked up.

"Tim, Brenna here. I'm afraid I have some bad news."

"What's happening? Where are you?"

"Sean Jamieson was shot tonight at the bandstand in the City Gardens. He's been taken to City General, and the doctors are working on him now."

Tim gasped. "How do you know this?"

Brenna wasn't sure how much she could tell him. "I happened to be at the Gardens tonight, and I found Sean in the bandstand. He'd been shot. I called nine-one-one, and he was taken to the hospital. I don't know how he's doing. The police are at the Gardens investigating. They'll be going to the hospital to talk to Sean later tonight if he can speak with them."

"If he can. Do you mean Sean might not make it?"

"I don't know. I have to go. I'll talk to you later." Brenna disconnected the call.

Emily had just pulled into the parking lot at Brenna's apartment building. She parked the car and turned to look at Brenna. "Are you okay? You sound as if you're fading."

"I'm really tired all of a sudden. I feel like a balloon with all the air draining out of it."

"K, let's get into your apartment. I'll put some coffee together, and you grab a shower. You'll feel better once you're cleaned up."

"You're probably right." Brenna opened the car door.

She and Emily climbed the staircase to the third floor and then entered her apartment.

Brenna walked into her bathroom and shook her head at her reflection in the mirror. No wonder everyone kept asking if she was hurt. There was blood on her neck, her hands, and all over her clothes. There was even a smear on her cheek. She peeled off her clothes, tossing them on the floor. They were going straight to the garbage. She wasn't going to bother trying to clean them. She never wanted to see them again. She got in the shower and made sure the water was as hot as she could stand it.

She scrubbed herself clean and washed her hair twice, even though it didn't need it. She couldn't block the events of the last few days. What had Sean been thinking? And who was he talking to? She didn't understand what was happening at the studio. At first, it had seemed Chef Mike's murder had been a terrible mistake. But the more she thought about what she had overheard, the note left in her apartment, and Mr. Harlow's poisoning, the more she believed the show was being targeted. The key was to find out who was targeting the show and why.

Emily had coffee waiting in travel mugs when Brenna came out of her bedroom. "Well, you look better. At least there isn't blood all over your face. I'm sure it wasn't easy for you to find Sean shot."

"If I had thought he was going to be in danger, I would have tried to stop him earlier."

Emily shook her head. "I don't think you could have stopped him. Here, sit down. You and I need to go over a few things before you go to the police station."

Brenna spent a few minutes bringing Emily up to speed on what had been happening at the studio, and she didn't hold anything back.

When she was done, Emily said, "I think you need to find another job. The studio isn't safe. Can't Jackie find something else?"

"I don't think I'm on anyone's hit list. I should be safe. I don't have a relationship with anyone at the studio."

Emily disagreed with her. "You found Chef Mike, and you found Sean. You're involved in everything happening there. We need to figure out a way to protect you if you're still going to work there."

"Well, there is increased security at the studio . . ."

"Right, and a lot of good it's doing."

"Oh, and well, there's something else I should tell you about."

Emily raised an eyebrow.

"Someone slipped a note under my door a few days ago. It was a photo of the cast and crew from the show's publicity department, and Chef Mike had a red X through his head. The note said, 'Who's next?'."

"Oh, for God's sake! Did you tell Detective Morris about this?"

"Yes. I called her right away. She and Bob have the note, and I wasn't to say anything about it to anyone. I haven't spoken about it. But, I thought since you're my lawyer, you should have this information."

Emily shook her head. "Do they have any idea who slipped this note under your door? And what are the police doing to make sure no one has access to your apartment? I have to say, I'm not thrilled with this development."

"Well, neither am I. But, I'm pretty sure I'm safe here. The door is locked, and no one should be able to get into my apartment. Dad came by and changed the locks to the building. I don't want to go home to mom and dad's because it would feel as if whoever's behind this is winning." Brenna scrunched up her forehead. "Come on. Let's get this sketch thing done. It's been a really long day."

THE DESK SERGEANT took their names and asked them to wait for a few minutes while he called for the artist. They didn't have to wait long until an officer came to get them. The officer called out, "Brenna Flynn?"

Brenna stood. "Yes."

"If you'll come with me to my office, we can get started."

Brenna and Emily followed the officer. She pointed to a couple of chairs. "Have a seat and make yourselves comfortable. We use a computer software program. It will generate a sketch based on what you can remember. Don't try to force anything; let it come naturally. Just tell me what you saw."

"The person I saw was wearing a mask, so I didn't see his face. How is this going to help?"

"We'll get the sketch down and see if we can nail down height, body type, and weight. Maybe even the shape of the person's head. If you remember the type of clothing the suspect was wearing, it will help too. There's always the possibility someone else saw this person, and the sketch may provide us with more leads."

Brenna gave as much detail as she could remember, and the officer was able to create a reasonable sketch of the person Brenna saw. They were able to include the shape of his head and the color of his skin, based on what she had seen of his ungloved hands. Brenna was able to provide information on his body shape and his height.

"You did well. You remembered a lot of helpful details. Does this look like the person you saw?"

"Yes. Wow, I'm impressed."

"Are we through here, Officer? If we are, I'd like to take Brenna back home to get some rest."

"Yes. Thanks for coming in. You did great." The officer escorted them out to the front of the building.

They got into Emily's car, and Brenna said, "Thanks for coming with me. It made it a lot easier having you there."

"Not a problem. Are you going to be able to sleep tonight? Do you want some company?"

"I'll be okay. I'm beat. I've been up since five-thirty, and it feels like today has been three days long. I wonder how Sean's doing."

Emily checked the clock on her instrument panel and turned on the radio. "The ten o'clock news should be coming on in a minute. They might have something about it there."

They drove in silence until the top of the hour, and the lead story was the shooting at the bandstand. The reporter indicated there had been a shooting and that police were on the lookout for the shooter. The victim was as yet unidentified and had been taken to the hospital with gunshot wounds. No further details were available.

"Well, that isn't helpful." Brenna was annoyed. "I'm going to call Bob and see if he can fill me in."

She pulled out her cell and placed the call. Bob answered immediately.

"Bob, I worked with the sketch artist, and she has an image she'll be sending out to you soon."

"Great. Why do I have the feeling there's something else behind this call?"

"I'm curious how Sean is doing? Have you got any word from the hospital?"

"He was going in for surgery, and then he'll be sedated for the night.

We've got a police guard on him until we can talk to him tomorrow. Where are you?"

"Em's going to drive me back to my car, and then I'm heading home."

"And what are your plans for the rest of the evening?"

"I'm going to get some sleep. Nothing else. I'm exhausted. It's been a long day."

"Fine. Make sure you stay home, and don't open your door unless you've checked the identity of the person on the other side."

Brenna sighed. "I'm not stupid. I know what I need to do"

"Are you working tomorrow?"

"Yes. I have to be in by seven tomorrow morning."

"Good enough. I'll likely see you at the studio sometime tomorrow. We'll get to the bottom of all of this soon. Keep an eye out and be careful."

Brenna filled Emily in on the conversation and on Sean's status. They had arrived at the parking spot where Brenna had left her car. There were still police working the scene, the lights from their vehicles flashing in the darkness.

"Are you planning on going to see Sean tomorrow?"

"Yes. I want to know what he was doing and who he was blackmailing. Or at least who he was meeting. But, right now, I want to go home and get some sleep. Thanks for going with me to the station and driving me back to my car."

"No problem. Can you give me a call when you get in your apartment? I want to make sure you're fine."

"I will." Brenna leaned across and gave her a hug, hopped out of Emily's car, and quickly got into hers and drove down the street.

CHAPTER TWENTY

Brenna's phone rang almost as soon as she walked into her apartment. She checked the caller ID. "Tim, what can I do for you?"

"I made it to the hospital before Sean went into surgery. It appears he'll be fine. The doctor said the bullet went right through his shoulder. He was very lucky, and if there's no infection, he should be able to come into work next week. It was fortunate you were there and able to administer first aid until the paramedics got there."

"That's a relief. I'm glad he'll be fine." Brenna kept walking through her apartment as she spoke with Tim. She was sure her place was secure, but she was going to check every room before she turned in for the evening. She was opening doors and checking in closets. All the lights were on.

"Brenna, where are you? What are you doing?"

"I'm home. I'm just going through my apartment to make sure everything is fine. I'm a bit spooked by what happened with Sean." She debated with herself. Should she tell Tim about the note? She had promised the police she wouldn't, and she wasn't sure who she could trust at the studio.

"That's understandable. Did you contact Mathew to tell him what happened?"

"No, I haven't had time. I'm just getting back from the police station. I had to work with a sketch artist."

"A sketch artist. Did you see the shooter?" Tim asked.

"I saw someone running away, but I didn't get a good look at their face.

The police wanted me to give the sketch artist whatever information I could."

"Oh. Well. Um, Mathew. I need to get in touch with him. I don't want him to hear about Sean on the news."

"They probably won't release his name if he's going to be okay. Isn't Mathew still at the hospital with Mr. Harlow?"

"No. Apparently, he left shortly after seven. I'll try to reach him. He may have shut off his phone to get a bit of a break. He does that every once in a while. You're still okay to come in tomorrow?"

"Yes, I'll be in at seven. We're doing postproduction, aren't we?"

"Yes. We'll need to have some contingency plans in case Sean isn't able to work next week. We'll have to wait to hear from the doctor tomorrow on his status."

"Fine. I'll see you in the morning." Brenna disconnected the call. She sent Emily a quick text letting her know she was home and fine.

She ran her hands through her hair. *What a night.* She could feel the adrenaline leave her body as the excitement of the evening dissipated. She knew she was too wired to sleep and wanted to catch the late news on TV to see if there was any news on Sean.

Brenna went to her bedroom and pulled out her favorite pajamas, washed her face, and then went to her kitchen. *No more ice cream tonight, but some wine might take the edge off.* She opened a bottle of Shiraz and poured herself a generous glass. She turned on the television and fell asleep on her couch, waiting for the news to come on.

A QUICK RUN and a hot shower in the morning gave Brenna the push she needed to deal with the day ahead. Either her couch was quite comfortable or she had been totally exhausted; didn't really matter because either way, she felt well-rested. Breakfast and a large coffee would get rid of any cobwebs in her brain.

She drove to the studio, planning her day. It was a postproduction day, but they would likely have to field questions from reporters on what was happening with the judges and the show. And now with Sean. She hoped his recovery would be easy.

Arriving at security, she noticed there were additional measures in place.

Carl Briggs was working the front entrance, but he was accompanied by another guard, this one a young woman, with her long blond hair pulled back in a braid. "Brenna, meet Charlotte. She'll be working with me on the front entrance for the next little while."

Brenna smiled at Charlotte. "Nice to meet you. I hope things go smoothly today. Are you the only two on security today?"

Carl said, "No, we have three more guards spread out in the building, and we have someone watching the video feed all day. That person is going to switch out between the three in the building. We've got the studio covered."

"What about outside?" Brenna asked.

Charlotte said, "The threat doesn't appear to be out there. But we do have cameras at every entrance, and the parking lot is under video surveillance as well."

"Tim hasn't asked for additional staff outside. Until he does, our company can't put anyone out there," Carl added.

"Well, I feel better knowing there are extra people here. Today's postproduction. It should be just the regular crew coming in. There may be reporters coming by, but Tim or Mathew will have to let you know how they're going to deal with them."

"Not a problem. If anyone shows up who isn't on the list, we'll make a call." Carl made a note as he told Brenna what the procedure would be.

She headed back to the studio and ran into Tim as he was coming out of his office.

"Morning, have you heard any more from the police?"

"Not yet. We have the postproduction meeting set for eight-thirty this morning. Can you make sure you're there?"

"Yes. Did you want me to get one of the cleaning companies in to clean up the studio again? I'm not sure if the regular cleaning crew was able to come in last night."

"They didn't. The police were still here, and they were turned away. Please take care of it this morning."

Brenna made a call to QuickClean.

"Marnie speaking."

"Marnie, Brenna Flynn from Studio One. I wasn't sure you'd be in this early."

"The phone calls come directly to my personal number. What can I do for you?"

"We've had an incident with one of the judges being ill. We need to have the set cleaned up and foodstuffs will need to be destroyed."

Brenna heard the flipping of pages, "We can be there this morning at ten. Will that work?"

"Perfect. Thanks. I'll let security know to expect you."

The postproduction meeting took place in the large conference room. Tim, Mathew, Margo, John, the floor director, and the two editors were present. Brenna made it to the meeting on time. As she walked in the room, she heard Mathew discussing what a sponsor had to say at their meeting the previous evening.

"They've expressed some concern about the issues we've been dealing with at the studio. Somehow, they've learned there have been items misplaced or stolen from the kitchens. The pantry appears to have someone who is changing things around. But those things are minor compared to Chef Mike's murder and Mr. Harlow's poisoning. Frankly, I had to work hard to convince this sponsor not to pull their campaign from the show. They're very concerned about their brand being associated with a show embroiled in a murder investigation. Now, with Sean being shot and involved in a police investigation, they have more concerns."

Tim ran his hands through his hair. "Mathew's recap is spot on. We have to, just have to, make this show work and prevent any other problems from coming up."

"We've made some additional changes to security. I'm confident the studio will be secure. As for what happened to Sean, well, I don't see how we can be held responsible for behavior outside the studio," Mathew replied.

"Tim, what's the story with Sean?" the floor director asked.

"Last night, Sean was involved in a mugging at the park. He was at the bandstand and was shot in the left shoulder. The shooter got away, didn't steal anything of Sean's, and hasn't been caught yet. Brenna happened to be at the park and heard the shot. She called nine-one-one and administered first aid to Sean. If she hadn't been there, Sean would be dealing with a longer recovery or worse. As it is, he's expected to be released from the hospital tomorrow, and he's made it clear he'll be ready to work for the next taping. There's no reason to believe Sean's shooting had anything to do with the show."

"How did the sponsor hear about the shooting?" Brenna asked.

"I'm not sure," Tim said.

There were a few more questions, and Tim answered them as best as he could.

"Okay, let's move on to the business at hand. The best way to keep our sponsors happy is to provide a quality product. Let's take a look at yesterday's show. John, over to you."

The team spent the next ninety minutes reviewing the tape.

At the end of the meeting, Tim said, "Thanks for the comments on how to improve the next show. I want to remind you all, Chef Mike's memorial service is tomorrow at four. It's being held at his restaurant. I've made sure there is a table reserved for the show. It seats ten people. If you can make it to the memorial, great. If not, we understand."

Mathew said, "Sunday is a much-deserved day off for everyone. Monday will be rehearsal for the next show. I hope everyone gets an opportunity to relax a bit."

"Brenna, are you okay? It must have been awful to find Sean." Margo said.

"Well, it wasn't the best way to spend an evening, but I'm glad I was able to help him. And I'm grateful he's going to be fine. I hadn't heard anything after last night. It's good news he's going to be released as early as he is."

"Are you going to Chef Mike's memorial?"

"Yes. I've known his family for a long time. And you?"

"I am. I think it's important to show respect for him and his family. It's so sad. He was killed just when his life was going in the direction he wanted. He was happy with his work, and he loved Vicky very much. I remember overhearing him talk to Chef Rosa about the upcoming wedding and how excited he was."

Brenna's phone rang. "Brenna Flynn here."

"It's Detective Morris. Bob and I are going to be at the studio later this morning. We need to review some of the security tapes from the last couple of days. Can you set it up for us?"

"Sure. I'll talk to the security team here and see how we can get it to you. I think we can send them electronically to you."

"No. We'll come there to review it."

"Fine. I'll touch base with you as soon as I talk to the security team."

"What's up now?" Margo asked.

"The police want to review the security tapes, and they don't want to have them sent electronically. They want to do it here. I better let Carl know. He can alert whoever needs to be told."

Brenna arrived at the security desk and cleared her throat.

Carl looked up from the monitor he had been watching. "Yes, Brenna. What can I do for you?"

"I just spoke with Detective Morris, and she informed me she and Detective McLean will be coming to the studio to view security tapes. I told her we could send them to the police station electronically, but they want to see them here. Who do I need to speak to about making sure they have access to the tapes and a location where they can view them?"

"I'll let the control room know, and they'll make sure to have the tapes ready for them. They can view them in the room next to the control room. There are a couple of monitors there."

"Great. I'll make sure to let them know."

Mathew came through the lobby. He was wearing a dark-blue blazer, blue dress shirt, and jeans, and his messenger bag was slung across his chest.

"Morning. How are things going today?" He stopped by security.

Brenna glanced at Carl, and he just shrugged. Charlotte was studying the monitor closely.

"What's up? Why the long faces?" Mathew asked impatiently.

Brenna said, "The police are coming here to review the security tapes."

"What tapes are they looking at?"

"Yesterday's tapes and the two previous days," Brenna said.

"Well, how are they going to know what's normal or not? They aren't part of the show's crew. I don't want any of the crew upset any further than they already are. It's a real challenge to put this show together. I'm leaving for another meeting with our sponsors and won't be back for a while, and I won't be able to be reached by cell either. At least not until after my meeting." He raised his left arm and glanced at his watch. "And I'm going to be late if I don't hurry. If the detectives need to speak with me, they'll have to wait."

He lowered his arm and walked out the door. There was something different about him this morning. But Brenna couldn't put her finger on it. She said under her breath, "Such a jerk."

Carl said, "You've got that right."

Brenna jumped. "I forgot you were here. I shouldn't have said anything, but he really does get under my skin."

"Don't worry. We won't tell anyone you feel the same as we do. Your secret's safe with us," Charlotte said.

Brenna chuckled. "Thanks. I better get to work. I'll chat with you later."

CHAPTER TWENTY-ONE

Brenna was setting up the deliveries for supplies for next week's shows. Her headset buzzed. "Brenna here."

"Brenna, QuickClean has arrived." Carl's voice boomed in her headset.

"I'll be right there." Brenna walked to the front and signed in Marnie and her team. As they returned to the set, Brenna said, "Part of the problem I have is some of the food was tampered with. Someone introduced poisonous mushrooms, and we aren't certain that other items weren't tampered with as well."

Marnie nodded. "I heard there were some problems. I know what has to be done. I've dealt with something similar, and I'm familiar with the FDA's rules and regulations. We'll make sure all the foodstuffs are removed and disposed of properly." Marnie gazed around the set. "You wouldn't think a cooking show would be such an issue. We rarely have to do anything like this."

"Have you worked on a lot of cooking shows?" Brenna asked.

"Not here. But I did some work on a couple in Chicago a while back. I think this is the first cooking show being done in Bayview. It must be costing a fortune in food. You do know everything has to be destroyed."

Brenna said. "I'm aware of that. Hopefully, this is the last time something like this will happen. And the show is getting supplies at a reduced rate. We do pay the suppliers a percentage of what it would normally cost, but they're listed as sponsors in the credits."

"Right, well, we'll get this cleaned up for you. It would be easier if we can come and go through the back. Who do we talk to about that?"

"I'll touch base with security. I don't think that will be an issue."

Brenna watched as Marnie and her team took in what needed to be done and then she went back to the front.

"Carl, the cleaning crew needs to be able to access the back door to get items in and out efficiently. Is that going to be a problem?"

Carl shook his head. "I'll make sure the cameras are recording in the studio and at the door. That way, everything is covered."

"Excellent. Thank you."

"Not a problem. Oh, Mr. Malone is coming in this morning, and he'd like to speak with you. Are you going to be here?"

Brenna frowned. "Yes, I'll be here all morning. Did he say why he needed to speak with me?"

"No. But I'll let him know you're in the back when he gets here."

Brenna stopped by the set on her way to the small conference room. "Marnie, you have access through the back door. I'll unlock it for you and then close it up when you're in the studio."

"Thanks, Brenna. I'll let you know when we're done. Where are you going to be?"

"There's a small office just off one of the conference rooms. I've set up my computer in there."

Brenna flew through the notes she had taken at the postproduction meeting. There were a few items she needed to address, and those were quickly taken care of. Once that was done, she took the time to call the hospital. She wanted to know how Sean was.

She was surprised to be put through directly to his room. "Hi, Sean. It's Brenna Flynn. Just checking in to see how you're doing today."

"Brenna. Thanks for the call. I'm doing well. The doctors are debating when they're going to let me out." Sean's voice was groggy.

"Really? I'm surprised."

"Well, I have you to thank for my speedy recovery. The police said you were there almost immediately and were able to give me first aid. I don't remember much of anything."

Brenna was silent for a moment. "You don't remember what you were doing at the bandstand?"

"No. I don't remember anything after leaving the studio."

"So, did the doctors tell you when you'll be let out?"

"They're thinking later this afternoon, depending on test results."

"Wow, that's quick."

"I have no intention of being stuck here. I've already told Tim I'll be back at work next week. I may have to wear a sling, but I'll make it work. Look, I have to go. Someone just came in. And thanks for your help last night. I mean that." Sean's voice had grown stronger over the call.

"You're welcome." Brenna was speaking to dead air. Sean had already hung up.

She shrugged. He was obviously doing well enough to be released.

There was a knock on the door, and she turned around.

Connor was in the doorway holding two cups of coffee. "Mind if I come in? I have coffee."

"Coffee will definitely gain you entry." Brenna smiled.

Connor came around to the table, took a seat, and handed her a coffee. "Cream and two sugars, right?"

Brenna took a sip. "Perfect. Is this from across the street?"

"Mmm, yes, it is. I didn't expect it to be this good. Wonder what they do to their coffee?"

"They roast the beans themselves and then grind them, twice." Brenna took a drink. "So, what's on your mind? I'm sure you didn't come here just for coffee."

"You're right. I heard you were the one who found Sean last night." Connor raised his eyebrows. "You seem to have made a habit of being first on the scene. What were you doing out at the bandstand last night?"

Brenna didn't answer right away. She watched him as she drank more of her coffee. "I overheard a conversation Sean had with someone on the phone yesterday. It sounded suspicious, and I thought I'd check it out."

Connor waited, and when Brenna didn't add anything else, he shook his head. "I spoke with Bob earlier this morning. He filled me in on what you told him last night. Look, I'm not one of the bad guys here. I'm trying to keep everyone safe. Information like this is important. You should have told either myself or contacted the police instead of going there yourself."

Brenna sighed. "Honestly, I didn't think much of it at the time. I was tired and in a hurry to get home. And if I had spoken with Detective Morris, there wouldn't have been a lot for her to go on."

Connor nodded. "I get that. How about from now on, if you see or hear anything that's remotely off, you call me. Immediately. Deal?"

"I guess I can do that."

"Now, do you have any idea who Sean was speaking with on the phone?"

"No, and I just spoke with him at the hospital. He says he doesn't remember anything about last night. Has no clue why he was at the bandstand."

Connor set his coffee cup on the table. "Hard to tell if he's faking or not. Some people suffer from traumatic amnesia, but he didn't get a head injury. Although, the stress of being shot could cause it as well."

Brenna got up and looked out in the hall to see if anyone was nearby. Then she sat down again and leaned closer to Connor. "I think he's lying. I think he knows exactly what he was doing at the bandstand. I think he'll get in touch with whoever he was blackmailing and try again." Brenna's brow was furrowed. "I know it was a man I saw running away. But I can't place him."

"Hard for us to tell if he's lying or not." Connor pulled up his phone and started typing something. "And you worked with a sketch artist. How did that go? Bob sent me a copy of the sketch."

"I remembered more than I thought I had. I was able to get the height and approximate weight down. And the shape of his head and skin tone as well."

Connor said, "The notes say he's just over six feet tall and his build was slim. Can you remember how he moved? Was he athletic, or did he run with heavy feet?"

"You know, he did move like he knew what he was doing. He was pretty light on his feet, and he was quick."

"That's good."

"Should I let the police know this?"

"I'll touch base with Bob this morning. They're coming in to look at some of the tapes."

"I wonder if it could have been Frank Simons. You know, the production assistant I replaced? He was arrested for drug possession, and from what Margo has said about him, he was athletic."

Connor looked at his phone again. "Well, he was arrested, and he's out on bail. The police checked on him last night. He was working out at the gym. At least eight people saw him there in the time frame Sean was shot. So, it can't be him."

"Is there any way to find out who Sean was talking to on his phone?"

"The police have checked his cell phone records, and there isn't any call either incoming or outgoing at the time you say he was on the phone."

"But I'm sure he was on the phone."

"He may have borrowed someone's phone, or he could have a burner phone. If that's the case, nothing will be traced back to him."

Brenna tapped her pen on the table. "It sounds pretty cloak and dagger to me."

"Well, if he was trying to blackmail someone, it would be. He certainly wouldn't be talking about it in front of others. Now, anything else that pops out at you that doesn't seem quite right here?"

"Hard for me to know since I just started here. Oh, do you know what's happening with Chef Aaron's knife?"

Connor frowned. "I haven't heard a lot more about it. He was brought in for questioning by the police. But he couldn't pinpoint the exact time the knife went missing."

"I wonder if someone took it while he was here. Each of the chefs had their knife rolls with them."

"Yes, but wouldn't they have kept the knife rolls with them all the time?"

"There was one time where they didn't. When they came in the pantry with me to show me where they wanted everything sorted."

"And how long were you all together?"

"Maybe ten minutes. It would be long enough for someone to take his knife. And Chef Aaron's kitchen is at the far end from the pantry."

"Well, there weren't any security cameras running at the time. Whoever would have done it would be been someone who wasn't afraid of being seen in the kitchen area. Any ideas?"

"It could have been anyone from the crew. Most people have legitimate reasons to work in the kitchen area. Lighting guys fixing the lights, Margo making sure everything is set up. Even Tim and Mathew come through once in a while."

"What about John, the director?"

"Yes, he does as well. Narrowing it down to one person at that specific time could be a challenge."

"Especially since it was the end of a rehearsal. Even Sean could have walked through."

Both were silent for a few minutes.

Brenna said, "You know . . ."

At the same time, Connor said, "The police . . ." Both of them paused, and then Connor said, "Go ahead. You were saying?"

"Thanks. I wanted to make sure you knew about the former classmate who came by when the chefs were opening their restaurants."

Connor looked through the notes on his phone. "I don't think I have anything about a classmate. Is this someone from the culinary school?"

Brenna filled him in on what she knew about the former classmate. She had just finished telling him what she had found online when there was a knock at the door.

"Morning, Brenna, Connor. Just checking in to see how you're doing, Brenna." Bob walked into the small office, followed by Detective Morris. The space filled up quickly.

"I'm okay. Have you got any more information on the person who shot Sean?"

Bob shook his head. "Nothing, and no one saw anything."

"I spoke with him this morning."

Bob's eyebrows rose.

"I called the hospital to see how he was doing and was connected to his room."

Detective Morris spoke up. "Did he tell you he can't remember anything about last night?"

"He did. Sounds awfully convenient to me."

Bob shrugged. "It happens. It's unfortunate, but I guess he believes he can't say anything else or he'll be implicated in blackmail."

Detective Morris said, "Brenna, I want to let you know that you're no longer a suspect in Chef Mike's murder. Although your security code was used, we're convinced that someone else may have used it."

Brenna sighed. "Thanks for that. Such a relief."

Bob asked, "Is there a way for you to change your security code?"

"I'm not sure. Sally gave me the code and told me it had been assigned by IT. I never thought to ask if I could change it."

"Okay. Well, we're off to look at the tapes from the last few days. Connor, thanks for arranging a space for us." Detective Morris turned to go.

They left, and Brenna smiled. "That was good news. Off the suspect list."

Connor looked at her. "Yes, it is. I'm curious, though. Who would know your access code?"

Brenna looked taken aback. "I don't know. The IT department, of course, and well, Sally gave me the code. And she also said the code was unique to me. That way, the security system could track who entered the building."

"If Sally knew your code, it's reasonable to think someone else could have it. She may keep a record of the codes on file. That could easily be accessed by someone looking for it. I meant to look into this last night, and I didn't have time. I'll do some digging around this morning, see what I can come up with." Connor got up. "I'll be in touch. Remember, if you hear or see anything suspicious, contact me or the police. Don't wait."

"I will, and thanks for the coffee."

As Connor left the conference room, Brenna sent a text to Emily.

> B: Talked to the police, no longer a suspect
> E: Awesome! This calls for a celebration
> B: Charlie's Pub?
> E: Sounds good. 7-ish works
> B: Perfect

CHAPTER TWENTY-TWO

Brenna got home a few minutes before six. Grabbing her purse and the tool belt, she bumped the car door closed with her hip and walked into the lobby of the house. She checked her mail. *Ha, I'm on a roll. No bills or lawyer envelopes to deal with today.* She hurried up the wide wooden staircase to the third floor.

Walking into her apartment, she appreciated the large windows looking over the treed lot behind the house. Her dining room alcove was in the octagonal-shaped tower on the west side of the house and, at this time of day, the light flooded her space.

She put her things away and made her way to the bedroom. Charlie's wasn't a fancy restaurant, but she wanted to change out of her work clothes. Opening her walk-in closet, she selected a light-blue sweater and a pair of black jeans. Laying them on the bed, she grabbed a quick shower. Makeup and hair were done casually and with a light hand. After getting dressed, she pulled on a pair of low boots and took her leather jacket out.

Glancing at the time, she took a look at her email account. "Still no message from that reporter, Mary Gilles. Maybe another short email to her will jog her memory." Brenna composed a brief message asking Ms. Gilles to connect with her if she had any information on Charles Mathews.

Brenna drove to Charlie's Pub. It was in the downtown area and would likely be busier on a Friday night than on a Monday evening. A short drive and Brenna found herself pulling into one of the parking spots just before seven.

She sent Emily a text.

> B: U at Charlie's?
> E: Just arrived. Where r u?
> B: Coming in now

Brenna locked the Jeep and hurried to the entrance. She opened the double doors and saw a few people ahead of her. She stood on her tiptoes, checking to see where Emily was.

"Brenna, I'm here." Emily waved her arm. She was ahead in the lineup, next to be seated.

"Sorry, my friend is waiting for me." Brenna made her way to the front.

"What took you so long?" Emily asked.

"I had to get an email out before I left."

"Table for two?" the hostess asked.

"Yes. Can we get a booth, please?" Emily asked.

They followed the hostess to the last booth on the left and waited while she gave them the evening specials.

A server arrived before they'd had an opportunity to start talking. "Did you want anything to drink?"

Brenna opened her menu. "I'll have a large Shiraz, please."

"And I'll have a vodka tonic." Emily looked at Brenna. "Long day?"

Brenna smiled. "Yes, but I did get good news."

"So, what email did you have to get out? Something for the show?"

"No. I told you about the classmate that came looking for work with the chefs a few years ago, didn't I?" Brenna waited as Emily nodded. "Right, Charles Mathews. Well, the reporter didn't get back to me yet, so I sent her a follow-up email."

"Do you think you'll learn anything from her?"

Brenna frowned. "I'm not sure. I'd like to know what happened to him after he left this area. The chefs wouldn't hire him, so I wonder if anyone else did."

"She might not know."

"That's true. But she did report on his death. She might have kept in touch with him."

"Have you talked to Kate lately?" Emily asked.

"Hmm, no, not since last night. Have you?"

Emily smiled broadly. "Yes, and you'll never believe what she's up to."

The server arrived with their drinks and took their food order.

"Okay, what's Kate up to?" Brenna took a drink of her wine.

"She's been at the hospital. With Sean."

"Doing what?"

"She was in the ER when they brought him in. And then she was assigned to his care."

"How did she manage that?"

"Not sure, but she told me she's going to be doing some private care nursing for him when he's released."

Brenna grinned. "Go, Kate!"

Their food arrived, and they dug into the meal. The two friends caught up on news from the last few days.

"Are we still going for our run tomorrow morning?" Emily asked as they were getting ready to leave.

"Yes. Do you want to do the Peninsula Trail?"

Emily winced. "I'm not sure I'm up for that hill."

"Come on. We'll take it easy. We need to start doing hills if we're going to run the 10K next month."

"You're right. What time do you want to meet?"

"How does eight work for you?"

"Better than six. I'll meet you in the parking lot at eight. You get some rest and try not to think about all that's happening. It's the police's job to solve this. You aren't the guilty party."

"I know. I'm hoping to get a decent night's sleep tonight. Thanks for meeting me for dinner. I'll see you in the morning."

"Sounds good."

THE NEXT MORNING was sunny and cool. Perfect running weather. Brenna drove the short distance to the Peninsula Trail. The trail followed Lake Superior along the west coast and continued down the peninsula. It was a bit hilly, but the ground itself was easy on the legs for running. The stunning lake views at the top of the trail made up for the challenging hill.

Brenna parked her Jeep in the lot and looked around for Emily. No sign of her yet, but Brenna was a few minutes early. She got out of the Jeep and stretched, using the hood of the Jeep for support. She was drinking water when Emily pulled in next to her.

"Sorry I'm late. My mom called just as I was leaving. She and Dad are in New York for the next week, and she wanted to touch base with me."

"That's okay. How are your parents, anyway?"

Emily's father was a cardiac surgeon and had recently retired. Her mother was a well-known landscape artist who was having a show in New York.

"They're good. Dad still isn't used to being retired, and Mom is so pumped about her show. They spent Thursday getting the paintings hung at the gallery, and Friday night, well, according to Mom, the reception was amazing. She sold eight of her paintings last night."

"Wow! I'm surprised she waited until this morning to call you." Brenna laughed.

Emily stretched her legs. "I don't think they've gone to bed yet. She sounded absolutely giddy with excitement. I'm so happy for both of them."

They made their way to the trail.

"Ready for this?" Brenna asked.

"As ready as I will be. Let's start off slow."

"No problem."

The path they took was well-worn and soft with pine needles scattered on it. They had been running easily for a few minutes when Emily asked, "How did you sleep?"

"Pretty well. Knowing I'm not a suspect anymore took a huge weight off my shoulders. I can't believe it took them that long to figure out I wouldn't have had a motive for killing Chef Mike."

"They had to look at the evidence. And, honestly, the security code wasn't a good item in your favor."

They were quiet for a few minutes as they climbed one of the hills. After running for about twenty minutes, they turned off the path and stood by the guardrail at one of the lookouts. The lake was calm, and the gulls were crying out searching for food. To the right, they could see Bayview City. The town was nestled around a harbor and boats were leaving the marina. The city planners had built the downtown core close to the waterfront, in a square. From the square, the streets radiated out. Cul-de-sacs were arranged neatly at the end of the newer subdivisions.

The university and the college sat at the west end of town, and the big box stores were located at the east end. North of the harbor was Pebble Island. A lighthouse was at the west end of the island, and a resort was located in the center. Access to the island was by boat only, and Brenna watched as a boat left the resort marina.

Brenna took a deep breath and let it out slowly. "I wonder if Connor has found out who had access to the codes for the alarm. He said he was going to look into that."

"He'll let you know or, rather, he'll let Bob and Detective Morris know. Have you heard back from that reporter?"

Brenna stretched her calf muscles. "Not yet."

Emily frowned. "We better head back to the lot. What do you think she'll be able to tell you about this person?"

They started a slow jog down the trail.

"I don't know. I'm hoping she can provide some more information about him."

They were quiet as they continued on their run.

They arrived at the parking lot, and Brenna opened her Jeep to pull out some water bottles. She handed one to Emily and took one for herself.

"Thanks. Tastes so good." Emily drank her fill.

Brenna leaned back against her Jeep. "Thanks for the run. It feels good to get out here."

"What time are you going to Chef Mike's memorial?"

"I'll be there by three-thirty. Are you going?"

"Yes. Are you sitting with the show or with your family?"

"I'm not sure. The show has a table reserved for ten people. Do you want to sit together?"

"That would be great."

"K. I'll see you then. I need to shower and get some errands done this morning."

It was almost noon by the time Brenna got home from running her errands. But at least there was food in her fridge for the next week. She still had to get laundry done. She'd deal with that after lunch. One of the features of the building was that each apartment had a stacked washer and dryer in its utility room.

Brenna made herself a quick lunch and checked her email as she ate. Still no message from Mary Gilles, the reporter.

CHEF MIKE'S restaurant was located close to the waterfront. Brenna parked in one of the new parking lots nearby. A quick five-minute walk and she was waiting to sign the guest book for the memorial. She took one of the pamphlets commemorating Chef Mike's life. There were a few photos, some bio information, and words of thanks from his family and Vicky. She looked around. Emily was speaking with a tall, well-dressed man. Brenna walked up to Emily and waited until she had finished her conversation.

"Looks like a good turnout for the memorial," Brenna said.

"He was well-known and well-liked. Brenna, I'd like you to meet Graham Rogers, a colleague at the firm."

"Good to meet you." Brenna held out her hand.

"And you. I should go and join my wife. She's sitting with a few of the partners. Emily, are you joining us, or are you sitting elsewhere?"

"Thanks, but I'll sit with Brenna."

They waited until he made his way to his table.

"You sure it's okay to sit with you?" Emily asked.

"Yes. Not going to be a problem." Brenna was looking around for the studio table. She saw Margo waving in her direction. "Margo's at the table; let's go grab a seat."

They wove their way to the table and, along the way, they said hello to several people they both knew.

"Phew, I forgot how many people I knew here," Brenna said.

Emily smiled. "Not everyone's aware you're back home. You've been kind of quiet since you've been here."

Margo stood. "Glad you could make it, Brenna. There's lots of room at the table. Tim reserved two tables."

"Oh, that's good to know. Margo Ryan, I'd like you to meet Emily Connors. She's an old friend of mine."

Margo held out her hand. "Nice to meet you. How do the two of you know each other?"

Emily shook Margo's hand. "We've been friends since kindergarten. Haven't lost touch in all the years in between, either."

"Nice. And did you know Chef Mike?"

"Yes. He was good friends with my brother and with Brenna's as well."

They sat at the table and looked around. The judges were there as well, sitting at their own table with their spouses. Brenna looked toward the entrance and was surprised to see Sean. Brenna stood and waved her hand. He nodded his head in her direction. Brenna was surprised to see Kate with him. Brenna nudged Emily. "Kate's here. With Sean."

Emily turned around. Sean and Kate were making their way to the table.

"Is there room for two of us?" Sean pulled a chair out for Kate and then sat next to her. They were across the table from Brenna.

"I'm surprised to see you here. When were you released from the hospital?" Brenna asked.

"Today at noon. And Kate here said she'd keep an eye on me this afternoon. She was one of my nurses at the hospital."

Kate said, "I worked the last couple of shifts, and he was one of my patients. We were supposed to meet for dinner last night. And I guess we did, only it was at the hospital." She rolled her eyes. "Not exactly fine dining."

Margo leaned forward. "Sean, do they have any idea who did this?"

Sean shook his head. "No. And I can't remember anything from the time I left the studio until I woke up in the hospital."

"Well, I did see someone running from the bandstand. I gave all the information to the police. Maybe they'll be able to find the person responsible." Brenna didn't mention she had overheard Sean's conversation. If he was going to stick with the amnesia story, Brenna wasn't going to bring up what she knew. But there was no way she was going to trust him. Brenna had some concerns about Kate spending time with him without all of the facts Brenna was aware of. She'd have to see when she could talk to Kate alone.

"Do the doctors have any follow-up for you?" Margo asked.

"I have to keep the wound clean and dry. It does make showering interesting, to say the least. I have to wear this sling. I'll be seeing the doctor in a few days, and he'll assess how well it's healing."

Tim, Mathew, and John arrived then. They expressed their concerns to Sean.

"I can assure you I'll be able to work the show next week. The taping on Tuesday shouldn't be an issue. I'm confident I'll be fine."

"Good to hear. Our sponsors were concerned you'd be laid up and we'd have to find a replacement." Tim sat.

"They'll be happy to hear you're out and about already," Mathew said.

John glanced around. "It's a full house for the chef."

Brenna said, "He was a pretty popular guy with a huge following for his restaurant."

Tim stood. "I'm going to get some drinks from the bar. It seems there's a variety of beer and wine available."

Margo asked, "Do you need help?"

"I can manage. There are a few trays there. Wine okay with everyone?"

Kate piped up, "Nothing but soft drinks for Sean and me."

"Right. I guess you're on pain killers, Sean."

Sean gave a half-grin. "Yes, and they're pretty strong. I'll be weaning myself off at the end of today."

Margo asked Brenna, "Do you recognize many people here?"

"I do. Most of the people are family and friends of Chef Mike's. This restaurant was always fun and busy. The food was fantastic. I wonder if Chef Tina will keep the menu the same or if she'll make changes."

Sean said, "There's quite the representation from the city. City councilors, university management, and some people from the restaurant industry too. There are a lot of big names here."

Brenna agreed with him. "It isn't just big names from the city. There are some major athletes here too. I know a lot of the hockey and football players ate here frequently."

She was looking around the restaurant as she spoke and noticed Bob and Connor standing by the front door. She excused herself from the table and made her way to see them.

"Hi, Bob, Connor. What are you guys doing here?"

"Well, I'm here checking out who's at the memorial. Detective Morris will be joining me shortly. I just ran into Connor, and we're comparing notes." Bob leaned back against the wall.

Connor raised his hands. "No ulterior motives. I'm here because I knew Mike. We went to school together. I saw Bob, and we just started chatting."

Brenna scanned the restaurant. "It's a good turnout. A lot of different people here. Bob, do you think you'll find anything out here?"

"You never know when you're going to get a break. Everyone has secrets. Remember what Aunt Rita says—everyone lies."

Brenna agreed. "Yes. And I suppose, in your line of work, you see it a lot."

"All the time. People forget something or, in some cases, make it all up. Then there are the ones who lie through their teeth anytime you ask them something."

"Do you honestly expect to see someone who could be Chef Mike's murderer here? Would the killer be arrogant enough to show up?" Brenna asked.

Bob shrugged. "The thing with criminals is they think they're smarter than most people—and especially smarter than cops. Some of them are good at hiding in plain sight. But we catch them. They slip up, or someone notices something different. And then it all comes together. We don't think Chef Mike's death was random."

"Did you find anything on the show's security tapes?" Connor asked.

"No. The tapes didn't record much in the studio and nothing in the pantry," Bob said.

"I told Tim and Mathew we'd be adding cameras to all sections of the studio. Otherwise, our hands are tied." Connor shrugged. "I can't do anything about the previous days, but from yesterday on, the security cameras are everywhere."

"Are they cooperating with you?" Brenna asked.

"Not as much as they should. I've made it clear they need to take the security more seriously, and to a point, they have. But they're reluctant to spend more money. I've come up with a few cost-effective solutions. I'll see what else they agree to."

Brenna was surprised. "You'd think they'd be ready to take care of the people they work with."

Bob shook his head. "It's all about the bottom line. Money talks."

Connor nodded to Brenna. "I've looked into who could have had your access code. It's unique. No one else has had it. So, that eliminates the idea you would have the same one as the production assistant who was fired.

Sally Marshall and the IT department would have it. I checked with Sally. She keeps a list of the access codes in the filing cabinet at the reception desk. It isn't always locked. So, anyone at the studio could have gotten ahold of the codes."

"Well, that isn't helpful, is it?"

Bob shook his head. "No, it isn't. We'll get to the bottom of this. Just need some patience. I have a feeling it's going to blow up soon."

The maître d' walked to the front of the room. "Ladies and gentlemen, thank you for coming today. If I could ask you to take your seats, we'll begin shortly."

Brenna nodded to Bob and Connor and went back to her table.

Margo leaned close to Brenna. "Do they have a suspect?"

Brenna shook her head. "Nothing more than what they had yesterday. And they didn't find anything on the security tapes from the studio."

The crowd turned around to face the front of the restaurant and watched as Chef Mike's family came in. In attendance were his parents, his two sisters, and their spouses. Chef Tina accompanied Vicky, his fiancée.

They sat at one of the reserved tables at the front, where they could see everyone. Brenna noticed most of them had Kleenex in their hands, and their eyes were red-rimmed. And although they were sad, they appeared to be pleased with the number of friends, family, and restaurant patrons at the service.

Vicky stood and walked to the small podium set up to the left of the family's table. Her long, dark hair was pulled back in a bun, and she wore a black pinstripe suit. She spoke eloquently about Mike and his life and of their plans to build their lives together. Then she said it was her hope the police would soon catch whoever had taken him away. She was composed while she spoke, not referring to any notes, her voice calm and steady.

Chef Rosa and Chef Aaron each got up to speak about Mike and how they knew him. The warmth they exuded about Mike didn't surprise Brenna. They had genuinely gotten along well and respected each other very much. Rosa's voice choked a few times, and she held back tears as she remembered Mike.

Kathy and Jo, Chef Mike's sisters, spoke last. They shared their memories of their brother growing up and the family's pride in him as he found his way into the culinary world.

Chef Tina stood at the podium and asked everyone to raise his or her glass in a toast to Mike. Everyone stood and toasted the chef with glasses of champagne provided by the bar staff.

Kathy, Mike's sister, then said, "Everyone, please eat and enjoy. We're here to celebrate Mike and everything he loved. Food was one of his big loves."

With that, the restaurant wait staff brought out platters of food and deposited one on each of the tables.

Emily and Brenna chatted for a while and had a bite to eat. Brenna noticed Sean was quiet while he ate. He appeared to be preoccupied. Tim and Mathew seemed to be arguing about something, but Brenna couldn't make out what it was.

Brenna realized Mathew was wearing the same navy-blue blazer he had worn yesterday. She didn't give it much thought until he reached across for some butter and she noticed one of the buttons was missing on his left sleeve. She stared at the remaining buttons on the sleeve; they appeared to be similar to the button the cleaning crew had found on the kitchen floor while cleaning up from Chef Mike's murder. She drew in a breath quickly and pulled out her phone. She was sure she had a picture of the button.

"Everything okay, Brenna?" Tim asked sharply.

"Um, yes. I had an alarm on my phone go off, but I didn't attach anything to it. I must have made a mistake with it."

Brenna didn't want anyone to notice what she was looking at on her phone; she hoped she had pulled it off. She checked her photos and found the one with the button. She enlarged the photo and quickly checked it. The button in the photo appeared to be the same as the buttons on Mathew's jacket. Brenna couldn't remember if the button had been missing when she first saw Mathew wearing his jacket.

CHAPTER TWENTY-THREE

Brenna glanced around to see if Bob was still in the restaurant. She couldn't see either Detective Morris or Bob anywhere.

Emily and Kate were chatting together, and Sean was checking his phone. Tim and Mathew were still arguing.

Brenna excused herself and made her way to the ladies' room. Her mind was racing. Could Mathew have been the person who killed Chef Mike? If his missing button was the one the cleaning crew had found, then that could place him in the kitchen when he shouldn't have been there.

She agonized for a few minutes. What should she do? At the very least, she needed to let Bob and Detective Morris know about this. It could be important. She composed a text with as much information as she could put together and then sent it to both detectives. One of them should be able to deal with it.

She came out of the washroom and almost ran into Sean.

"Sorry, Brenna. I was looking for the men's room."

Brenna pointed down the hall. "Just another couple of steps will get you there."

She made her way back to the table.

Emily looked up as Brenna sat down. "Everything okay?"

Brenna smiled. "Yes, I'll talk to you about it when we leave." Emily raised her eyebrows. Brenna shook her head and mouthed "Later."

Emily nodded.

Mathew's phone pinged with a text message. Everyone at the table looked at him. Mathew didn't look happy.

Brenna asked, "More problems with the sponsors?"

Mathew frowned. "Hmm, no. This is personal. Someone I haven't heard from in a long time." Mathew turned to Tim. "I'm going home. I'm pretty tired from this week and plan on getting a good sleep."

Tim checked his watch. "Sounds good. I'm going to pay my respects to the family, and I'll talk to you later. Everyone, it was good of you all to come. I'll see you on Monday morning. Brenna, I may send out a script I'm working on to you tomorrow. If you could send it to everyone who needs it, I'd appreciate it."

"Sure. I'll watch out for it."

Tim's phone pinged with a message. Brenna looked in his direction. He checked the message and scowled. He put his phone away and then made his way to the family's table to pay his respects.

Brenna and Emily got up to leave the table. Sean had just returned to the table.

Brenna turned to Emily, "I need to speak to Kate about what happened last night. Can I meet you in a few minutes?"

"Not a problem. I'll wait for you out front."

"Kate, could I speak with you for a minute, please?"

"Oh, sure, Bren. Sean, are you okay to get to the door?"

"I'm fine. I'm going to speak with the judges."

"What's up?" Kate stood watching Sean make his way to the judges.

Brenna didn't want to upset or worry Kate, but she wanted Kate to know what she had overheard and seen. "It's about Sean. There's something you need to know about what happened at the bandstand."

"Do you know what happened? 'Cause if you do, you should say something to the police."

"I've already spoken with them. I'm going to tell you, but I don't want you to repeat it. Especially not to Sean." Brenna took a few minutes to fill in some of the blanks Kate was unaware of. "Please, Kate, if you're going to spend time with Sean, you need to be careful. I don't think what happened was a mugging that went wrong. Sean was blackmailing someone, and that person shot him. And whoever that person is is still out there. The police haven't found him. I checked with Bob earlier. I want you to be aware of this and to be careful when you're with Sean."

Kate said, "And the police have no leads?"

"None." Brenna was watching Kate.

Kate sighed. "Darn. I thought he was one of the good ones. I promised him I'd help him out this afternoon, getting him back to his place and making sure he's okay on his own. I'm still going to do that, but, knowing what I know now, well, I'll be extra cautious. I won't be staying any longer than I should. And I'll follow up with him later with a call instead of a visit."

"I'm sorry. But I couldn't let you go blindly with him."

Kate held up her hand. "Brenna, you have nothing to apologize for. I appreciate you caring enough about me to tell me. I'll deal with this. Not to worry." She smiled. "I better get Sean back to his apartment. I think he's in for a surprise if he thinks I'm spending more time with him than I said." Kate leaned into Brenna and gave her a hug. "Thanks. I'll talk to you later tonight. I promise."

Kate went off to get Sean, and Brenna hurried to meet Emily.

Emily was waiting just outside the front door. "So, how did she take the news?"

Brenna shrugged. "You know Kate. If she says she's going to do something, she does. But now she knows what I know. She'll take Sean back to his place, but she isn't going to stay long. And she'll be more watchful too."

"What are your plans for the rest of the day?" Emily asked.

"I need to get some meal prep done for next week. I can't keep eating out like I have been. And if I haven't heard from that reporter, I'm going to see if I can find her number."

"Are you going to your parents' place for dinner tomorrow?"

"Yes. Mom's trying to get all of us over for a meal. Why don't you join us?"

"I just might. Let me call you in the morning, and we'll figure things out."

"Sounds good. I'll talk to you later."

BRENNA CHANGED her clothes as soon as she got home. Wearing heels was something she didn't do very often, and her feet hurt. She pulled on her favorite jeans and a green Henley T-shirt. She put her hair back in a messy bun and slid her feet into a pair of ballet flats. *Heaven*. She walked into the kitchen.

She opened her fridge and took out some ground turkey and onions. Walking to her pantry, she picked up some breadcrumbs, garlic, salt, and pepper. Brenna put the ingredients on her island and turned on the television. She started making meatballs while listening to the news. There wasn't anything new to report on Chef Mike's murder, but the station had sent a reporter to the memorial.

The reporter had interviewed some of the restaurant's staff and had tried to get a statement from Bob. Brenna chuckled as Bob did his best to avoid the reporter. By the time the news was over, Brenna had forty-eight meatballs ready to be cooked. She slid them in the preheated oven, set the timer, and then washed her hands.

She glanced at the clock. Time to check on her email. Maybe Ms. Gilles had responded. She poured herself a glass of wine and sat down with her laptop.

She checked her email and found a response from Mary Gilles. She quickly got to the point and said the student in the photo was the same person who had been killed in a shooting a few years ago. His name was Charles Mathews. His mother, father, and an older brother named Timothy survived him. His parents were retired and lived in Chicago. His brother, Timothy, worked in the television industry.

Mary had included her phone number in her signature in the email. Brenna sat back and thought carefully about what she had learned. She still had more questions than answers. And certainly nothing she could take to the police.

She decided to call Mary Gilles to see if she could get more information out of her by talking to her.

"Gilles here." Her voice was rough, a smoker's voice.

"Hi, this is Brenna Flynn. I just read your email, and I hope I can ask you a few questions."

"Sure. I don't know what else I can tell you about Charles but go ahead."

"It isn't about Charles. It's about his brother, Timothy. Do you know how old he would be?"

"He was a good five years older than Charles. I would think he'd be close to forty by now. Why are you asking?"

"I have a few questions first. I promise I'll tell you why I'm asking shortly. You said he worked in television. Do you know where and in what capacity?"

"He was working in New York, but not at any of the larger studios. It was one of the independents. They specialized in documentaries. At the time of Charles's death, he had been working on a documentary on bullying in the workplace. He was one of the producers."

"Do you know if he's still in New York?"

"No, he left shortly after his brother died. He refused to answer any of my questions about his brother's death. His parents were concerned about him. He was very angry about Charles's death. You see, Charles was an addict. And he was killed while making a drug deal. His brother seemed to think he could have prevented Charles' death. And I don't know where he is now. With his parents in Chicago, I would think he'd be close by."

"One more question. Can you tell me which restaurants Charles had applied to try to get work in Bayview City or Ann Arbor?"

"I'm not sure which ones for certain. I do know he looked up three former classmates who were just starting out. They were each starting their own restaurant in Bayview City. I remember the city because it was a smaller city. Not a big one like Detroit. He might have been fine working there. Now, what's this about?"

"I'm working on a cooking reality show in Bayview City. The three chefs on the show are three of the students Charles went to culinary school with. Charles went to them looking for work. One of the chefs, Mike Jones, was murdered earlier this week. I'm the one who found his body. There's someone on the set that reminds me of Charles Mathews, at least from what I can see from his pictures. It's frustrating there isn't a clear picture of his brother, Timothy. The executive producer of our show is named Tim Harris."

Mary inhaled sharply. "Charles's mother's maiden name was Harris. Do you have a photo of this Tim Harris?"

"I do. It's a publicity still from the studio."

"Send it to me, and I'll let you know if it's the same person."

Brenna went to her laptop and quickly sent the photo to Mary. "It's on its way." She waited while Mary opened the file.

Mary said, "He does look very much like the Timothy Mathews I attempted to interview a few years ago. He's changed a bit. He's wearing glasses, and his hairstyle is different. And he's lost some weight as well. But I'm pretty sure it's the same man."

"Thanks so much for this. I need to connect with the police and let them know. They'll need to look at him more closely." Brenna was in a hurry to get off the phone. This might be the break the police were looking for.

"Not a problem. Glad I could help. Let me know how this all turns out. It would be great to get a story out of this."

"I'll keep in touch. Thanks again!" Brenna disconnected the call and was trying to put a call through to Detective Morris when her cell rang. She picked up the call without checking the caller ID. It was Tim.

CHAPTER TWENTY-FOUR

"Brenna, you're not going to believe this, but Chef Rosa was just brought to the hospital. The doctors think she's been poisoned."

"What! How did it happen? Is she going to be all right?"

"They think it was in the wine sent to her house from the studio. Fortunately, she only drank one glass. Her partner saw she wasn't feeling well and called for help right away. It's a good thing her partner doesn't drink, or they'd both be in bad shape."

"What do you mean? Wine from the studio? I know I didn't send anything out for delivery to Chef Rosa. There was nothing about that in the paperwork I was dealing with yesterday. Margo didn't mention it either."

"Well, according to Abby, Chef Rosa's partner, there was a bottle of wine sitting on their front porch when they returned from Chef Mike's memorial service. The note with it said, "With Sympathy from The Crew." They both assumed it came from the studio."

"Have the police been notified?"

"Abby called nine-one-one, and the dispatcher sent out the ambulance. I don't know if the police were sent."

Brenna heard the blare of sirens. "Tim, where are you?"

"I'm at the hospital, with Abby. She called to let me know. We're waiting to see how Chef Rosa is going to make out."

"You haven't spoken with Detectives Morris or McLean?"

"No, I haven't."

"Well, I'm going to touch base with Detective Morris. If the wine was tampered with, this could have something to do with Chef Mike's murder. Do you know if anyone has spoken with Chef Aaron or Chef Tina?" Brenna remembered the note slipped under her door. Could this be an attempt on the other chefs? This might have been an attempt on the other chefs.

"I haven't spoken with either of them. Why?"

Brenna thought quickly. With the information she had learned tonight from Mary Gilles, she didn't trust Tim. "If the wine came from the studio, it would make sense Chef Aaron and maybe Chef Tina had a delivery as well."

"Do you think this is related to the show?"

"I don't know, but I do know the police need to be informed. And I'll call Chef Aaron and Chef Tina to check on them."

"Well, I think we would have heard from them if there was a problem." Tim's voice was tinged with impatience.

"Maybe not. If they had wine that was poisoned and they were alone, they could be in serious trouble."

She heard a sigh. "Honestly, Brenna, I'm not sure of anything anymore. I can't reach Mathew, and I may need some help dealing with the media on this if it gets out. Can you come to the hospital?"

"I'm going to touch base with Detective Morris, and I'm going to check with the other two chefs." Brenna's oven timer began to ding. "Tim, I'll be at the hospital as soon as I can."

She pulled the meatballs out of the oven as she called Chef Aaron. His phone rang a couple of times before he answered.

"Chef Aaron, it's Brenna Flynn. Have you received a bottle of wine tonight?"

"Yes. I was surprised because it's from my vineyard. I was just about to open it and have a glass."

"Don't! I need you to call the police. Do not open that bottle. Chef Rosa received one, and she drank from it. She's at the hospital now. The doctors are saying she was poisoned."

"Oh no, no, no! Is she going to be all right? Where's Abby?"

"I don't know how she is, and I've been told Abby's at the hospital with her. Chef, I need you to call the police right away. I have to talk to Chef Tina as well."

"Right, I'll call them straight away, and then I'm going to the hospital. I need to make sure Rosa and Abby are okay."

Brenna disconnected and called Chef Tina. It took her longer to answer her phone, and Brenna was almost ready to hang up.

"Chef Tina, it's Brenna Flynn from the studio. I need to know if you received a bottle of wine today as a delivery?"

"Hmm, no, I didn't. Was I supposed to?" Chef Tina sounded puzzled.

"Well, the studio didn't arrange for any deliveries to be made." Brenna debated if she should tell her about Chef Rosa. Better to be overcautious. "You need to know Chef Rosa received a bottle of wine tonight and is in the hospital. The doctors believe the wine was poisoned. Chef Aaron received a bottle as well, but he hadn't opened it yet. If you do get a bottle, please call the police right away and don't open the wine."

"What on earth is happening? Who is doing this and why? Is Rosa going to be all right?"

Brenna gave her the same explanation she had to Chef Aaron. As she finished up her call, she reminded Chef Tina about not opening the wine should she get a bottle.

She hung up and took a breath. Her hands were shaking, and her heart was racing. The next call she made was to Detective Morris to alert her about what was happening.

"Morris here."

"Detective, it's Brenna Flynn. Did you know Chef Rosa is in the hospital?"

"Yes, I just received a call, and I'm on my way to the hospital."

"I just spoke with Chef Aaron. He received a bottle of wine as well. He hadn't opened it yet, and I told him to contact the police."

"I'll contact our officers and have them go to Chef Aaron's and retrieve the bottle. They'll take it to the lab. Do you know if anyone else got a bottle?"

"I don't think so. I checked with Chef Tina, and she hadn't received one."

"I've just arrived at the hospital. I'll talk to you later."

Brenna quickly put the meatballs in a container, covered them, and put them in the fridge. She grabbed her leather tote, put on her jacket, and hurried out of her apartment. Before leaving for the hospital, she called

Mathew. "Come on, answer." Mathew's phone went to voice mail. "Mathew, it's Brenna Flynn. We have a problem with Chef Rosa. Please call me or Tim right away. It's urgent."

She drove to the hospital as quickly as possible. She pulled into the parking lot and ran toward the emergency room. Arriving in the emergency room, she saw Bob, Detective Morris, and Tim. Detective Morris approached her as she came through the doorway.

"Brenna, do you remember seeing anything about a delivery to the chefs for tonight?"

"No. And that would be something I would be responsible for. Unless Tim or Mathew ordered it separately."

Tim said, "I didn't order it, and Mathew didn't mention it to me. I just checked with Margo, and she didn't send anything out either."

"Could it have been one of the sponsors?" Brenna asked.

"Don't know why they would, but we can always follow up with them to find out." Tim turned to Bob. "Unless the police need to check on it."

Bob said, "We'll check on everyone connected with the show. The wine was from Chef Aaron's vineyard, and the chefs are familiar with it. Chef Rosa thought it was from the studio. Chef Aaron thought it was from his staff at the restaurant."

"What about Chef Rosa? Where is she? And do we know what she was poisoned with?" Brenna asked.

Detective Morris said, "Chef Rosa is being treated for a fentanyl overdose. Not a pleasant experience, but she'll be all right at the end of it."

"Fentanyl? How did that happen?" Brenna was shocked by this turn of events.

"The fentanyl was mixed into the wine. Then the bottle was re-corked and sealed. Neither Abby nor Rosa noticed anything different about the bottle. There was a lot of fentanyl in the bottle, though—enough to kill." Bob's phone rang, and he stepped away to answer it.

Tim took out his phone and moved toward the lobby.

Brenna noticed Abby, Chef Rosa's partner. She was sitting off to the side by herself. Brenna walked over and sat down next to her. "Hi, Abby. I'm Brenna Flynn from Studio One. How are you doing?" she asked.

"Oh, right. I remember you. You were at the house a few days ago." Abby pulled her cardigan closer. Her face was pale, and her blue eyes were filled with tears. "I've been better. It was pretty scary to see her go down as quickly as she did. I knew she was tired, but she has never, ever passed out on one glass of wine."

"Well, your quick thinking saved her life—and Chef Aaron's as well. He received a bottle of the wine."

"Who would do this? And why? None of them has ever hurt anyone." Abby's hands waved as she spoke.

"I'm sure the police will figure it out. Do you know how the bottle was delivered to the house?"

"When we got home from the memorial, it was sitting on the doorstep in a basket with a note. There was nothing to show how it had been delivered. None of our neighbors remembered seeing a delivery truck around the house, either."

Brenna thought for a minute. "Do you have any idea who would give you wine?"

Abby shook her head. "It doesn't make sense. We thought it was from the studio because of the note. Rosa opened this bottle because it was from Aaron's vineyard. We know the wine."

Brenna put her hand on Abby's arm. "Hang in there. Chef Rosa was lucky you were with her and you got help so quickly."

The doctor came out looking for Abby then. "Abby, if you can come with me, Rosa's awake."

Abby rose from the chair and hurried to Rosa's bedside.

Brenna was relieved to hear Rosa was better. She walked back to the others. "Chef Rosa's awake. The doctor just came for Abby."

The detectives headed toward the emergency room door.

Brenna sat in the waiting area. A few minutes later, Tim returned and sat across from her.

Brenna asked Tim, "Where's Mathew?"

"I haven't seen him since the memorial. I called him after I got here and left a message, but I haven't heard from him. I'm surprised he isn't here yet."

"I called him before I drove here and left a message as well. He hasn't gotten back to me either."

The detectives returned from Rosa's room in time to overhear the conversation.

"Is it normal for him to not answer a call or return a message?" Bob asked.

"Sometimes he shuts off his phone when he's tired and needs sleep. I know he's been putting in some late nights. I'm sure he's fine. I'll catch up with him in the morning," Tim said.

Bob shook his head. "Given what's been happening, I think we need to make certain he's okay tonight. I'll send a unit to check on him right now. Do you have his address?"

Tim reluctantly provided him with Mathew's address, and Bob made the call.

"A unit is on the way. Once they get there, they'll let us know what's happening."

Brenna asked Tim, "Did you contact the PR agency?"

"Yes. They're sending someone down tonight to work with me. Probably Margaret. We'll have a statement ready for the press if we need it."

"What do we do now?" Brenna asked.

Bob said, "You do nothing. It would be best if you went home, but knowing you, you won't." Bob put his hands on his hips and looked directly at Brenna. "The bottles of wine will be processed as quickly as the CSU team can get to them. It would be great if our would-be killer left fingerprints that we could find in the database, but that's probably wishful thinking." Bob's phone rang, and he excused himself.

After a few minutes, Bob returned to the group.

"Mathew didn't answer his door when the uniforms got there. They checked with his neighbors, asking if they'd seen him. One woman said she saw him earlier when he came back from the memorial service, but she hadn't seen him since. His car is in his parking spot. The uniforms got the building manager to open the door. They found Mathew in his living room, barely responsive. There was a bottle of wine from Chef Aaron's vineyard on the coffee table. He's being brought to emergency. Uniforms are securing the scene."

Brenna gasped. Tim didn't say anything.

"There was no note with the wine, but uniforms found what they think could be a suicide note in his living room. I'm going over there now to take charge of the investigation. Detective Morris, can you keep an eye on things here?"

She agreed. "I'll keep you informed."

Brenna walked out with Bob. "What does this mean? Is Mathew responsible for everything that's been happening?"

"I won't know anything until I get to the scene, and hopefully we'll be able to talk to Mathew later on."

Brenna grabbed Bob's arm. "Wait. I received some information tonight from someone I connected with. I think Tim Harris may be involved with what's been happening."

Bob stopped walking and faced Brenna. "What exactly do you mean? What information?"

Brenna filled him in on what she had learned from Mary Gilles. "I know it isn't proof, but there's something there. I know it."

"Can you send us the information you have?"

"I can, but it will have to wait until I get home. I don't have the information on my phone, and I can't access it until I get to my laptop."

"When are you going home?"

"Tim wants me to stay here and help him deal with the PR person."

"I don't want you alone with Tim. If he is the killer and thinks you have information on him, you could be in danger. I need you to get home right away and send us that information."

CHAPTER TWENTY-FIVE

Brenna went back inside the emergency department. She glanced around, searching for Tim. "Where did Tim go?" she asked Detective Morris.

"I don't know. I didn't see him leave. Why?"

Brenna filled her in on what she and Bob had talked about. "I'm going to do as Bob asked and get the information to you both."

"I'd feel better if you call and let me know when you get to your apartment. How far is it to your place from the hospital?"

"About ten minutes. Why?"

"If I don't hear from you, I'll connect with you."

"I'll call when I get home." Brenna left the hospital and hurried home.

She pulled into her assigned parking spot at her apartment and noticed the light in the lobby was out. She made a mental note to let her father know. The outside lights were functioning.

She unlocked the door, entering on the first floor, and walked up the stairs. She stopped and looked over her shoulder, half expecting to see someone coming up behind her. *There's no one there. Just get in the apartment, and you'll be fine. Bob and Detective Morris are waiting for the information.*

Her phone rang as she arrived at her door. She put her key in the door. "Hello."

"Brenna, Detective Morris here. Bob spoke with Mathew. Tim came by to see him earlier tonight. He says that Tim brought a bottle of wine to celebrate Chef Mike's life. They sat in the living room, and Tim poured out two glasses, but Mathew doesn't remember Tim drinking any. The uniforms say there was just one glass on the table, but if Tim is the killer, he could have cleaned up after himself. Where are you?"

"I just got to my door. I'll be sending the files to you and Bob in a few minutes."

"Right then. Be careful. That PR woman showed up at the hospital a few minutes after you left. Tim wasn't anywhere in the hospital or in the parking lot."

"I will." Brenna disconnected the call and opened her door. She entered her apartment, and as she began to close the door, someone rushed toward her. She tried to shut the door, but he pushed on the door hard, and Brenna fell backward onto the floor.

He slammed the door and reached down to grab her. Pulling her up off the floor by her hair, he whispered in her ear, "Shut your mouth, and I might let you live, you interfering bitch."

He pushed her toward the living room and into a chair. Standing over her, he pulled a gun from his jeans. He pointed the gun at her chest.

"Well, this is an interesting development. What are you thinking? I can see your brain running a mile a minute trying to piece this all together. Where's your computer? You told the cops you had all the evidence against me. I want it, and I want it now!"

Brenna didn't say a word. She had to keep it together. She was worried about what he was going to do next. She had been right. Tim *was* the killer.

He waved his gun at her. "Come on. Speak up. Where's the computer?"

Brenna's eyes moved to the right where her laptop sat on the dining room table. She cleared her throat. "It's on the table."

"Don't move."

Tim walked to the table. While his back was turned, she yanked her phone out of her jacket pocket and hit the call return button, then put her phone on the chair and adjusted the throw pillow to hide it. Tim came back with the laptop.

"Turn it on and open the files."

Brenna opened the computer, turned it on, and waited for it to boot up. "What are you going to do?"

"You're going to get rid of the evidence you have against me. Then I'll decide what I'm going to do with you."

Brenna thought if she could keep him talking and stall a bit with the files, it might allow Detective Morris to get to her. Her number was the last one used on her phone. She hoped Detective Morris had picked up the call and hadn't disconnected.

"Tim, I don't understand why you're doing this. What did the chefs do to you? And what did I ever do to you?" Brenna raised her voice as she questioned Tim.

Tim sighed and paced the apartment, all the while keeping the gun in his hand. "Really? You don't understand why? Well, I'll tell you why. First of all, you're really nosy. You ask a lot of questions about things that don't concern you. You couldn't leave well enough alone. You had to keep digging into Chef Mike's past."

He stopped pacing and faced her, pointing the gun at her again, his hand shaking. His voice grew louder as he became more agitated. His face was red, and a vein throbbed in his forehead.

"But you didn't learn everything about him and his two buddies. Those chefs thought they were too good for anyone else. They were the ultimate bullies at the school. They poisoned the teachers against my brother. Then, when he heard they were opening restaurants, he thought they might help him out by hiring him. They wouldn't even look at him. They had heard about his little problem in Ann Arbor. It was all a mistake. He told me about it. It wasn't his fault."

Tim started pacing again.

Brenna was watching him carefully. Maybe she'd be able to get away.

Tim became more agitated by the second. His voice cracked as he spoke. "Chef Mike was the worst. He made sure Rosa and Aaron didn't hire Charles. He reminded them of all the mistakes he made in school and how the critics in Ann Arbor blamed Charles for the poisoning incident."

"They didn't know you?" Brenna asked.

Tim stopped his pacing and glared at her. It was as if he had forgotten she was there. Then he grunted. "Huh? No, they'd never met me. I wasn't able to go to his graduation from culinary school. And they didn't go to his memorial service. But I knew all about them. Charles used to confide in me when he was at school about the problems he was having. And as for the Ann Arbor restaurant, well, he was just trying to spice up the dish with fresh, wild mushrooms. He didn't know they were poisonous."

"How did you get Chef Mike to meet you at the studio? And how did you get my code for the door?"

"I'm the executive producer. I have access to everything in the studio, including everyone's security codes." Tim snorted. "As for getting him to the studio, I told him I had a problem with the way the kitchens were set up and needed his expert advice. I told him I'd meet him in the back lot after he was through at his restaurant. He never questioned me. His ego was that big."

Brenna looked at him. His eyes were wild, and his gaze jumped from one item to the next. She glanced to the table next to the chair. Photos of family and friends covered the tabletop. Her stomach pitched at the thought she might not see them again.

Her spine stiffened. *Not happening*, she thought to herself. *I've overcome too much in the last six months to let someone else take control over me*. She was through with people thinking she was a victim. A surge of strength and determination coursed through her. She hadn't felt that in a long time. She wouldn't let Tim get away with this. If she kept him talking, Detective Morris would hear everything. Maybe even a confession.

"What happened with Sean? I take it you're the person who shot him?"

Tim cackled. "Sean thought he was so clever. He saw me go in and put the mushrooms in the pantry, and he overheard me talking to my contact for the fentanyl. He thought he could blackmail me, get the money, and then leave for work on the West Coast." He snorted. "What a hack. It was easy to get him to the bandstand. Greed does that to people, you know. I'm going to get him when I leave here. He's at home and on medication. It won't be difficult to get rid of him."

Brenna shuddered. "What did you do to Mathew?"

"He's such a patsy. So simple, really, to lead around. He thought he was oh so very important to the show and the sponsors. He was nothing more than my fall guy."

Tim stopped in front of Brenna.

"The button the cleaning crew found? Well, it came off one of Matthew's jackets. Too bad the police didn't make the connection. They really are dense. I had to make sure I got rid of him."

Tim resumed his pacing.

"I knew he was tired after the week he'd been through. He's not very strong physically or emotionally, you know. When he told me at the memorial he was going home to rest, I knew I could get to him. I stopped in to see him. I brought the wine and suggested we toast Chef Mike. He was tired, but I knew he wouldn't say no to me. I poured myself a glass, but I didn't have any of the wine. It only took one glass for him to feel the effects of the fentanyl. I'd put a lot in his bottle. Too bad. If he'd had two glasses, he might have died right away."

"What about the suicide note?"

Tim looked at her for a moment. "That was easy. I had the note in my pocket. I waited until he fell asleep and made sure the note was on the table next to the wine. Then, I cleaned up my glass and put it away. I wasn't going to leave fingerprints. I had wiped the wine bottle clean of my prints before heading to Mathew's, and I wore driving gloves. I'm not stupid, you know." He waved his gun in her direction. "Come on, quit stalling. Get me those files."

"I'm having difficulty accessing them. I saved them to the cloud and can't get online."

"Don't be stupid. Put the computer on the table and turn it around so I can see the screen. And stay in your chair."

Brenna leaned across and placed her laptop on the low coffee table, turning it to face him as he had instructed her. The Wi-Fi connection icon had a red line across it.

"Fix it, now."

"I'm trying. But I have to reboot my router."

"Fine. Where is it?"

"In the kitchen."

"Get up, slowly, and I'll follow you."

Brenna did as he told her. This might be her only opportunity to escape. She started walking, then stumbled and almost fell. Tim reached toward her to grab her.

She leaned back into him and, using her elbow, hit him in the stomach. Then she stomped on his foot. Turning around, she hit him in the nose with her palm. He dropped the gun and raised his hands to his face. She kneed him in the groin.

He lay curled on the floor, bleeding from his nose and gasping for breath. Brenna kicked the gun away from him and then hurried around him to pick it up.

Someone banged on her door.

CHAPTER TWENTY-SIX

"Police, open the door now!" Her door burst open, slamming into the wall as Bob and Detective Morris came through the door, guns drawn.

"I'm fine. I'm okay. Tim's on the floor, and I have his gun. About time you guys got here!"

"Are you sure you aren't hurt?" Detective Morris hurried to Brenna's side as Bob reached Tim.

"I'm a little shaken up, but I'm okay." Brenna held out Tim's gun. "Can you take this? I think it's the gun he used on Sean."

Detective Morris took the gun and set it aside. "We'll tag this into evidence."

Bob leaned over, grabbed Tim by the arms, and pulled him to his feet. "Tim Harris, you are under arrest for the murder of Mike Jones, the attempted murder of Sean Jamieson, Mathew Smith, Aaron White, and Rosa Cavalli." He said to one of the uniformed officers who had accompanied them, "Make sure to read him his Miranda rights. I don't want him getting away on a technicality."

Brenna was standing by the hall table and overheard the officer recite the familiar phrase, "You have the right to remain silent . . ."

Tim lifted his head and glared at her as the officer walked him out of the apartment. "I would have gotten away with it if it hadn't been for you and your interfering."

Brenna shook her head and let out a deep breath.

Bob walked over to her and pulled her into a hug. "Are you okay? Really?"

Brenna wrapped her arms around him for a moment and then nodded her head. "I'm fine. Shaken up a bit. He pushed his way in the door and knocked me down and then pulled me up by my hair. I have a headache, but I'm not hurt." She tightened her arms around him and then stepped back.

Bob said, "You're pretty good kid. Calling Clare was quick thinking on your part. She heard everything he said and recorded the call. We probably won't be able to use the recording in court, but we have all kinds of information. Before we start asking you questions, do me a favor and call your dad. He called me while I was on my way. One of your neighbors let him know there was trouble."

Brenna grabbed her cell phone and made the call. "Dad, I'm fine. It's okay. Bob and Detective Morris are here. They caught the guy, and I'm okay. I am."

She and her father spoke for a few minutes, and then she hung up.

"Is he okay?" Bob asked.

"He's better now. But he's on his way over. He wants to see me and know that I'm all right."

Bob snorted. "Yeah, I can imagine he wants to see you."

Detective Morris had been working with an officer to secure the apartment. "Brenna, I'm going to ask you some questions. I know that's the last thing you want to do. If we can get through them tonight, it will be easier tomorrow."

"If I can have a few minutes, I'd like to call Emily and have her here with me when I talk to you."

"Not a problem. We'll wait until she gets here to proceed."

They walked to the other side of her apartment while she contacted Emily.

"Okay, Em will be here soon. And Dad should be here soon, too. I'm going to make some coffee."

While Brenna busied herself making the coffee, Bob and Detective Morris had the CSU team photograph and deal with the scene. Bob talked to one of the officers at the door and told him to make sure Emily and Brenna's father were permitted upstairs.

Brenna's father, Dan Flynn, arrived in five minutes. "Brenna, are you all right?"

"Dad! I'm okay. Just shaken up."

Dan ran up to her and took her in his arms. "God! You scared us half to death!"

"Sorry. I was pretty scared too. But I got him. I remembered the self-defense move you taught me when I was a teenager."

Dan's eyes misted over. "Good. I hope you hurt him?"

"I did." Brenna smiled at her father. "I'm making coffee. Do you want some?"

"I do. And I better talk to your mom, let her know you're safe."

Brenna poured coffee into a carafe and set out mugs, sugar, and cream on the kitchen island. As she got that done, she heard Emily in the hallway. "I'm Emily Connors. They're expecting me."

Brenna hurried to the door. "Officer, it's okay. She's my lawyer."

Emily was in the apartment in a flash. "Are you all right?" her gaze traveling up and down Brenna's frame.

"Shaken up, but otherwise, I'm good. Come on. Bob and Detective Morris need to talk to me."

They walked to the kitchen island, and Emily helped herself to some coffee.

Dan wrapped up his call and poured himself a cup. "Bob, I'll be here until you and Detective Morris finish taking Brenna's statement. I'll make sure her apartment is secure before I go home."

"I understand, Uncle Dan. Emily, have a seat. We'll take some time to go through the events of this evening, and Brenna, you'll need to sign your statement tomorrow."

"Do I go to the station to sign my statement?"

Detective Morris pulled out her notebook. "It would be better if you did. It won't take long, and you won't see Tim while you're doing it."

"That's fine. Let's get started."

Detective Morris questioned Brenna on what happened during the evening. Brenna was able to recollect the events calmly and factually.

When Brenna was through, Bob asked, "Do you have the information on Tim for us?"

"Yes, it's on my laptop." Brenna got up and grabbed her laptop. She found the files in her inbox and forwarded them to both Bob and Detective Morris.

Detective Morris opened the attachment. "Good information here. This should make our jobs easier. If I have any further questions, I'll let you know. We'll get out of here so you can get some rest. If you need to talk to anyone about what happened here tonight, here's the name of a counselor with our victim services department. And you can connect with me anytime. Here's my personal number."

"Thanks for that information. I think I'll be okay." Brenna took Detective Morris's card and tucked it in her jeans.

The crime scene technicians had completed their work while Brenna had spoken with Detective Morris.

Bob and Detective Morris left.

Dan walked to the door and checked the lock. "I'm going to fix this up tonight. I have tools in my truck. I'll be right back."

"Thanks, Dad."

Emily started cleaning up the coffee things. "Bren, I'm going to spend the night. I don't want you to be alone."

"That would be great. Thanks."

Emily loaded the dishwasher and wiped down the kitchen island. "Do you want a glass of wine?"

"Yeah. That would help. I'm going to send a message to Mary Gilles and let her know her information helped." Brenna opened her email account and composed a brief message. "I'm letting her know she can call me tomorrow morning if she has any questions."

Brenna finished the message and shut down her laptop. Emily handed her a glass of Shiraz.

"Thanks." Brenna took a large swallow of wine. "I'm so glad this is over."

Dan arrived with his tools. "Brenna, this will take me ten minutes. I'll get out of your hair then. Emily, I take it you're spending the night?"

"Yes, I have a feeling we'll be talking into the morning."

"Perfect. And Emily, we'll expect you at the house for dinner tomorrow evening." Dan started working on the door.

"What happens to the show?" Emily asked.

Brenna shook her head. "I don't know. I'll have to wait to hear from Mathew what his plans are. If the sponsors pull out, the show will fold."

"I bet there's still a lot of interest in the show. Yes, there's been a huge scandal, but that might give the show some notoriety," Emily said.

"Maybe not the notoriety the sponsors want." Brenna shrugged. "I can't worry about it now. I'm glad Tim is behind bars. I hope he stays there for a long time."

Dan came into the living room, "I fixed the lock. No one will be able to get in unless they have a key. You're certain you're okay?"

Brenna stood and gave her dad a hug. "Dad, I promise I'm fine. Em and I are going to talk things out tonight. And, I'll get some sleep. I can already feel the adrenaline leaving."

Dan kissed her cheek. "Okay. Your mom and I are a phone call away. If you need anything, let us know. We'll check in on you tomorrow."

Brenna followed him to the door and made sure it was locked when he left.

Emily was putting a frozen pizza in the oven. "I thought we'd have something to eat while we talk. I know I can't sleep yet."

"Sounds like a plan. I have to talk this out, or I won't be able to rest."

"Are you going to talk to the counselor Detective Morris told you about?"

"I'm not sure. I saw someone in Wayhaven when Dave died."

"I didn't know that. Was it helpful?"

"I worked out some of the feelings I had to deal with." Brenna took a drink and sat on the couch. "Dave had me fooled. I knew nothing about his gambling debts. He was going out a lot more, but I believed him when he said it was for work. I felt betrayed when I learned he was in debt to the mob and that he had kept it from me."

"Well, that's understandable. He broke your trust." Emily sat across from Brenna on the loveseat.

"It wasn't just that. It was the fact he was running drugs for the mob." Brenna shook her head. "Em, the mob! I just couldn't believe that. I still can't wrap my head around it. And the police, well they didn't believe I didn't know anything. They all thought I knew about it, that I had his list of contacts for the drugs and with the mob."

"You must have been scared. Why didn't you call me for help?"

"Honestly, I didn't want you involved." Brenna took a drink of wine. "I contacted our family lawyer we had used for our wills, and she recommended a good criminal attorney. She was a big help. Made the police back off since they had no evidence I was involved."

"It wasn't just the police, it was the FBI as well, wasn't it?" Emily got up to check on the pizza.

"They were the scary ones. They kept talking about federal prison if I didn't cooperate."

Emily pulled the pizza out of the oven and let it rest on the cutting board. She got two plates down. "What finally got them to stop looking at you?"

"My lawyer got them to see Dave had kept everything in separate accounts. He kept the money in his name alone. The drug transactions and his contacts were in a different email account and on a different phone."

Emily sliced the pizza and set the plates on the coffee table. "He was living two lives."

"He was. I don't know how he kept so much from me. I didn't just feel betrayed. Because he died, I couldn't vent my anger to him. Dave and I always communicated well. Or we had until two years before he died. So, I've carried around a lot of anger. The counselor I saw gave me some coping mechanisms, and they worked—to a point."

"And then you lost your job. Honestly, Brenna, I'm not sure how you kept going."

Brenna swallowed her pizza. "I didn't have a choice. And there's still a lot unresolved. The FBI is still working to bring someone in for drug running and money laundering. The only thing resolved is that they understand I wasn't involved in Dave's actions. I still hear from one of the agents. He checks in on me every couple of weeks."

Emily frowned. "Why?"

"He wants to make sure the mob doesn't come after me. The house in Wayhaven is still on the market, and someone broke into it a few months ago. They were obviously looking for something. My real estate agent contacted me. Whoever went in ripped the couch and the mattress and put holes in the walls. Dad, Jim, and I went to Wayhaven to fix it up. Dad insisted on putting in an alarm system complete with cameras. That's stopped any other break-ins. That was when the FBI agent started contacting me."

Emily let out a breath. "Good grief! That's not a good situation. No wonder your dad is keeping close tabs on you."

"It's better than it was. The police in Wayhaven have been patrolling the street the house is on more often. That's helped me learn to trust the police again. The FBI agent isn't contacting me to harass me anymore. Now, he's actually checking on me."

"Anything else I should know about?" Emily asked.

Brenna smiled. "I can't think of anything else. I'm hoping the situation is resolved soon with the mob. Trust is hard to build. It feels as if there's a wall I have to climb over when I meet new people. I can't just forget what happened with Dave, but I do have to learn to live with it and move forward."

They stayed up late talking about what happened, and they drank the full bottle of wine and devoured the pizza. It was almost two in the morning before they turned in for the night.

CHAPTER TWENTY-SEVEN

The next morning, Brenna was having coffee when Mary Gilles called. "Brenna, Mary Gilles here. I saw your email. Is now a good time to talk?"

Brenna put her cup down. "Now will work. Our discussion last night about Charles Mathews gave me the information I needed to connect his brother Tim to Chef Mike's murder. I wasn't positive it was him until he broke down my door getting to me."

Mary drew a sharp breath. "Are you okay?"

"I am."

"What can you tell me about last night?"

Brenna filled her in on the events of the previous evening. "The last I heard was they were going to charge Tim with the murder of Chef Mike, the attempted murder of Chef Rosa, Chef Aaron, Mathew Smith the show's producer, and Sean Jamieson, the show's host."

"I'm going to be running a story on this. It ties in with Charles' story. I'll be contacting his parents for their statement. Thanks for your help on this."

"You're welcome. I feel sorry for their parents. One son dead and the other one on murder charges."

Brenna hung up and finished her coffee. She was getting breakfast organized when the phone rang again. This time it was Mathew.

Emily walked into the kitchen while Brenna was on the phone with Mathew. "Who was on the phone?"

"Mathew. He's responded well to the emergency treatment at the hospital. He's still groggy and will be in the hospital until tomorrow. The doctors are being cautious. It looks as if the show is going to continue. Mathew spoke with Sean this morning, and Sean's assured him he's ready to go back to work. The chefs and judges have contacted Mathew as well and let him know they want to continue with the show. He has to get the sponsors on board, and he's going to talk to them later today."

Emily doctored her coffee. "Do you think the sponsors will want to continue?"

"I'm not sure. Mathew can be persuasive. If the chefs and judges are ready to continue, I don't think the sponsors will want to back out. It could look bad on them."

"And what about Sean? Is he being charged with blackmail?"

"Mathew didn't say anything about that. I'd have to ask Bob or Detective Morris."

They ate breakfast and began clearing up the kitchen. Brenna told Emily about the phone call from Mary Gilles.

Emily shook her head. "Those parents are going to have a tough time. Did Ms. Gilles say when the piece was going to come out?"

"No, and she didn't say what paper she was working with either. I hope she lets me know."

"You can reach out to her later today, see what she'll tell you."

Brenna's phone rang. "Hi Brenna, it's Detective Morris. Can you come to the station to sign your statement?"

"I can go in the next thirty minutes. Does that work?"

"That'll be great. Just ask the officer at the desk for me."

Brenna hung up. "I have to go sign my statement. I told her I'd be there in thirty minutes."

"Not a problem. Let me clean up the dishes, and you go grab a shower. I'll drive you to the station and then back here."

"Thanks. Are you coming to dinner tonight at mom and dad's?"

"I plan on it. Are you okay if I go home after the police station?"

"Yes. I'll be fine. I need to get myself organized for next week. And I might even take a nap."

Twenty minutes later, they were on their way to the police station.

THE OFFICER at the front desk called Detective Morris down, and she arrived in a few minutes.

"Thanks for coming in Brenna, Emily. If you'll come with me, this won't take long."

Brenna read the statement and verified it was what she had given the night before and then signed it.

"So what happens now?"

Detective Morris put Brenna's statement away. "Tim talked to us last night, but it didn't take long for him to contact a lawyer. The DA's office will have a strong case. Will you testify when the time comes?"

Brenna closed her eyes briefly. She wouldn't let Tim get away with what he had done. "Yes. I will." Brenna picked up her tote bag. "I better get going. Thanks, Detective."

They shook hands and Brenna left with Emily.

Emily dropped Brenna off at her apartment. "Are you sure you're okay to go in?"

Brenna sighed. "I am. I have to do this today. I don't want to let anyone or anything keep me from being comfortable in my home. Do you mind waiting until I'm in my apartment? I'll text you to let you know I'm in."

"No problem. I'll wait until I hear from you."

"Thanks." Brenna leaned and gave Emily a hug. "You're the best friend I could ask for."

Emily smiled. "I know. And you're going to remember that next week when you treat me to dinner to celebrate all of this being over and done."

Brenna laughed. "Pick a day. I'll look forward to it."

Brenna hurried up the steps and noticed her father had already replaced the inside light in the lobby. She went up the stairs and paused for a moment before opening her door. There was no sign Tim had pushed it open or the police had slammed through it. Her dad had made sure of that.

She unlocked her door and walked into the apartment. Standing in the hallway, she took in the kitchen, dining room, and living room. Everything looked normal. Brenna let out a breath she hadn't been aware she was holding in. Her shoulders dropped at least an inch, and the stress seemed to flow off her. Grabbing her phone, she sent a short text to Emily.

B: In my apartment. Everything is good. See you at dinner tonight.

E: Awesome. Can't wait for your mom's cooking.

Brenna busied herself with getting laundry done. She made a list of chores to get done. Keeping busy and making sure she was organized would ensure some peace of mind.

Her phone rang. A glance at caller ID showed her it was Jackie Randall.

"Brenna are you all right? I just got off the phone with your mother." Jackie's voice shook.

"I'm fine, honest I am. It's been a crazy week. And I spoke with Mathew this morning. He's the producer of the show. The show is going to continue. And I'm going to stay with the show."

"You can't be serious. I thought you'd be ready to leave there."

"Well, I haven't had a lot of time to learn about the job, but what I've done, I've enjoyed. Most of the cast and crew are great. It's only six weeks. I'm going to see it to the end."

"Fine. We'll talk tonight at supper at your mom and dad's."

"See you there." Brenna hung up. She wasn't sure Jackie believed she still wanted to work with the show, but Brenna wasn't a quitter.

Brenna finished up her to-do list for the next few days. She got up to make a coffee, and her phone rang again. She didn't recognize the number and was cautious when she answered.

"Brenna, it's Lori Hastings. I'm calling to see how you are."

"Lori. I'm fine. I take it you heard from Mathew?"

"He called the farm office just before lunch. I have to say I'm surprised he's going to go ahead with the show. Ken and I spoke about continuing to sponsor the show, and we've decided we'll stay on as sponsors."

"I'm glad to hear that. Did you want me to let Mathew know?"

"No. I'm sorry. I'm not explaining myself well. We've spoken with him. I wanted to let you know I'm sorry you went through what you did with Tim, and I'd like to reconnect with you again. We were good friends in school."

"I think that would be great. But it's not your fault about Tim. He fooled a lot of people."

"Okay. Let's make plans for lunch sometime this week. I can't do dinner but would love to catch up with you over lunch."

They chatted a few more minutes and made tentative plans to meet later in the week. Brenna hung up. *Well, something positive might come from this last week. Catching up with Lori will be good.* Brenna smiled as she got her coffee and grabbed her latest book.

LATER THAT AFTERNOON, Bob dropped by to bring Brenna up to date on Tim.

"Tim's charged with Chef Mike's murder and the attempted murder of the judges, Sean, Mathew, and the other chefs. And with assault and forcible confinement of you. We found all kinds of evidence in his home. I guess he didn't think he would be a suspect. He's ignoring the advice of his lawyer and is talking to us about everything he did. It's a flood of information. The DA will not go after Sean for blackmail, provided Sean agrees to testify against Tim."

"Does Sean understand the consequences of what he did?"

"He seems to. His lawyer made it quite clear to him he should take the deal and consider himself lucky."

"I'm sure Tim knew exactly what he was doing all the time. When he told me what he did and why, he was cold and calculating."

Bob agreed. "Tim fell apart after his brother died. He felt responsible for him and believed he had let him down. He and his brother had talked after Charles returned from meeting with the three chefs. Charles had nothing good to say about them, and he kept telling Tim how they had treated him in school. Tim never forgot what his brother said, and he blamed the chefs, and himself, for Charles' death. Anyway, we have Tim solidly on Chef Mike's murder. And all the attempted murder charges will stick."

"I'm curious. How did he get Chef Aaron's knife? That's what he used, wasn't it?"

"He told us he picked it up when you asked the chefs to join you in the pantry to give you a diagram of where they wanted the supplies kept. He didn't need long to grab it, and Chef Aaron's knife roll was still on the counter."

Brenna's mom called her shortly after Bob left. "Just checking in with you. How are you doing?"

"I'm good, Mom. It seems like a nightmare, but I'm okay."

"When are you arriving for dinner?"

"Does around four work? And Emily is coming as well."

"That's perfect, and Emily's welcome anytime. Bob's coming, and he's invited a couple of friends as well. We're expecting a crowd. Your brothers and their families will be here too."

"I'll be there soon. Don't let them eat everything in sight."

Brenna tidied up her apartment and then hurried into the shower. She was just out of the shower when she received a text from Kate.

> K: At work, just heard what happened last night. Are u ok?

Brenna shook her head. Everyone was worried about her.

> B: I'm good. Shaken up last night, but I'm good now. Chat tomorrow?
>
> K: Yes, off tomorrow all day.

Brenna glanced at the clock; she'd have to hurry to get to her parents on time. She took extra care with her makeup, making sure it concealed the bags under her eyes. A dark-blue sweater and a comfortable pair of jeans took care of the rest. One last look in the mirror and she said, "Pretty good. That should keep everyone happy."

She sent Emily a text.

> B: Heading to my parents. Meet me there for dinner.
>
> E: I'll be there in fifteen.

The drive to her parents' house didn't take long. Her brothers' cars filled the driveway. Brenna parked on the street. *Mom was right, there's a crowd for dinner.* Emily pulled in right behind her.

They walked to the back of the house together. Brenna opened the gate to the fenced-in yard. Two of Brenna's brothers were in the yard throwing a ball with a Golden Retriever.

Emily noticed the dog. "Did your parents get a dog?"

"I don't think so. They didn't have a dog earlier this week. Maybe Jim got it for the boys."

Brenna and Emily climbed the steps to the large, covered deck. Her father, Bob, and Connor were sitting on the deck drinking beer. To the left of the deck, Brenna noticed three of her nieces and nephews playing on the playground equipment her father had put up last year.

"There you are. Your mom's been waiting for you. She keeps checking the street every five minutes." Her dad got up and wrapped her in a hug. "You cannot scare us like that again. I swear you're responsible for every gray hair on my head."

The familiar scent of her dad's aftershave brought a lump to her throat, and she had to swallow hard before answering. "Dad, this one wasn't my fault. And thanks for the repairs you did to my door last night."

"Uncle Dan, I have to agree. This time it wasn't her fault." Bob chuckled as Brenna and Emily took a seat.

"Do either of you want something to drink?" Dan asked.

"I'm good for now, Dad."

"I'll have a soft drink. And I'll get it. I know where they are." Emily walked to the built-in fridge under the bar. "Anyone need a refill while I'm up?" Everyone shook their heads.

Connor leaned over to Brenna. "I hear you have a mean elbow."

Brenna's brow furrowed and then cleared. "Oh. That. I guess I do. Dad taught me a few defense tactics when I started dating. I hadn't used them in a while."

"I have to say, I'm glad you're all right. You've had a rough time this week."

"I think I was angrier than anything else when it was happening. I couldn't believe someone would do what Tim had done and think he could get away with it."

"There are some nasty people out there."

Brenna agreed. "How are you settling in Bayview? Is it good to be back?"

Connor took a swallow of his beer. "I've been busy getting my business underway. I'm glad to be closer to my parents and my sister. My sister got married a few years ago, and she just had another baby. I enjoy being an uncle."

"And how's the business going?" Dan asked.

"It's growing. I offer a variety of services, including cyber security. That's made my business stand out."

Cecile came out on the deck. "Brenna Marie Flynn! What are you doing out here?"

Bob laughed. "All three names. You're in trouble."

Brenna flushed. "Mom, I just got here."

"Come on in. We've been waiting on you to get our celebration going."

Brenna looked at her dad. "Who else is here?"

"Well, your brothers and your sisters-in-law, your nieces and nephews, Rita and Ian, and Jackie Randall."

"For heaven's sake! It's like what we have for Thanksgiving." Brenna's jaw dropped.

"And Clare Morris is stopping by. She doesn't know a lot of people in town. It'll be good for her to meet the family," Bob added.

Emily linked her arm through Brenna's. "Come on. I'll help you face the crowd."

Brenna smiled at Emily. Cecile held the door open, and they walked into the kitchen.

"There she is!" Rita called out.

The family spilled into the large family room just off the kitchen. Cecile, Jackie, and Rita passed around platters of appetizers. Dan opened bottles of wine, and Bob got soft drinks out for the children. Jim, Brenna's oldest brother poured beer. Clare arrived a few minutes later, and everyone welcomed her.

Dan raised his glass. "Everyone, if I can have your attention please." He waited a moment while the noise level died down. "I want to take a minute to say thanks to Bob and Clare for being there when it counted for Brenna." Cecile led everyone in loud clapping and cheering. Dan waited once more and then continued. "Brenna, I'm grateful you weren't hurt by what happened last night or earlier this week. Your mother and I have one request. In the future, leave the investigating to the professionals."

There was laughter from everyone. A few questions were asked. Cecile raised her hands. "Okay, why don't we have Brenna tell us what happened last night. And Bob and Clare can fill in where they can?"

Brenna looked at Bob. "Is that okay?"

"Brenna can talk about what happened to her and her involvement in the situation. We'll need to be more circumspect about what we say."

Brenna found a seat in one of the large chairs. The dog that had been playing outside had followed everyone in and sat at Brenna's feet. She told her family what had happened and how she had put the pieces of the puzzle together. She didn't spend a lot of time talking about what happened when Tim pushed into her apartment. She didn't want to relive that moment.

Bob and Clare filled in where they were able to.

Brenna's oldest brother, Jim, raised a glass. "So glad you're safe. Now, on behalf of the family, please leave the police work to Bob, Clare, and the Bayview Police Department."

Everyone raised their glass in a toast.

Brenna glanced at the dog lying next to her. The dog looked at her, smiled, and then thumped her tail. She licked Brenna's hand as Brenna reached down to scratch her ears. "Whose dog is this? Jim, did you get a dog for the boys?"

Jim shook his head.

Brenna's mom and dad looked at each other. Her father scratched his head. "Now, Brenna, don't get upset with us. With all that's happened in the last few months, we thought it might be good if you had a dog. One of my contractors had this dog, and she's a great dog, but his son is allergic to dog hair. He asked if I knew anyone who could take her. She's well trained, housebroken, loves to run, and is a great guard dog."

Her mother added, "And look, it seems as if she knows she belongs with you. She hasn't left your side since she came in."

Brenna was rubbing the dog's head. The dog rolled over and exposed her belly for a belly rub. "I'm not sure how I'll be able to take care of her. My hours at the studio are long."

Brenna's mom said, "If you take her out for a run in the morning, I don't mind going over at lunch and taking her for a walk. That should take care of her during the day. You'll be home in the evenings for dinner, and she'll be great company. You'll see."

Jim spoke up. "And if she's too much work, we'll see about taking her. But it would be great if you tried it. We all think you need a guard dog. Mysterious notes and people pushing their way in wouldn't have happened if you'd had Jake there."

"Jake? I thought she was a female?"

"She is, but the contractor's kids wanted to name her Jake. She's a year old and accustomed to her name. It might be difficult to change it now," Dan said.

Jake sat up and put her paw on Brenna's knee. She looked straight at Brenna.

"I'd have to be heartless to turn her away. She's beautiful and well-behaved, too. Let's see how things work out."

They sat in the family room and got caught up on family news. It was interesting to hear what her nieces and nephews had been up to.

Jackie Randall came and sat next to Brenna. "Brenna, you're sure you still want to work with the show? I can find another temp contract for you," Jackie said.

Brenna said, "I'm good. We'll figure something out once this contract is over. Something that doesn't involve murder."

Jackie chuckled. "I'll do the best I can."

They all gathered around the table for their meal. Brenna looked around at her family and smiled. She was home. Maybe the future would be brighter.

Acknowledgements

Writing a book is a solitary process, but there are many people who help.

Dave and Corina McLaughlan, who connected me with Kim Bondi and Vince Deiulis. Kim and Vince answered my questions on reality television and on the work production assistants do daily. Any errors or omissions are mine.

The original writers' group from the Timmins Public Library: Jessica T and Jessica F, Vero, Kaitlyn, Janice, Diane, Colleen, and Ed. You all consistently gave encouragement, feedback, and friendship.

Nobody understands a writer like other writers.

My beta readers: Louise, Ann, and Debby. You read through the original draft. You were brave! Thanks for your feedback and comments, they made the book better.

Aline de Chevigny, you are my friend, mentor, and a most excellent critique partner. Thank you for your feedback and constructive criticism.

Stephanie and Jay, Greg and Claire, Mame and David, your unwavering support means so much.

Thank you to my editor, Kimberly Coghlan for her work and to ColbyMyles.com for my beautiful cover.

To my agent, Dawn Dowdle of the Blue Ridge Literary Agency. Thank you for believing in this book and the characters as much as I did and for finding it a home.

Manufactured by Amazon.ca
Bolton, ON